# The Hanging of Dr. Hanson

Miscarriage of Justice or Fitting Finale of a Fool?

## Bentley Gates

Savant Books
Honolulu, HI, USA
2014

Published in the USA by Savant Books and Publications
2630 Kapiolani Blvd #1601
Honolulu, HI 96826
http://www.savantbooksandpublications.com

Printed in the USA

Edited by Zachary M. Oliver and Daniel S. Janik
Cover by Dennis Krull



13-digit ISBN: 9780988664067
10-digit ISBN: 0988664062

# Dedication

This novel is dedicated to the American judicial system, which, despite its faults, remains the greatest in the world. It is equally dedicated to those participants who suffer unjustly under this auspicious system—those who are misidentified, perjured against, wrongly convicted, or who have suffered from a prejudiced jury, lacked sufficient counsel at trial or have been made to endure inhumane conditions while imprisoned.


# Acknowledgements

As an author and historical researcher, I must acknowledge the scribes—those individuals who record the mundane, day-by-day, year-after-year. Their persistence in creating and maintaining chronicles for an unknown posterity is invaluable. Some have left doodles to evince their boredom; others have slipped in pieces of paper with notes meant to explain confusing or contradictory entries. Whether the record-keepers were governmental, military, judicial, volunteer historical societies, or keepers of family histories, every document discovered was valuable in garnering the information needed to reconstruct this story. Profound gratitude is expressed to all such scribes, relentless in keeping their journals accurate and safe, without whose contributions, additions and annotations this novel would never have been conceived.

# RELEASE.

(IN DUPLICATE.)

## Headquarters, Camp Chase, Ohio,

June [illegible] 186[illegible].

By virtue of an Order received from [illegible] dated at [illegible] 186 , [illegible] resident of [illegible] County, and State of Kentucky, Prisoner at this Post; after having complied with the requirements of, and subscribed the following Oath and Declaration, is hereby released from confinement. [illegible]

DESCRIPTION.

| Complexion. | Hair. | Height. Feet—Inches. | Eyes. | Age. | Whiskers. |
|---|---|---|---|---|---|
| [illegible] | [illegible] | 6 | Blue | 30 | |

**THE UNITED STATES OF AMERICA, SS.**

I, [illegible], do solemnly and voluntarily swear that I will support, protect and defend the Constitution and Government of the United States against all enemies, whether domestic or foreign, and that I will bear true faith, allegiance and loyalty to the same, any ordinance, resolution, or law of any State Convention, or Legislature, to the contrary, notwithstanding; and further, that I do this with a full determination, pledge and purpose, without any mental reservation or evasion whatever, and will neither directly nor indirectly give aid or information to the enemies of the United States, and will not advocate or sustain, either in public or private, the cause of the so-called Confederate States. So help me God.

This Oath is taken, and Pass accepted, with the full understanding that if the party receiving it be found hereafter in arms against the Government of the United States, or aiding or abetting its enemies, the penalty will be death.

Hanson Bumgardner [illegible]

Sworn to and subscribed before me, this 2[illegible] day of June, 186[illegible].

[illegible]

Major Battalion Governor's Guards, Commanding Post.

# Author's Note

When reading "The Hanging of Dr. Hanson" one should remember that the years surrounding the Civil War (1861-1865) were marked by significant change. New technologies sprang up that would significantly alter individual and social behavior. New ways of thinking and communicating were introduced. Formulated medicines began taking the place of homemade remedies. Railroads made travel less difficult. New manufacturing methods were introduced and rapidly improved upon. The Mexican-American War (1846-1848) ended and the nation began prospering. People migrated steadily from the farm to the city, a phenomenon that continues to this day.

However, during this same time, the nation was being pulled apart by forces that could not be suppressed. People's positions regarding federal powers, states' rights, and slavery split, entrenched and became unmovable. Cultural differences between the North and South sparked heated discussions and deadly behavior. "Free-Staters" following John Brown's urgings became involved in guerrilla clashes later known as "Bloody Kansas." These encounters continued throughout 1859 claiming fifty-six lives, and polarized the nation further. National divergence over these issues soon overshadowed and influenced every aspect of life.

Hanson Bumgardner was a real person, as can be seen by the

Loyalty Oath he signed later in life, who lived through those tumultuous years. During his life, Bumgardner was a gigolo, drunkard, preacher, doctor, thief, counterfeiter as well as a son, brother, husband and father. Today, his actions would likely label him a "survivor," assuming a myriad of different roles during those chaotic times. Like many, he turned to crime to survive the Civil War, continuing his criminal activities afterwards. Despite renouncing the taking of life throughout the war and afterwards, he was, in the end, adjudicated a murderer.

Long after his 1866 trial, there were those who questioned the conviction. Despite the overwhelmingly adverse conceptions by the people of the county about his guilt, Bumgardner remained adamant that the murderer was one of the John Woods gang. Although admitting he was a member of the Woods Gang, Bumgardner blamed the other members of the gang for the actual murder and insisted he was framed.

Researching what Hanson Bumgardner said on the gallows was difficult and time-consuming. The notoriety of the trial and the many records surviving the war helped immensely in my reconstruction of his life. Federal records, state records, and county historical societies proved excellent sources for piecing together the story. As with all good historical fiction, care was taken to present this tale as realistically as possible. Though sometimes confusing, dates and facts were kept consistent with historical data. On the other hand, the actual conversations, thoughts and motivations of the characters portrayed are, by necessity, fictional.

Insofar as possible, the people mentioned in the novel were real people. Sheriff Hicks never again ran for election to the position. Sen. Knowles, who served as defense attorney, was re-elected several times.

The district attorney, Col. Alban, retired, and his assistant, Thomas Ewart, took over the role. The affable Maj. Longwell, whose humor raised the spirits at Camp Chase, died as indicated of smallpox, as did his wife. There are but a few truly fictional characters in the novel, and these were used sparingly. An excellent example is the episode of Hanson's service to the Partisan Rangers. No records exist to support his claim of being forced into servitude with such a group. However, most records regarding such rangers were destroyed in the last days of the war. Billing's Partisan Rangers Regiment is a fictional unit based on known facts regarding such groups operating under warrants from the Confederate States Congress.

The rancor of today's politics mimics that which occurred prior to the great American conflict of Bumgardner's time. Hopefully, Hanson Bumgardner's successes and failings will provide some guidance to future generations as to how to endure the turmoil of similar cultural divides.

# Chapter One

The jingling of heavy cast iron keys aroused Dr. Hanson Bumgardner in his jail cell in Marietta, Ohio. He slowly opened his eyes to his final day as the heavy, four-inch-thick plank door of his cellblock creaked open. Diadana Hicks, the wife of County Sheriff Jackson A. Hicks, slipped in, carrying a wooden tray with his special breakfast. The day before, Bumgardner had chosen steak and eggs for his last meal. Famous for her culinary expertise, Diadana had personally prepared the sumptuous meal she presented to him early this morning.

Inhaling a preview of the breakfast awaiting him just outside his cell, Hanson swung his legs down and sat upright on the wood-and-canvas-web bed he had occupied since September 1866. Stretching his arms upwards, he exhaled in a long moan.

"Is it Friday already?" The question came from the adjacent cell.

"Yup. Friday, February fifteenth, 1867," Sheriff Jackson Hicks replied, as he turned the key in Bumgardner's cell door lock. "Well, Hanson, this is your big day."

Looking at the sheriff, then the others around the cell block, Hanson broke into one of his famous, beguiling smiles and chuckled. Ambling nonchalantly to the long common table, he sat down before his hearty meal. "I don't know how big a day, Jackson, but it is certainly my last."

Not quite sure how to respond, Sheriff Hicks placed a package wrapped in brown paper tied with jute on Hanson's bed and exited the cell. "The suit your family provided," Hicks said to Hanson in subdued voice, flicking his thumb over his shoulder at the parcel.

"My thanks to them. Tell my brother…"A single heavy bong from the clock in the town square interrupted his reply.

"That makes eight-thirty," advised the Sheriff, answering the unasked question about the time before it arose. Facing Hanson square on, he waited for the man to finish his interrupted statement.

"Tell my brother to deliver my body to Union Church for interment," Hanson said before returning his attention to the sumptuous breakfast before him.

"Yup, I understand," Hicks mumbled and turned away.

Hanson placed each bite slowly into his mouth, consciously savoring its taste. This was to be his last meal before crossing over to the other side. Hicks went from cell to cell, opening each door, and the other prisoners joined Hanson at the table. Their breakfasts of oatmeal with a pat of butter and a cup of coffee looked comparatively meager. "Gonna miss you Doc," one of the inmates said sadly to Hanson.

"Ha!" Bumgardner scoffed between bites, "But I will not miss you, sir!"

A chuckle rippled through those assembled in the room.

Hanson chewed slowly, inviting his senses to soak in each exquisite taste. Finished, he placed his fork on the metal plate, dabbed his lips with the napkin, cleared his throat, and turned to speak to those sitting around the table.

"Fellow prisoners! Let me be clear that I am an innocent man. I have lived my life trying mightily to walk the righteous path, and am sitting here before you because of the lies and deceit of the companions I chose in life. Turn from demon Satan to the Lord! Repent your sins before God and man as I have. Leave behind those who would draw you down."

Turning towards a young inmate named Jeremiah, Hanson addressed him directly: "Jeremiah, you have confided in me the desire to take Jesus Christ into your heart. Your petty thievery may require your presence here for a year, but I implore you, young sir, to change your heart now! Doing so will make your wait bearable and lead you to a happy, fruitful and productive life once your debt to society is paid."

"Sure, Doc. Sure," Jeremiah replied, staring at the tabletop, embarrassed by Bumgardner's admonition in front of the other prisoners.

Hanson returned to his cell and picked up the package. The clock on the square tolled nine times while he unwrapped the suit of clothes. It was a modest suit, made of dark linen, neatly pressed. Pulling up the pants and buttoning the fly, he noticed the fit was snug. "Well, there's no time for alterations," Hanson said with a laugh, breaking the tension in the cellblock where only open-bar cells separated the men. The men welcomed the laugh to ease the anxiety they each felt.

Dr. Hanson, the name Hanson Bumgardner once resisted but now preferred, looked up to the creaking cellblock door to see the sheriff's brother, Chief Deputy Thomas Hicks, escort in reporters from the Marietta Times and the Marietta Register. One shook off the water that accumulated on an umbrella from the rain, falling steadily throughout the morning.

"Good morning, Mister Fields. I'm glad to see the Times

represented. Oh, and Mister Sibley, I see the Register has again sent their legal expert to watch over the proceedings," Dr. Hanson remarked. His comments were upbeat, surprising most in the room given the circumstances prompting the occasion.

"Your story sells papers, Hanson," Fields replied in a similarly jovial tone, tapping the raindrops from his bowler hat.

Hanson replied, "No doubt, sir. Then perhaps you would consent to give my widow a portion of the proceeds my story has made possible for your gazette."

Dr. Hanson's dark comment momentarily stopped all activity in the room. Realizing that the comment held humor only for him, he raised his hands, palms up, smiled and said, "Perhaps you would share the same with *all* of the prisoners here whose stories have helped your circulation grow." The doctor's disarming frankness and charming smile courteously put everyone at ease. Catching the lightheartedness their peer was trying to share, the prisoners chuckled as the newly admitted guests navigated to seats.

Dr. Hanson continued dressing, adding, "Throughout my life, I have always believed that clothes make the man. In my time, I have paid as much for a suit as most would pay for a horse. The suits often earned me more than would any horse."

Hanson slipped into the shirt, pleased to find the cuffs had buttons, as he owned no cuff links. Trying on the jacket, he confirmed the fit and presented himself to the assembly who nodded their approval. Removing the jacket, he placed it carefully upon the bed and searched through the brown paper wrappings. He found nothing else.

Flinging the paper into the air, he questioned aloud, "What? No tie?" and looked comically around the room. "Oh yes. For a moment I forgot: Sheriff Hicks has a special necktie waiting for me outside."

Hanson forced a laugh and waved his arms to encourage the others. Some joined him in macabre laughter; most glanced at each other in disbelief at the cavalier way Dr. Hanson Bumgardner was acting in the face of the awaiting horror.

Picking up paper and pen, he went to the central table and began composing a letter. The room went silent, then quiet conversations cropped up throughout the cellblock as Dr. Hanson penned a letter to his mentor, Thomas Brown, in Virginia. Folding the letter into the shape of an envelope and sealing it with candlewax, he placed it to the side and started another. This one was to his wife, Sue. Tears slowly formed in the corners of his eyes, eventually flowing down his cheeks as he wrote. Blank pages were quickly filled. As he completed the third, the town clock tolled ten, the sound obliterating the pen's scratching.

At the last toll, Hanson stopped writing, stood and began pacing the cellblock. He brushed aside the tears, now apparent to all, and rubbed his forehead with thumb and forefinger as though it might aid his thinking. After several minutes of pacing in what appeared to be deep meditation, he sat again and continued his letter. This time, he seemed anguished, carefully considering each word, every nuance. The final page took an hour to complete.

Shortly after the clock on the square struck eleven, Dr. Hanson leaned back in the wooden chair, reread the letter, and, appearing satisfied, read it aloud to all assembled. Sheriff Hicks had to fight back tears, listening to the emotional letter, which did not decry his pending death, but rather lamented the harsh life his death would impose upon his three sons and daughter. The letter ended with instructions to his family. Several minutes elapsed as each person in the room reflected pensively upon his own mortality. Bumgardner at last folded the letter into an envelope, sealed it with candle wax and passed it to the sheriff. Rising, he once again addressed the men about him with a broad smile. "Gentlemen, have any of you a cigar? I have the habit and not much more time to enjoy one."

Fields rose, handed the prisoner a cigar, and struck a match. Puffing several times and letting slip a gratified groan, Dr. Hanson slowly exhaled, blowing a huge cloud of blue smoke into the air.

"Ah, yes. This mortal pleasure I will surely miss," Bumgardner admitted as he pulled his chair against a wall and sat, leaning it back on two legs. Puffing again with unrestrained pleasure, he repeated the comment as he continued to enjoy the panatela. Leaning his head back against the wall, his eyes glazed over in a fixed stare at the ceiling while smoke drifted lazily around his head. A long period of silence followed, and time itself seemed to drift leisurely on the blue streamers meandering upward, curling towards the ceiling.

At last he spoke.

"Yea, though I walk through the valley of the shadow of death, I will fear no evil, for Thou art with me," Bumgardner quoted from the Bible, at last breaking the silence. "Come sing with me," he asked those present, standing and walking the length of the cellblock while moving his hands as though conducting a choir with the cigar as his baton. He led them in his favorite hymn from the Standard Psalm Tune Book, "Lord It Belongs Not to My Care."

As he listened to the hymn and studied the doctor's face, Sheriff Hicks was again impressed. He had taken care of this prisoner since the man's September arrest and had grown to like him. Hanson had spent many an evening telling tales about his unusual life, and in the process, they had become *like* friends. They remained "like friends" only because they stood on different sides of the law. Had Dr. Hanson stuck to medicine, they might have been close, even best friends.

Tears welled in everyone's eyes as Hanson, the inmates and guests sang the last refrain, "But 'tis enough that Christ knows all, and I shall soon be with Him."

Clearing his throat, Sheriff Hicks said, "Yup. Almost noon, Hanson…"

Hanson returned to his cell, picked up the wrapping paper, folded it neatly and laid it upon the bed, placing the twine in its center. He pulled on his new suit coat and straightened it, smoothing out the creases with his hands. He groomed his hair back several times with a brush and then tossed the brush on the bed.

"May I speak with the Reverend?" Hanson requested. The local Methodist preacher who had been ministering to the prisoner since Hanson's trial began in December stepped into the cell. Dr. Hanson knelt and whispered a prayer with the Rev. William M. Mullenix they shared only with God.

Finished, Hanson rose from his knees, exited his cell and again addressed the men in the common area of the cellblock, this time in a tender voice. "Boys, my humble thanks for you all. You all have been good friends to me, God bless you. God knows your condition; I don't. My wish is you all may come to God. I have been pardoned by Him. You may be unjustly dealt with, but if your peace is made with God, all will be well. God bless you." As he spoke, Dr. Hanson, Jeremiah and the prisoners wept openly.

"It's time for witnesses and reporters to go to the yard surrounded by wooden walls where the gallows stands," the sheriff directed and they quickly complied, walking silently in single file behind a deputy and out the cellblock door.

Moments later, three deputies entered the cellblock and

surrounded Hanson. While they waited, the sheriff walked out to the gallows and back to confirm the path was clear, as he had practiced. Then he cuffed Dr. Hanson's hands behind him and draped a black hood over Hanson's shoulder. Together, the group shuffled *en masse* down the hall, then turned a corner and marched down another hall across a meeting room and through the open door where Hanson caught his first glimpse of the gallows.

Heavy gray clouds overhead cast solemn shadows over the scene on this remarkably warm February day in Ohio. The air hung heavy with moisture and the yard looked like a muddy pit. Sporadic rain throughout the morning had completely soaked the ground, requiring the deputies to place boards around the perimeter. The spectators were huddled together in small groups on the boards. A double width of clean boards led to the base of the gallows.

Stepping outside into full view, Hanson paused to survey the scene, his eyes resting on the simple wooden casket waiting under the gallows to receive his body. With a nudge, the group of deputies directed him on to the base of the steps where they paused. Only Sheriff Hicks, Deputy Hicks and Rev. Mullenix were to ascend with Hanson onto the platform.

Gripping the railing, the reverend placed a foot on the first of the steps while Sheriff Hicks removed the cuff on Hanson's right hand to allow the condemned to do the same.

"Careful, Hanson, grab the rail," Sheriff Hicks cautioned, maintaining a hold on the left handcuff as Hanson began to ascend. "The steps are wet."

Hanson laughed ironically. "Yes, it wouldn't do if I were to deprive the State of Ohio of the pleasure of my execution by accidently slipping and breaking my own neck."

This was the first under a new Ohio law requiring closed executions. The new law allowed a maximum of thirty official witnesses and the next of kin to be present. Hastily constructed twenty-five-foot tall wooden walls surrounded the gallows to provide a visual barrier, and not as one might first assume, to prevent escape.

Bumgardner slowly climbed the steps to the platform sixteen feet above the earth. Once there, Reverend Mullenix assisted Hanson to a corner. As he joined them on the platform, the sheriff's face was grim, revealing his abhorrence to this most dreadful aspect of his official duties. No previous Washington County Sheriff ever faced the grievous task entrusted to him today.

Sheriff Hicks walked alone to the trapdoor with its three large sandbags resting in the center to perform a final inspection. He looked high above at the four-by-twelve-inch horizontal wooden beam supported by two upright posts that ran the width of the platform, visually inspecting the length of rope hanging from the horizontal beam. He checked the hangman's noose to confirm it was properly tied. Death was to be delivered by a swiftly broken neck. The thought of this eloquent man strangling slowly at the end of the rope repelled the sheriff.

Walking to the table on the far side of the platform, the sheriff laid a leather pouch upon it. A foot away, a metal hand lever, salvaged from a war-damaged steam engine, jutted forty inches up through a slot in the floor. Completely absorbed in his work, Hicks grasped the lever with both hands and yanked it towards him, triggering the trap door. It clanged open and the sandbags fell below with a sloppy splash. Several witnesses who had been talking together gasped, believing the execution had just been accomplished. After the initial shock, the fact that it was a prelude of what was soon to come percolated through the audience. Two deputies below the platform reset the trapdoor.

Dr. Hanson rolled up onto his toes to look over the fence. Anxiously peering east, his look of anticipation turned to one of disappointment. Seeing Hanson's despair, Rev. Mullenix bowed his head and quietly invited Hanson to join him in quiet meditation. Hanson paused, then rolled back onto the soles of his feet, and together they said the Lord's Prayer aloud.

The clock in the square struck twelve, evoking a look of pain on the sheriff's face. Sheriff Hicks nervously poured a glass of water from the pitcher present on the table and heaved an audible sigh before downing the water in one protracted gulp. Replacing the glass, he picked up the leather pouch and removed several papers. Reviewing them, he selected one, returning the others to the satchel.

Stepping to the front of the gallows, Hicks looked down on the gathered spectators, drew in a deep breath and in a strong baritone voice began reading the sentence. "As to the State of Ohio versus Hanson Bumgardner on the count of murder in the first degree: Hanson Bumgardner, on December 20, 1866, you were found guilty by a jury of your peers of the premeditated murder of John Thomas Eubanks on or about September 15, 1866. The jury so finding, Judge E. A. Guthrie of Washington County, Ohio, declared and sentenced you to be put to death by hanging on Friday, February 15, 1867 between the hours of ten in the forenoon and three post-noon. On Thursday February 14, Governor Jacob Dolson Cox, replying to a clemency plea, declined to commute the sentence. The laws of the State of Ohio having been complied with, the sentence will now be carried out."

Sheriff Hicks took another deep breath and looked at Hanson who appeared to be looking east over the fence towards the hills of

West Virginia just beyond the Ohio River.

"Hanson Bumgardner, do you have any last words?"

Verbally pulled from his faraway thoughts, Hanson replied in a resolute manner, "Yes, Sheriff, I do have some thoughts." Stepping forward, a handcuff dangling loosely from his left hand and the hood still draped over his shoulder, he surveyed the crowd. Seeing familiar faces, but not the ones he had hoped to see—the ones out there somewhere who he hoped might still make it back in time to speak on his behalf—he began. "I never killed any man. In these, my last moments, I feel interested in leaving a true record behind.

"I am the first of the family against whom such a charge has ever been brought…"

# Chapter Two

In the autumn of 1845, fifteen-year old Hanson Bumgardner was walking the streets of Clarksville, Virginia, with five friends including Beth Thompson. Hanson looked with his sparkling blue eyes at Beth making it apparent to everyone that she controlled him more than he controlled her or himself. "Here, Beth, have some more butterscotch candy," Hanson offered his pretty girlfriend, pulling some candies wrapped in yellow wax paper from his pocket.

She inspected several pieces. Selecting one, she grabbed it and ran ahead of him, laughing and teasing the lovestruck boy. Over a shoulder, she shouted, "Com'on everyone! Let's go over to Criss' General Mercantile and get some more candy."

A spontaneous footrace began to the store, Hanson outrunning everyone. He stopped at the hitching post out front and watched as they caught up.

"*You* can't go in," Charles Tyler, one of his friends, taunted.

"You shouldn't've cussed out ole' man Criss," Sam Hough, another of his friends, remarked to young Bumgardner.

"Maybe I shouldn't, but he was being mean to Beth," Hanson retorted.

"Yeah, well, it's his store, so he sets the rules," Charles shot back.

Beth held the door open for two girlfriends, tossing a coy smile at Hanson, before following them inside. The two other boys jumped onto the wooden porch and disappeared into the store after them.

Hanson leaned against the hitching post, pulled a coin from his pocket, and began to roll the coin from one knuckle to another, then between his fingers, finally making it disappear. Sleight-of-hand tricks interested him, and he knew that only through constant practice could he be dexterous enough to fool anyone.

"Hanson," an urgent voice cooed in a stage whisper.

Young Bumgardner looked around, but saw no one. Then he heard his name again, only louder.

"Hanson! Over here! It's me, Polly."

Hanson looked to the side of the building to see Polly Blackmon. He smiled, then slowly approached. "Polly. It is a pleasure to see you."

"Come quickly," Polly urged, backing away from him into the alley where she'd been hiding.

Young Hanson had to speed up to catch her. "Slow down, girl," he said jokingly as if speaking to a horse. "Steady, there. What is it you want?" He stared questioningly into her eyes at a look he had never seen before.

She stepped up to him and playfully wrapped an arm around him. "This is what I want," she whispered in his ear, reaching across his muscular chest with the other arm and pulling his face to hers, kissing him on the lips.

"But...but you're John Franklin's girl," he sputtered between kisses.

As she leaned closer against him, he quickly reconsidered as they shared a breath, their lips almost brushing. He took her face in his hands and kissed her with a newfound passion. They kissed several more times, their breathing increasing, then he turned and hugged her tightly. At this, she pushed him away and backed up.

"I *am* John Franklin's girl. But I wanted to kiss the most handsome boy I've ever known. Nothing more, nothing less. You're a nice boy, Hanson, but you're not the kisser John Franklin is." With that, Polly turned, skipped deeper down the alley, and disappeared around a corner. Confused about what had just transpired, he returned to his position at the hitching post to practice his coin tricks while awaiting his companions.

He didn't have to wait long. The pack reappeared, gathering on the porch around Charles who was holding a small brown paper sack filled with peppermint candies. Charles offered Hanson one, but, as Hanson already had a half-eaten piece of butterscotch candy in his mouth, he declined the offer. The friends fell into step and began walking down the street, jostling each other and joking as they enjoyed the sweets melting in their mouths.

Inside the store, Mr. Criss returned to dusting, and noticed that the lid on the butterscotch candy jar was askew. Moving to the window he looked out at the teens walking away and noticed that Hanson Bumgardner, the boy he had forbidden to enter his store, held a candy up in the air that glinted gold in the sunlight. Quickly, he tossed his broom against the wall and rushed out the door, chasing after them, shouting, "Hey! You!"

Beth laughed and took off running, inspiring them all, including Hanson, to do the same.

"Why are we running?" Hanson shouted from within the group.

"Stop them!" Mr. Criss shouted over and over.

Hearing Mr. Criss' desperate shouts, Sheriff John Davis rushed from between two buildings in front of the teens, extending his arms.

"Whoa!" Davis commanded and the teens skidded to a dusty stop in front of him. "What's all this fuss about?"

The teens seemed confused, when Mr. Criss approached and grabbed Hanson by the arm. "This one!" Criss accused Hanson. "This one stole candy from my shop!"

"I did not!" Hanson replied, angrily denying the allegation.

"I sold some peppermint candies to this bunch, and, after they left, noticed the butterscotch jar lid askew. I didn't notice any adults in my store while they were buying the peppermint candies. He must have snuck in while I was distracted and pilfered the butterscotch candy jar. I told him before, when he cursed at me, that he was never to set foot in my store again. See if he has any butterscotch candies on him!"

"Okay, Hanson. Let's see what's in your mouth." Davis leaned forward and sniffed loudly. "I smell butterscotch. Empty your pockets, Hanson."

Hanson turned out his pockets to reveal several coins, a top, a jackknife and a yellow wax paper packet with a few butterscotch candies in it. The sheriff shook his head. "I'm placing you under arrest for theft."

"But Sheriff Davis, these were given to me by my father early this morning. I…" Hanson began to protest.

"Save it, Bumgardner. Everyone knows you've had a grudge against Mister Criss since he threw you out of his store," Davis said as he proceeded to take Hanson into custody.

"Beth, tell them I offered you a butterscotch before you went into the store."

The other teens, intimidated by the sheriff's badge, remained silent. Beth looked morosely down at her feet and muttered, "If my daddy gets wind of me being here..."

"Charles," Hanson interrupted. "Please ride back to Ten Mile and get my dad." Charles nodded and took off towards where he'd left his horse. They rest watched meekly as Sheriff Davis directed Hanson to a small jailhouse located across from the courthouse.

Hours later, Hanson's parents, Addison and Jane Bumgardner, arrived at the sheriff's office.

"I can't believe you arrested my boy based on a flimsy allegation by Criss," Addison declared in disbelief. "That man has been after Hanson for weeks, ever since Hanson cussed him out."

"I know about the cussing match, Mister Bumgardner, but this is different; Mister Criss claims this was theft."

Hanson protested from behind the cell bars. "Father, I wasn't even in the store!"

Addison asked what needed to be done to take the boy home. "Why hasn't bail been set?" Addison asked.

The answer only brought more grief.

"Because Circuit Judge Edwin Duncan won't be here 'till Tuesday, and William A. Harrison, the prosecutor, who needs to make a decision as to whether or not to prosecute this, is also away. Hanson will just have to stay here 'til then," Davis said, shrugging.

Hanson spent the weekend in jail, Sheriff Davis allowing him out during the day to sweep the jail and courthouse. Hanson's friends came by, but wouldn't speak to him, for fear of being presumed guilty by association. The increasingly angry young Hanson Bumgardner, for his part, underwent a profound learning experience. He recognized he was being used by everyone.

Tuesday morning, Addison and Hanson met with Prosecutor Harrison. After listening sympathetically to father and son, Harrison explained his predicament. "Mister Criss has decided to make an example of Hanson, and has filed formal charges. I have no choice, Addison."

"Fine. Then let's get on with it," Addison said with disappointment.

Later, on their way into the courtroom, Mr. Criss passed Hanson and said with a sneer, "This courthouse was built in 1812 and still has a whipping post out back. I will be reminding the judge of that fact."

The entire proceeding took less than ten minutes to present to Judge Duncan. The case against Hanson was circumstantial, at best. Addison then testified about giving Hanson the butterscotch candies he had in his possession that day. The storekeeper's case finally fell apart when the teens, now sworn to tell the truth, testified that Hanson had offered to share the butterscotches with them *before* they went to Mr. Criss' store. The teens also unanimously testified that Hanson had stayed outside that day, having been previously barred from the store by the storeowner. Judge Duncan decided in Hanson's favor and ordered his immediate release.

Addison, upon hearing the verdict, strode over to Mr. Criss and growled, "We'll not be shopping at your concern any further, sir. And, upon my vow, I assure you that folks in this county will not be allowed to forget your actions in this matter. They can decide, as we have, whether to take their business elsewhere. If there is justice in this matter, it will be served by your eventual bankruptcy."

# Chapter Three

It began to drizzle again in Marietta, Ohio, as Hanson stood on the gallows platform and continued with his life story, trying to buy time. He noticed the reporters using the new shorthand writing system to record his remarks.

"You boys be sure to set down my words correctly," he admonished them gently. "You had it wrong about me being a bushwhacker; please get the facts correct this time." He took several steps forward, cleared his throat, and began anew. "I was next involved with the law at seventeen in Ritchie County, Virginia…"

At seventeen, Hanson was trim and muscular. His jet-black hair attracted the eye of many a young lady. The beguiling nature of his warm smile captivated those around him. He walked confidently with a stride just short of swaggering.

In spring of 1847 on Good Friday, Hanson coaxed his sorrel into a gallop on the road to Harrisville, Virginia. He'd spent his weekends for the last two months cutting and hauling firewood to purchase an Easter dress and bonnet for Rebecca, his current girlfriend, a striking beauty with light brown hair and playful blue eyes. Three weeks ago, Hanson had accumulated just enough money to order the dress from the Burlingham and Rexroad store in Harrisville. One of the owners,

Henry Burlingham, promised delivery just in time for Easter.

Arriving at the store, he saw the other owner, Daniel Rexroad, locking the doors.

"Oh sir! I am so glad to catch you before you left. I've come to pick up the dress I ordered. It arrived, didn't it?" Hanson asked anxiously.

"Yes, I saw today it in the back. But, young man, I have had a bad day and have taken ill. Won't you please come back on Monday?" Rexroad replied without looking at the young man's eager face.

"Oh, sir. Please. The dress is for Easter Sunday; Monday will be too late. I have already paid your partner for it. See? Here is the receipt. You need only deliver the goods." Hanson slipped from his horse and waved the receipt at the merchant.

Rexroad paused, coughing long, and coarsely. "I tell you I am ill. I am not well enough to reopen the store; you should have been more punctual."

*"I should have been more punctual?"* Hanson echoed. "Sir, the item in question was ordered three weeks ago! The clock in your own store shows ten minutes before five. I've made it here with time to spare! I ask again, I beseech you, to make a young lady proud to promenade on this Sunday in the dress ordered from your store."

Rexroad was considering the young man's words when a bout of coughing seized him. Leaning on the hitching post for support, he coughed uncontrollably until his face turned beet-red and a long string of sputum drooled from his mouth. "No, no. I cannot. I am, as you can see, too ill." He wiped his mouth on his sleeve and began shuffling away.

"You can't leave me here," Hanson pleaded.

"I can and I must. Good evening to you, sir," Rexroad said,

coughing in fits as he followed the sidewalk home.

Frustrated, Hanson slapped the reins around the hitching post and sat heavily on the wooden sidewalk in front of the store, trying to figure out what to do. Looking about, he noted he was the only person on the street at that moment. Rising and checking that the front door was locked, Hanson slipped down the side of the building and found a window in the back that was open several inches. Raising the window further, he climbed into the building, hoping to bring his problematic adventure to a quick and successful end. Luckily, the folded dress with bonnet on top lay on a storeroom counter. He delicately placed the hat in a hatbox, and carrying the box in hand, draped the dress over his arm and headed out the window.

Halfway out, the window sash slid down, pinning him half-in and half-out. Despite his best efforts, he was stuck. The sheriff happened to be making his nightly rounds and noted the commotion in the alley.

"Halt!" Sheriff Noah Rexroad shouted.

"I am going nowhere, sheriff. I'm stuck." Hanson said, chuckling at his predicament, holding up the hatbox and dress in explanation.

"Yes, sir, and you'll be stuck in jail for quite a while for breaking and entering," Sheriff Rexroad remarked, clucking his tongue disapprovingly.

"But, Sheriff," Hanson retorted, "I paid for this. The storeowner is ill, so he closed shop early, and wouldn't open the store so I could pick up what was rightfully mine to give my girl to wear on Easter Sunday."

The sheriff was incredulous.

Hanson offered dryly, "If that son-of-a-jackass had cared more about his customers and less about himself, everything would've been okay."

"Well, it's not okay, son," Sheriff Rexroad replied. "You're under arrest."

Hanson hung his head in frustration. "But it was the shopkeeper who…"

"That 'son-of-a-jackass' shopkeeper, who just happens to be my brother, didn't force you to break in."

"Yes. Of course. Just my luck…" Hanson sighed in resignation.

The sheriff lifted the window sash, freeing Hanson to fall to the ground. Shaking his head at the ridiculousness of the situation, Sheriff Rexroad helped him up and, doing his duty, snapped on a pair of handcuffs.

Just then, Daniel Rexroad came coughing around the corner. "I wondered what was going on when I saw his horse still out front from my bedroom window. Put this young devil in jail, Noah!"

The sheriff chuckled, picked up the dress and hatbox as evidence, and led Hanson to jail.

On Monday, the Circuit Prosecutor made the rounds in Harrisville. It was William A. Harrison, the same prosecutor whom Hanson had faced in Clarksburg. Harrison arrived early at the jail to interview the prisoners, recognizing Hanson Bumgardner. "Mister Bumgardner, what crime brings us together in jail this day?"

"No crime, sir. I merely retrieved what was mine and was unlawfully denied me." Hanson answered smartly.

"How so?"

Hanson showed Harrison his receipt for the goods marked 'Paid in Full'. "This is proof of my ownership of the goods in question. It is the same proof I presented to the merchant upon my arrival at the store. I arrived just before closing hour, but Mister Rexroad denied delivery of my prepaid purchase." The evidence together with

Hanson's self-confident demeanor seemed to impress Mr. Harrison, so Hanson continued. "The shopkeeper claimed to be too ill to reopen the store and allow me to take possession of the dress and bonnet in question, despite knowing the purchase was intended for Easter Sunday."

Hanson leaned forward towards Harrison and lowered his voice. "Yet, after I went in through an open window to get the goods, the same 'gravely ill' shopkeeper returned and demanded I be jailed. I had no other goods upon my person save the items I ordered and paid for in advance. If the man was healthy enough to return and accuse me, why couldn't he simply allow me to take my goods and go? Why didn't Mister Rexroad explain to the officer that I did not steal those goods, but had paid for them in advance and waited weeks for their delivery? Instead, he insisted his brother jail me for an offense precipitated by his own actions."

Harrison smiled at the oratory skills of the young man before him. As Hanson was about to continue, he noticed a man standing at the cellblock door. It was Henry Burlingham, Rexroad's partner.

"I have been asked to appear on behalf of my ill partner and the aggrieved, Burlingham and Rexroad. Irrespective of the reasons, this kind of behavior is most appalling!" Burlingham exclaimed.

"Appalling though it may be, I am curious how stealing one's own property is a crime," Harrison opined.

"Dear sir! I refer not to the actions of this esteemed customer, but that of my wrongheaded partner. Thanks be to God he is too ill to appear today, as the last time we talked, he was calling for this young man's crucifixion. I would blame his ill nature in this matter on the severity of his illness, as he is generally a most agreeable man."

"The last time I looked, trespassing was not a capital offense warranting crucifixion. Furthermore, the time sensitive nature of the merchandise clearly forced the hand of the prisoner to take action upon his own. He did not break the window, but entered through an open portal, and removed only those goods for which he had prepaid. With your consent, Mister Burlingham, I propose dismissing all charges," Harrison suggested.

"Agreed. I consider the matter closed, sir."

"Then, I'm free to go?" Hanson interjected.

"Yes," Harrison confirmed.

"I'll just take the dress and hat then, and be on my way," Hanson said, looking at the sheriff.

To Hanson's surprise, Sheriff Rexroad held up both hands palms out, and said defensively, "I informed Rebecca Cole on Saturday about the situation, and she picked up the dress and bonnet later that evening. I thought you wanted her to have them to wear for Easter. She is to bring them in for evidence later this morning."

Hanson shook his head in disbelief, then smiled. He was pleased his girlfriend had been able to wear the dress and hat on Easter Sunday after all, even if without him present.

The sheriff unlocked the cell and stood to the side, while Mr. Harrison and Mr. Burlingham looked on, each of their faces lit with a broad smile.

In the waiting area, Hanson's younger brother, James, and his father, Addison, sat on a bench, awaiting the trial. Their eyes focused on young Hanson as he entered the room. "I'm free to go," Hanson relayed to them, "Thanks for coming. I'm glad the message got to you."

Choking back tears, Hanson was embracing his father when, suddenly, the courthouse door burst open and a short, pale, skinny man barged in. Hanson recognized him instantly as Joseph Cole, Rebecca's father.

"Here!" the man yelled, flinging the dress and the hatbox at Hanson. "Here's the damned dress. She waited till today to tell me it's stolen property. She looked like a harlot in it anyway." Pointing a bony finger at Hanson, he added, "Don't you ever speak to my daughter or set foot on my property. You are a known criminal, and have been adequately warned under the law. Stay away from my daughter and family or I will kill you!" Cole turned and stormed out of the courthouse, slamming the door behind him.

"Hanson Bumgardner, you certainly evoke an emotional response from people. You should harness that talent and apply it towards a clearly positive endeavor," William A. Harrison commented offhandedly in the aftermath of the drama.

"Thank you for the advice, sir." Hanson said amiably.

On the gallows, as he finished the story of the Easter hat and dress, and his second entanglement with the law, Dr. Hanson shifted his weight awkwardly, and looked at Sheriff Hicks, who was standing solemnly, arms crossed. Hanson had come to respect the sheriff and knew the feelings were mutual. "Your efficient handling of my execution is duly noted, Sheriff Hicks. Everything is, as it should be, in perfect order. I compliment you." Hanson returned his gaze to the news reporters who were exchanging information and flashed his signature smile. Clearing his throat to regain their attention, he pressed his index finger to his lips.

# Chapter Four

With all eyes back on him, Dr. Hanson resumed his soliloquy. "At nineteen, I married a girl from Ritchie County; Reed was her name..."

Hanson smiled as he watched his new bride, Sara Reed-Bumgardner, straighten the drapes in the apartment they'd rented in Belpre, Ohio. Fine furniture crowded the small apartment. The furniture and a hundred dollars cash comprised the dowry that Hanson had been told would be in the thousands. Looking at the furniture, he nodded, bleakly acknowledging their value, but wishing, nonetheless, they had more cash to navigate the beginnings of married life.

Hanson smiled again as he watched Sara bend over to hem the drapes. Noticing him watching, she teased, "Excuse me, Mister Hanson Bumgardner!"

He grinned along with his attractive wife, the grin concealing his worry about finding work. He had hoped to find a position in sales or shipping along the Ohio River, but, despite his efforts, three weeks had passed without a substantive offer. Sara had, in desperation, taken a position cleaning rooms in a local hotel, her pay being barely sufficient to pay their bills, but leaving little for anything else.

Eyebrows raised, young Sara looked to her dashing young

husband for his approval on the length of the drapes.

"Yes, Missus Hanson Bumgardner. Yes, they are perfect!"

Despite their marital bliss, as the days passed, Hanson became increasingly frustrated at not being able to financially contribute. Discouraged and unsure why he was unsuccessful in finding work, Hanson cursed in frustration to the only ear that would listen. "Dammit, Sara, I have skills that any merchant would desire, but cannot find one in need!"

Sara tried to reassure her husband. "Hanson, sweetheart. The other cleaning ladies say there are opportunities down at the river docks for laborers."

"But Sara! I am not a laborer! Do I look like a mule or slave? No, my mind is my strength, not my brawn."

"Still, it would help greatly if we had more money. Any amount would be providential just now," Sara replied patiently.

"True, but it will be better in the long run if we must conserve our funds and survive until I find suitable work," Hanson contended, rejecting the thought of doing simple labor.

"I didn't marry you just to survive, husband, but for us as a family to thrive. I had thought you the heir to the Jacob Bumgardner Rye Whiskey clan!" Sara tossed back, angry that her new husband wouldn't listen to reason.

"I never claimed that!"

"No, but you implied it, and later didn't deny it!"

Several months and many arguments later, Sara arrived home a half-hour early, hot, sweaty, and tired from her long day of cleaning. Carrying her canvas bag of groceries up three flights of stairs, she turned to walk down the hall to their apartment. The apartment door opened, and a giggling middle-aged woman emerged from inside. The woman looked to Sara infinitely more attractive in her finery than Sara did in her rumpled work clothes. Sara immediately noted the woman's mildly disheveled hair, and the slight disarray of her clothes. Hanson followed her from the apartment and stopped abruptly when he noticed his wife staring angrily at him.

Sara swiftly covered the distance to the doorway, announcing her presence as she approached with a loud, "Ahem!"

The woman standing next to her husband gave her a haughty look, and sneered. "Hanson, it appears your cleaning woman has arrived. I am glad we were able to finish our social intercourse uninterrupted by house staff." Pulling a delicately embroidered handkerchief from her sleeve, she held it to her nose with practiced aplomb.

"This one definitely needs a bath. I question whether she will leave your apartment clean or not, but either way, I warrant her odor will remain." The woman wrinkled her nose, turned back to Hanson, and continued. "I'll send a man around tomorrow for the table." Pulling from her purse a small nebulizer of perfume, she spritzed it in the general direction of Sara.

"Well, I never!" Sara growled.

"Perhaps you should," the woman said contemptuously as she walked briskly past Sara and disappeared down the stairs.

"Who is *SHE?*" Sara demanded.

"*She* is Emily Ebenezer, wife of Edgar Ebenezer, the shipping magnate on Scott Street. I interviewed with him today for a dispatcher position. When I mentioned my tired feet, she offered me a lift back to the apartment, nothing more." Hanson flashed his winning smile.

He leaned forward to kiss her, but Sara pulled away. "And what kind of lift did she provide you, pray tell, to make it upstairs and into our apartment?" Sara countered.

Hanson pulled back and stared at his enraged wife. Hard work had aged the pretty young girl he had married barely a year ago. Sara's slender fingers were thin and calloused; her face was drawn from worry about their bills. "None, sweetheart, she…"

"*SHE* what*?"* shouted Sara. "I don't want to hear about *SHE!*" Sara pushed past him and dropped the grocery bag loudly on the table.

Hanson watched from outside the apartment as she poured water from the pitcher into a glass. Her once enviable hourglass figure had filled; her arms and legs had noticeably thickened. "Calm down, Sara. I happened to mention that odd table, there," Hanson pointed at an old and worn occasional table relegated to a corner position. "and that we have no matching piece. She expressed an interested in purchasing it."

"No, Hanson! That came from my grandmother who brought it from England! We cannot sell that one!"

"But, Sara, I thought…"

"No!"

"But four hundred dollars seemed…" Hanson let the amount hang in the air between them.

"What?" Sara asked, surprised by the dollar figure, yet appalled at Hanson's audacity.

"She offered, and I accepted, four hundred dollars for the table." Hanson stated.

Sara fell backwards onto the sofa with a soft whumph."Four hundred dollars?" she asked, her anger visibly moderating.

"Yes, dearest. With this, we can stay afloat for quite a while. She wanted to send someone with the money to pick it up tomorrow, but I told her that, if you objected, we would not release it."

"When I saw you with her and her hair and clothes..." Sara

acquiesced.

"You saw her reaction to my having caught her, preventing her from falling after tripping on a floorboard, nothing more, darling," Hanson reassured his wife.

"Four hundred dollars..." Sara said, wistfully pondering the large sum. "We could move back to my family's farm. With this, we could buy some land of our own."

"No, Sara. We needn't move. Mister Ebenezer will hire me, of that I'm certain. Things will get better now. You'll see."

With his wife's approval, Hanson sold the table, but the job with Ebenezer Shipping was not forthcoming. The whole incident left Sara suspecting Hanson was attempting to cover up an illicit sexual affair. Despite Sara's growing accusations of infidelity, and the increasing offers from women of hidden liaisons with him, Hanson remained steadfast and did not stray from his marriage vow.

Nonetheless, as the months passed and the money dwindled, Hanson began to accept day labor jobs, enduring the indignity, until a note made its way to his door. Reading, then re-reading it several more times to be certain he'd understood it, he thanked his good luck:

*A position has become available which will engage your considerable talents and provide excellent compensation. Please come to my office at 840 Elm Street at 2:00 this afternoon to discuss.*

*Yours,*

*E. Ebenezer*

This was just what he'd been awaiting. That afternoon, as he made his way to the address, he felt a great weight lifting from his shoulders.

Following Elm Street away from the riverfront, the buildings slowly shifted from business to residential. When he had at last located the address, a single story residential building in desperate need of repair, Hanson felt confused. This was surely not the home of a wealthy shipper. After rechecking and confirming that he was at the indicated address, he knocked on the door, then paused to check his suit.

"*Entrée*," a female voice from inside the house said in French. Hanson pushed open the door and stepped into the entry. Unlike the exterior, the interior was pin-neat and tastefully furnished.

"Lock the door and come here," the voice instructed, this time in English.

Hanson, eyebrows raised, locked the door and followed the hall to the back of the house, his wits heightening as he progressed. Halfway down the hall, he noticed a nook with an occasional table identical to the one he'd sold Mrs. Ebenezer.

"In here," the voice continued, and Hanson stepped into the back parlor room to see the silhouette of a woman reclining upon a fainting couch. Heavy drapes covered the windows, darkening the room and making it difficult to see.

"Missus Ebenezer?" Hanson questioned, peering about as his eyes strained to adjust to the dim light.

"Yes, Hanson. Come in." The voice was soft, inviting, urging.

When his eyes had fully adjusted, he noted Emily Ebenezer on the couch, wearing black puffy house slippers and a red and black corset underneath an open silk housecoat.

"Missus Ebenezer?" Hanson questioned again, feeling distinctly uncomfortable. "I...I thought I was being summoned for employment."

"Well, Hanson. This *is* for a position—a private one between you and me." She rose from the couch, the pale white of her inner thighs catching the faint light enticingly.

Startled, he stepped back. Emily continued towards him and seized his collar to end his retreat, gazing at Hanson with the same look that Polly Blackmon had in Clarksburg years before. Older and more experienced with women, Hanson recognized the look in her eyes and the tone of her voice.

Emily pressed her lips to his.

"But...but we're married," Hanson protested, adding between breaths, "to different people!"

"Then, this is perfect," she whispered. "Neither of us will be tempted to reveal the relationship, eh?" She ran her professionally manicured nails through his thick hair and pulled him to her for another passionate kiss.

"But...but...my wife...my work..." Hanson stammered.

"I have had you placed on my husband's payroll. Your job is to keep a wealthy, unloved woman from being lonely." Emily again pressed her lips to his and forced her tongue into his mouth.

Hanson again pulled back, uncertain, yet clearly intrigued. "But I...I love my wife," he sputtered.

Emily wetted her lips with her tongue. "And I love my husband, too. I just need more than he can provide. If you're so willing to sell your services to my husband to satisfy his business needs, why do you hesitate to do so for me and my needs? You will be my 'dispatcher'. The pay will be the same, but I will require much less. Edgar would have you working from eight until six daily; I will require your services for only four hours two mornings a week. Being regularly employed and contributing money to support your family isn't 'cheating'," Emily Ebenezer reasoned.

Knowing that if he continued without regular work he would

eventually lose Sara, Hanson reconsidered. *It is a 'dispatcher' job of sorts, and I need not describe the specific job tasks I perform to Sara,* he thought. *Our situation is desperate. I must find work to recapture her love and respect.*

He assured himself that he would engage in the proffered employment only until he found a more worthy one. It was, after all, an offer of employment, and, as with any good employee, he would be bound to earnestly follow Emily Ebenezer's instructions, whatever they might involve, in order to please his employer.

*There are distinct benefits to such a position as well*, Hanson reasoned and sighed, giving in to her offer, his own twisted logic, and the carnal passion of the moment.

# Chapter Five

Eleven weeks later, Hanson and Emily were relaxing in bed following a particularly vigorous encounter when her husband, Edgar Ebenezer, burst into the room.

"Ah hah! I knew I had no warehouse along this part of Elm," he shouted incredulously to no one in particular. In the darkness, he hadn't yet recognized the extent of the situation he had happened upon, but seeing Hanson jump up from the bed and hastily attempt to dress, Edgar quickly realized he'd been cuckolded. "Scoundrel!" he shouted.

"Edgar!" Emily shouted back, pulling the bedsheets over her nakedness as she reached for her pantaloons. She shrank back under the covers when she saw her enraged husband digging furiously into his vest pocket for the derringer he always carried.

"Mister Ebenezer! Wait! You have to understand. We don't love each other. You see…" Hanson attempted to explain.

"Oh, so this is just for your fun? You bastard! Am I then to be denied the consolation that she loves a younger, more muscular, and more handsome man than me?" Edgar shrieked, withdrawing the single-shot derringer, cocking and aiming the gun at Hanson who raised his hands futilely in front of his face in defense. As Edgar pulled the trigger, Emily threw a pillow at her husband's arm, causing the shot to miss Hanson, and instead shatter the boudoir lamp. Slivers of colored glass splayed about.

Ebenezer tossed the spent derringer aside and rushed at Hanson punching him solidly in the abdomen. Hanson, struggling to hold his pants up, grunted and staggered backwards from the force of the blow. Edgar, using all of his bulk and weight, slammed into Hanson pinning him against the wall.

Emily, having donned her pantaloons and bustier, threw a water pitcher at Edgar. Barely missing him, the pitcher shattered on the wall next to Hanson's head, showering both men with water and shards of porcelain.

Edgar, his fury uncooled, grasped Bumgardner's wrist in both of his hands and slung him towards the opposite corner wall. Hanson's back met the wall with a thud. While he slowly slid down it, Ebenezer rushed over and kneed him in the groin. Barely conscious, Hanson gasped for breath.

Suddenly Emily jumped on Edgar's back shouting, screaming and striking him on his bald head. "You bastard!" she screamed. "You never make love to me anymore, and you expect me to be celibate as a nun? Your damned money means more to you than I do. That's the real reason you're here, isn't it? To find out about the extra warehouse you were being billed for! That's really why you're so angry, isn't it?"

Edgar began turning in circles to try and shake the frenzied woman off while she continued to pummel him on the head and shrieked louder. In desperation, he dashed her against the wall.

Seizing the opportunity, Hanson grabbed the remainder of his other clothes and headed for the door. Freed of Emily, Edgar intercepted him, directing his weight to Hanson's side and cracking several of Hanson's ribs. Hanson stumbled, and grappled painfully with Edgar until the two slammed into the single draped window. With a violent rip and crash, glass, men and drapes came to rest inextricably entwined in the filthy back alley.

Both lay stunned for a moment. Trapped in the drapes, Hanson looked up to see Emily, standing in her housecoat, looking down at him through the ragged opening that had once been a window.

"My boots! Throw me my boots!" Hanson shouted.

Ebenezer moaned loudly while Hanson pulled and kicked frantically at the drapes tangled around his legs. Getting up on his knees to catch the boots, he felt a crashing blow to the back of his head and fell down flat. Looking sideways, Hanson saw Edgar on his knees crawling towards him seeking to repeat the blow with a stone he held menacingly aloft.

Hanson flipped over and began crawling backwards, crab-style, as fast as he could from Edgar. Suddenly, a boot flew past his ear, the heel of which smashed squarely into Edgar's right eye. His other boot landed close by, kicking dirt into Edgar's twisted face.

"There are your boots. Run! Hurry!" Emily shouted from above.

Hanson acutely felt the need to run. A small crowd of people was already gathering to investigate the commotion. Hanson grabbed the nearby boot and slipped it on. Edgar was rolling and moaning on the ground on top of the other boot that had knocked him senseless. It took several tries, but Hanson eventually recovered the boot from beneath Edgar and hurriedly pulled it on.

Standing, Hanson grimaced as he slipped into his shirt. He had just begun pulling up his suspenders when a policeman seized him from behind.

"Hold there!" the officer commanded, grabbing and pinning together Hanson's arms from behind. "What's this, now? What's going on here?"

"Arrest him!" Edgar blurted out, holding a hand over a swollen eye.

"Mister Ebenezer! What happened?" the officer inquired, recognizing the well-known shipper.

"He..." Edgar gasped, "he raped my wife, then assaulted me!"

"He didn't rape me, you bastard! And *you* assaulted *him*!" Emily shouted from the window opening.

Ignoring Emily's entreaties, the officer stated calmly to Hanson, "You're under arrest," then to Edgar Ebenezer, "I know you will appear, if need be," then back to Hanson, "but you're going to have to come with me, as I don't know you."

News of the altercation spread quickly around town. Hanson was left in jail pending bail. Several days passed before Sara finally came to visit and, when she did, she was painfully brief about the matter.

"Is it true you were having an affair with Missus Ebenezer?" Sara asked pointedly as she sat and placed a hand on the cold iron bars separating her and her husband, visually examining her battered, forlorn-looking husband.

"No. I was merely her employee, and was that day performing official duties," he pleaded in honest belief that without emotional involvement, there could be no affair.

He reached out to take her hand, but Sara pulled away. "I knew the first time I saw her at our apartment," Sara said, her voice wavering as she pulled a lace-trimmed handkerchief from her purse to dab the tears rolling down her cheeks.

"Sara. Darling. I need money and a lawyer. I didn't attack Mister Ebenezer, he attacked me, but he has filed charges against me for assault with a deadly weapon. I don't know how a boot can be considered a deadly weapon, and, in any event, I didn't throw it. His wife did," Hanson said, vigorously defending himself to his wife.

"I don't care!" Sara replied angrily through her tears. "I don't care who threw the boot! What has come between us…" she hissed, "…isn't the fight. It's the affair."

"But, don't you see…?" He began, only to be interrupted.

"You will have an attorney, Hanson. I will see to that," Sara growled and stood. Turning to the guard, she regained her composure and spoke sweetly to the young man in uniform. "I am *finished* with the prisoner. I should like to go now."

Two days later, Mr. John Greene, Esquire, visited Hanson Bumgardner, who was still in jail. "I have been employed by Sara to represent you, Mister Bumgardner. I have discussed this matter thoroughly with the prosecutor who has agreed to accept a plea of guilty to a lesser charge…"

"I am not guilty!" Hanson interrupted indignantly.

The lawyer raised a hand and continued, "The prosecutor will reduce the charge from 'assault with a deadly weapon' to 'simple assault' if you will agree to plead guilty. The sentence will be a five dollar fine and five days in jail. As you have already served the jail time and Sara has paid me the monies for the fine and my services, your release will be forthcoming, should you agree to the terms."

"Thank you, Mister Greene," Hanson agreed, realizing that this proposition was probably the best he could hope for.

That afternoon, Hanson appeared before the magistrate and pled guilty. After the hearing, he walked back to his and Sara's apartment to find a wagon waiting outside loaded with the furniture from Sara's dowry. Her father, Jonathan, and brother, Edward, were securing the load with rope.

"Hold up," Edward commanded, stepping between Hanson and the apartment house door.

"I need to talk to my wife. Please step out of the way," Hanson asked trying to maintain as pleasant a tone to his voice as possible.

Jonathan Reed stepped forward to join Sara's brother, leather satchel at his side. Pulling out several documents along with a small vial of ink and a stubby quill pen, he said, "She's done with you, Hanson. We're all done with you. These are divorce papers. She has already signed them and paid the fees. Now you need to sign them. Then, it will all be over, and you can go your way. Let go of Sara, Hanson, to start a new life without you."

"I need to talk to Sara," Hanson interjected.

"She doesn't want to talk with you. She left with her mother yesterday for Ritchie County," Jonathan Reed informed him.

"Is there nothing I can say then?" Hanson asked, his voice breaking.

"One day you will learn that it is what you *do,* not what you *say,* that matters in life," Jonathan Reed observed.

Hanson nodded and, with a heavy heart, signed the document.

# Chapter Six

Rain began lightly tapping on the platform about him. Hanson bowed his head, ashamed of his past actions. From his position on the gallows platform, he looked out upon his audience, drew a fresh breath, and shrugged. Once again his eyes drifted in hope to the distant horizon and beyond. What he hoped to see was his salvation coming towards him, but was rewarded with a gray lifeless haze. His hope failing, he acknowledged the truth of the sad end of his first marriage but assumed no blame. "Over time she had become increasingly unkind; so I found it beneficial to grant the divorce. Despite her unkindness, I was heartbroken, gentlemen, and took to drunkenness..."

Hanson, as if in a dream, entered the apartment to find little besides his clothes and a shot glass etched with an oddly fateful logo: "J. Bumgardner's Famous Rye Whiskey." That particular brand of whiskey soon became his closest companion, as he roamed from town to town presenting himself as a representative of his distant uncle's distillery.

In Virginia, on one beautiful afternoon, he walked into a bar along the Richie County border. Glancing about, he spied several bottles of Bumgardner's Famous Rye Whiskey displayed behind the bar. As he had done so many times before, he approached the bartender and spoke to him with a somewhat haughty attitude. "Sir, I am Hanson Bumgardner of the Bumgardner whiskey family. I'm here today to sample your stock to assure the family that it meets the quality to which our reputation is accustomed."

The bartender examined the man standing before him warily. The man's clothes were expensive, but worn and in need of cleaning.

"Good sir. I note your hesitation," Hanson baited his quarry. "Observe." He retrieved the etched shot glass from his coat pocket. "Would I have possession of this were I not whom I purport to be? Should I advise Jacob or his son James that you decline the quality testing and no longer wish to carry our brand in your establishment?"

"Oh no," the bartender replied, retrieving a half-filled bottle from under the counter and pulling the cork. "Here, allow me to pour you one."

Hanson set the shot glass on the bar and waited impatiently for the bartender to fill it. He lifted the glass to the light, peering through the caramel-colored liquid as he swirled it gently. He sniffed the amber liquid several times, then sipped from the glass, swishing the burning liquor back and forth in his mouth before spitting it into a spittoon on the floor. Then, he downed the remainder in a single gulp.

"An excellent blend, indeed," he said, nodding towards the several bottles displayed behind the bar. "I will need to sample each one," he added mechanically. Noting the bartender's furrowed forehead, he cocked one eyebrow and added, "to assure they have not been watered down, sir."

"You have a practiced eye, sir," the bartender replied. "Those are empties that I fill with colored water. When customers try to pilfer a bottle, they generally aim for one of those. I keep the bottle from which I serve under the counter. I have a barrel of Bumgardner's in the back from which I fill my under-the-counter bottle."

"I'll need to sample from that barrel, then," Hanson said in a business-like tone, while plotting to require the tavern owner to rotate the barrel several times in order to "assure the co-mingling of the liquor." Doing so would require several additional tastes, all for quality assurance.

"I think not," a gruff voice spoke from behind him. Hanson turned to see three men crowding around him. "We've been following you, *Mister Bumgardner*, if that is indeed your name. Me and the boys here are from the distillery. We told James Bumgardner that we were gonna find you and talk with you about this 'quality sampling' program you've been conducting." Their looks, however, indicated the men had no intention of talking.

"Good sirs. James told me himself…" Hanson began in rehearsed explanation.

"Naw, he didn't. He said you'd claim such and maybe even produce papers to back your story. You see, we're fed up with you using their good name. Your free ride is over," the largest man replied, cracking his knuckles. Two men immediately grabbed Hanson, lifting him from his feet and shuffling him towards the door.

"Hey! Who's gonna pay for the drink?" the bartender asked.

"Oh, he's gonna pay. Come outside and watch if you like!"

Hanson struggled, but with little effort the massive men carried Hanson to the center of the street, and threw him hard on the ground. Then they pummeled and kicked him until he lay limp and bleeding but still breathing.

The lead thug went back into the bar, retrieved the shot glass, and stood imposingly above the disheveled man lying in the street. "James said to make sure we didn't kill you, so that's our gift to you. Never present yourself as a representative of the Bumgardner whiskey business again, or you may not be so gifted the next time. You understand?" The man towering above Hanson hurled the shot glass against a tree, shattering it into thousands of shards.

Bleeding, ears ringing, his bones throbbing, Hanson nodded his understanding.

"Good!" the leader grunted before kicking Hanson in the stomach a final time. The three thugs clapped each other on the shoulders and shook hands for a job well done, then mounted their horses and rode away.

Hanson drew each breath slowly and painfully. Unable to stand, he crawled in the dusty street to the nearest building, a Methodist Episcopal Church, and leaning heavily against the building, passed out.

Standing under the hangman's noose years later, Hanson looked up toward a part in the clouds. The light rain stopped, the excess water spilling from the edge of the gallows to the mud below while he continued the enigmatic narration of his life in a softer, gentler voice: "It was there, in the depths of despair, that I met the only daughter of Eleven Riddle. She was a beauty, physically as well spiritually." The quiver in his voice revealed the depth of love he still felt for Elizabeth. "She was my soul, my love, my life…"

Two men jostled Hanson awake and placed him in a wagon. He tried to resist, but it was simply too painful. An angelic voice reassured him that he would be alright. He felt the wagon jolt and rumble ahead as he slipped back into unconsciousness.

It seemed like several days passed before he cautiously opened his left eye, his right one still swollen shut. He had no idea how long he'd actually been out, or where he was, but he could feel a layer of cool refreshing sheets above his naked body, and from the softness beneath he deduced he was in a down bed. His entire body throbbed and ached. Trying unsuccessfully to recall what had happened to him after the beating, he slipped back into sleep.

The next morning, he awakened to the enchanting face of Elizabeth Riddle. Her younger brother, Jim, slipped from behind her in between them to inspect Hanson's injuries in more detail.

"Good morning, sir," Elizabeth said sweetly from behind her brother.

"Um…good morning Miss…uh," Hanson replied, attempting to peek around Jim's bulk and see the source of the compassionate-sounding voice.

"Elizabeth, Elizabeth Riddle. This is my brother, Jim," Elizabeth said, pushing her brother gently aside and introducing the two.

"Good morning to you both. Where am I?" Hanson asked.

"At our family farm along Spruce Creek. My father is Eleven Riddle," Elizabeth answered.

Hanson thought hard, his head still aching from the drubbing he suffered, until he finally recalled the family name of one of the earliest colonial settlers of Virginia. They had been there since before the Revolutionary War. The family enjoyed a reputation of wealth and benevolence.

"It is not right to beat a man in the street like that. We have laws against sending paid ruffians to hurt someone, irrespective of what the person might have done," Elizabeth opined.

"Honestly, I think their actions were largely of their own accord. I don't believe the Bumgardners would do such a thing," Hanson said, sitting awkwardly, and in the process, finding new places that hurt.

"Well, you can rest here for now," Jim said. "What is your

name?"

"Hanson Bumgardner."

"Really? So you truly are a Bumgardner?" Elizabeth asked.

"Yes, from Harrison County."

"I know Mary Bumgardner from Ten Mile. Are you related?" Jim jumped in.

"She is my sister. My father is Addison Bumgardner."

The Riddles contacted Addison who brought Hanson home to recover. Over the next six months, Hanson regained his health and courted the beautiful Elizabeth Riddle. Jim acted as chaperone for the couple.

"Now I have two handsome angels to watch over me," Elizabeth said as Hanson and Jim accompanied her to church one Sunday morning.

"It is a glorious day God has granted us," Hanson professed joyfully.

"Hey! That's my line, Hanson!" Jim shouted, playfully shoving Hanson.

"Thanks be to the Almighty for bringing us together," Hanson said in a soft voice. "I could not have a better friend than you, Jimmy, or love anyone as much as I love you, Elizabeth."

As the three progressed towards the church, Hanson slipped one arm around Elizabeth's waist and the other around Jim's who, in turn, placed his own around Hanson's shoulder. Suddenly serious, he stopped. "I cannot swear off all alcohol consumption, but swear to never again over-indulge," he pledged to Elizabeth. Elizabeth, taken aback for a moment, smiled and laughed, accepting his promise and its implication regarding a life together.

As days passed, Hanson decided his rescue was an epiphany, later reasoning it was a call to the ministry. As it was a Methodist Episcopal Church where the epiphany began, and it being the denomination in which his Uncle George Bumgardner served as minister, he decided this was the denomination into which God was calling him.

That night, sitting on the hickory porch swing and talking with Elizabeth, Hanson said, "My uncle, George Bumgardner, is a minister in the Methodist Episcopal Church in Iowa and also works as a surveyor. I have decided to move to Iowa and apprentice under him."

"But, what about me, or rather…us?" Elizabeth asked, surprised at the firmness of his decision.

"You cannot accompany me, Miss Riddle," Hanson replied, "but you can join me as Missus Hanson Bumgardner, if you will." Hanson pulled a small silver ring from his pocket and paused it above the tip of her ring finger.

"Oh yes, Hanson, I will marry you!" Elizabeth replied joyfully.

A few short weeks later, they left Virginia together in a small wagon, trailing a saddle horse behind. Approaching a rise, Elizabeth turned her eyes back towards the home and family she was about to leave behind. "Though I'm nursing the heartache of leaving family, I am nonetheless joyful to be with you," Elizabeth said, returning her gaze to Hanson and squeezing his arm. She was already anticipating her wondrous life in the service of God together with her new husband, and the adventures promised by the frontier ahead. "I am so happy to be with you, Hanson."

"You are the better half of me, I confess," Hanson said, his blue eyes glowing down at her with love.

The wagon hit a rut throwing them closer together on the seat, and Hanson slipped his free hand about her waist, pulling her tightly against him as they laughed together.

# Chapter Seven

Settling in Iowa nearby his Uncle George and Aunt Sarah Bumgardner, Hanson took a job with a store making deliveries while he studied for the ministry. George wanted to introduce Hanson to the Muscatine Indians to whom he ministered, but they rarely showed. "I guess I'll have to work harder to get them to come to church, since I can't talk you into going to their village," he laughed. "Witnessing to the heathen is an important part of the ministry, Hanson," George gently reminded.

"I know, Uncle George," replied Hanson, "but my studies with you and the Bishop seem to be leading me to the church pulpit. Together with my job, it leaves me no time."

Leaning back, George smiled broadly and exhaled. "And you are becoming a better church preacher every day!"

The new year of 1857 found Elizabeth in her eighth month of pregnancy. Hanson came in to the house, the cold January wind following, stamped his feet and shook the snow off his heavy jacket. "This has been the coldest day I have ever lived through," he declared. "But, I earned three extra dollars today making special deliveries for the General Store."

"My! Three dollars! That's wonderful, Hanson," Elizabeth

replied.

"Yes. One dollar goes to the church building fund, leaving two for us to share." Hanson looked over his shoulder at his wife. She looked pale and frightened. Removing his outer garments, he knelt at her side. "Are you okay?" he asked, taking her hand in his.

"Um hum," she murmured through gritted teeth, attempting a smile.

"Elizabeth, what's wrong?" Hanson asked with growing concern.

"Pain. Too early. I have more than a month to go, but I am already having birthing pains."

"I'll go get the midwife," Hanson said, rising and reaching for his garments.

"No, husband, please stay," she pleaded, urging him back down beside her. "Hanson, something is wrong inside. A woman knows, and this…Oh!" she cried, her body cringing, tears forming in her eyes.

"What? What can I do?" Hanson asked, feeling the icy grip of panic.

"Nothing, my handsome angel. Be calm. The Lord will protect me," Elizabeth stated, attempting to soothe her distraught husband between what was becoming increasingly frequent hard contractions.

Within the hour, Elizabeth had delivered a girl. They named her Susan, after Elizabeth's mother. Hanson and Elizabeth praised God in prayer and song for the life of their daughter. Baby Susan cried in unison, suckled hungrily, then drifted off to sleep.

Elizabeth struggled to recover after giving birth. The premature child was healthy, but slight. During the next couple of days, the baby nursed vigorously, and the mother's strength visibly waned. A local midwife prescribed cow's blood to replace the blood Elizabeth continued losing, but to no avail. Fourteen days after giving birth,

Elizabeth Bumgardner died.

Her death devastated Hanson.

"I don't know what to do," Hanson shared softly with George one evening.

"Several times previously, you mentioned you felt called to go west to spread the word of God to the gold towns of California. Perhaps this is part of a greater plan to send you there," George offered by way of comfort.

"Yes, Uncle George. Perhaps it is, after all," Hanson wistfully replied. "But, first I must return to Virginia and spend some time considering this advice. Two mothers and two fathers there eagerly await meeting their new grand-daughter."

The next day, Hanson packed his belongings, packed the necessary provisions and located a wet-nurse wanting to return to the East to travel with him and the baby. Along the way, he sang hymns and repeatedly asked God why He'd taken Elizabeth from him. Eventually, Hanson came to believe that Elizabeth's death was a sign from God for him to go to California. The Lord, he reasoned, had taken Hanson's dearest earthly love in order to free him for the ministry with the conviction only a devout belief can engender.

Hanson, baby and wet-nurse arrived safely at Ten Mile to discover his father, Addison, in poor health. "Cancer" Addison's physician called it. Few had ever heard of this particularly fulminant form of consumption.

Hanson’s mother, Jane, was willing but nonetheless hesitant about taking in her granddaughter, Susan, in light of her husband's illness and Hanson's plans to travel alone to the western frontier. Her husband's condition already required her constant attention and had to remain her primary concern. Susan's care thus remained an unresolved matter in the Bumgardner home.

One afternoon, while Hanson sat on the porch, rocking his baby daughter, Elizabeth's brothers, Jim and Sam Riddle, rode up. "Jimmy! Sammy! Now you're are a sight for sore eyes!" Hanson called.

"How are you doing, Hanson? How's my little niece?" Jim asked smiling widely as he dismounted and approached.

"She's a sweetheart," Hanson answered, looking lovingly at his daughter.

"May I hold her?" Jim asked as Jane Bumgardner opened the house door to see who had arrived.

"Jim, Sam. Good to see you!" she said happily, standing on the porch and watching the men exchange the baby.

Jim cradled Susan Bumgardner in his arms and cooed at the infant, his eyes wet with tears. "I can see Elizabeth in her face…" His voice faltered in mid-sentence and trailed away.

Hanson stood and leaned against a porch post, resting his head forlornly on his forearm. Smiling back at his two young in-laws holding his precious daughter, he whispered, "Lord, give me strength to persevere."

Sensing the heaviness in both her son and his wife's two brothers, Jane stroked the baby's face lovingly and, with the practiced hand of a mother, dabbed away the tears from Jim's cheeks.

Looking up from baby Susan to Jane, Jim pledged, "Jane. I promise that if you will keep and nurture this child, as long as I live, you and she will want for nothing. I make this solemn oath before Almighty God that I will take care of the both of you, even if Hanson follows God's call to California."

"That comforts me greatly, Jim," said Hanson, crossing the porch and wrapping his arms around Jane, Jim and the baby.

"It comforts me, as well, Jimmy," Jane added, kissing the strong young man's cheek.

"You can count on me, too," Sammy added, blushing crimson when Jane kissed him, too.

At the mention of California, Hanson's brother, James, joined them from inside the house. He clearly had something important on his mind that he couldn't keep silent any longer. "Brother. You need to stay here to take care of your own, not pursue some imagined ministry."

"James, James, we've been through this before, I..." Hanson began to say.

"Did you not hear me, James? I will stand for the child. I will act as father if Jane and Addison become unable to care for him. Or, if you prefer, I will gladly take her now to our farm on Spruce Creek, where we Riddles will raise her," Jim responded.

"Thank you, but no, Jim. She is a Bumgardner. We should raise her, but I believe her father should do the raising..." James replied, casting an irritated glance at Hanson.

"War is coming!" Addison Bumgardner interrupted in his booming voice as he stepped onto the porch. "The fighting has started at last in Kansas by John Brown's men. Slavery is the issue, and I fear that the coming war may be so terrible that many of us will not survive. You must stay, Hanson, to protect your daughter, our family and the Union!"

"Father!" Hanson exclaimed. "I want nothing of war. I have pledged myself to serve the Lord. I believe he has called me to..."

"Yes, son," Addison interrupted again, wanting to hear nothing of it. "You've said so before, son. But James is right. You must stay here and raise your child, and should you be called, you must stand for your country!"

Hanson's brother, James, continued. "You have tried many different ways to earn a living, Hanson. Why not stay and farm with us? You know the old saying by John Heywood: 'Many hands make light work'. Then, if our nation calls either of us, we can enlist together."

"No. No war. The Lord's work comes before all other," Hanson replied, now resolute in his conviction.

"Hogwash!" Addison declared. "What makes you so pious? You are the only Bumgardner to have stained the family name by being arrested. And not once, but twice! You only recently decided after waking up from your latest drunken stupor that this was your calling. No! It's not right! You must stay!" Addison had become so agitated, he began coughing.

"Father, I respect you, but I *am* called," Hanson said emphatically as his mother led his father back into the house.

"No!" Addison yelled over his shoulder angrily between coughing fits.

"Maybe you should spend a few days with us, Hanson," Jim Riddle offered. Sam nodded in agreement.

Hanson accepted their offer and took Susan with him to the Riddle farm. He spent a couple of days with them before he packed his horse and left for California. After Hanson left, Jane reluctantly decided that it would be best if the Riddles raised baby Susan.

# Chapter Eight

"It is the greatest regret I bear," Hanson said from the gallows to his captive audience. "That the last words I had with my Father were angry ones."

One of the men looked up at Sheriff Hicks, pulled out his pocket watch, and pointed at it as he raised his eyebrows. Hicks scowled at him and nodded back towards Hanson as if to say, *Let him talk.*

"I headed for California anticipating a stay in Muscatine, Iowa, to finish my studies with Uncle George and Aunt Sarah…"

At the nearest town, Hanson purchased a black suit with a staid upright collar in anticipation of his new profession, believing that clothes made the man. He did not purchase the white clergy collar insert, as he wasn't yet ordained. A large black, round-crowned, wide-brimmed hat with a black satin hatband, called a preacher's hat, topped off his ensemble. Attired in this garb, and looking like a kind of traveling minister known at the time as a "saddleback preacher" or "circuit rider," he headed west, intent on completing his studies and dispensing God's graces to the uncouth gold miners in California. His days along the way were full, liberally sharing the fruits of his calling with fellow travelers.

In Indiana, he stopped to water his horse at a small stream.

Suddenly, a scream arose from a nearby covered wagon. Fearing the worst, Hanson called out defensively, "Hello there! I am Pastor Bumgardner. Is anything amiss?"

A man covered in sweat and wearing a huge grin appeared at the back of the wagon and called back, "On the contrary! I am a father! Hoorah!"

"God's blessing upon you and your family," Hanson returned, greatly relieved.

"A minister, you say? What a godsend," the man cried. Looking back into the wagon, he said, "Sally, your prayers are answered, for there is a minister right here to bless our child!" After pausing to hear her response, he shifted his gaze back at Hanson. "Come! Come! Give our new son your blessing."

It was Hanson's turn to pause. Up to now, he had simply shared the joy of his calling with others, but this time he was being called upon to act as a fully ordained minister. "It is not my blessing that matters, good sir, but those of the Lord," he replied cautiously, adding, "But I should be most happy to ask for His blessings for your son."

Hanson climbed down from his horse and into the covered wagon where mother and child were resting but awake. Cradled atop a makeshift mattress amid stacks of household goods, the young woman radiated motherly happiness.

Hanson knelt and prayed, "Dear Father in Heaven, Lord of the Faithful, God of the Righteous, hear our prayers. We beseech Thee to bless this young soul You have so generously given to this man and this woman. Bless this family that they might arrive at their destination safely. Give them Your guidance and be a light, illuminating the path they should follow. Bless this child…" Hanson stopped and looked over at the man. It was unlikely this new family would come across an established church with a fully ordained minister anytime soon. "What name shall I christen him?" Hanson asked, coming to a personal decision.

"William Charles Wilson, after my father and my uncle," the man replied.

"Bless this child in life, giving him the strength to resist temptation, the knowledge to know right from wrong, and place a love in his heart for his earthly parents as well as his Heavenly Father. I christen thee William Charles Wilson in the name of the Father, the Son and the Holy Spirit."

"Thank you, Reverend. Thank you," the woman said, smiling although exhausted.

*Reverend*, thought Hanson proudly. God moved the woman to call him thus, he reasoned, therefore, God was, in effect, ordaining him to do His work henceforth on His behalf.

Rain poured from the brim of his hat as he plodded across the Illinois prairie during the autumn of 1857. Continuing with stoic resolve on to Iowa, he slowly convinced himself that God was telling him that what he really needed was experience rather than study. Furthermore, it reinforced his perspective that, despite what his father and brother had said, his journey was no fool's errand.

He reined his horse to examine a river he needed to cross that raged before him. Having been informed of a safe ford, he followed the swollen river south in search of a crossing. Suddenly, over the roar of the water, he heard a voice howl.

"Help! Help!"

The cry seemed to be coming from the river.

Sitting up in his saddle to gain a better view, Hanson scanned the waters, hoping to locate who'd called out. A waving arm appeared then disappeared below the waters. Spurring his horse, he raced to the edge of the embankment and called out, "Hello! Where are you?"

"Here! Help!" the voice cried again, and Hanson glimpsed a man clinging desperately to a log hurtling downstream in the swift waters. Hanson spurred his horse downstream, determined to get ahead of the log. Seeing at last a sign marked, 'Ford Area', he directed his mount into the water. Much of the water at this crossing was being naturally diverted underground. There, in the lessened but still formidable current, Hanson searched for the hapless traveler.

Spotting him, Hanson shouted, "Here!" to get the man's attention. As the man looked up, Hanson tied one end of rope to the saddle horn and tossed the remainder at the man. Fortunately, the throw was true and the man caught it. Hanson spurred his horse against the charging current towards the shore. Horse, rider and victim struggled mightily, the horse finally making its way up the embankment. From there, Hanson, still atop his horse, wrapped the rope around both arms and pulled the man from the water onto the shore.

"Are you alright, sir?" Hanson asked, dismounting and walking over to the man. To his surprise, the traveler was an Indian dressed as a white man.

"Thanks you for saving me," the man said, coughing water from his lungs. "I am Wakoa of the Muscatine." The Indian coughed up more water. "I thought to make north ford, but water too swift. Lost… horse… wagon…everything. Went that away," he said, pointing weakly downstream.

"You speak very good English, Wakoa. My name is Hanson."

"Yes. I am Christian. Minister and wife spend many hours teach my people English."

"Your people?" Hanson inquired.

"My people," Wakoa repeated. "I Chief of Muscatine."

"The minister and his wife are to be commended."

"They not far from here. I go there. They help," Chief Wakoa said.

Hanson shared his horse with Chief Wakoa. After making their way through several bouts of foul weather, they arrived at a crossroads that Hanson recognized.

Chief Wakoa laid his hand on Hanson's shoulder and pointed in the direction of one dirt road. "Go here, Reverend George…"

"…is a mile and a half down the road!" Hanson finished the Chief's sentence. "Reverend George Bumgardner is my uncle!" Hanson revealed excitedly. "I am Hanson. Hanson *Bumgardner*."

"Praise God! I cannot believe! Saved twice in life by a Bumgardner! One saved soul, other saved life," Chief Wakoa declared happily.

Wakoa's rescue was cause for a grand celebration for he was indeed chief of his tribe, and Hanson was acknowledged a hero. The generous man told his people the story of the bravery of the Christian minister, Hanson Bumgardner, who was sent by Almighty God to save their chief from the clutches of the angry river.

Several weeks later, Uncle George sat with Hanson on the Muscatine church stairs, enjoying the sunset with Chief Wakoa and several other converts. "You know, it's dangerously late in the season to begin a journey across the Great Plains, Hanson," Uncle George offered. "I shudder to think of you riding alone on horseback all the way to California. You would at least benefit from a wagon and supplies."

"I have wagon. I help you this time," Chief Wakoa added, wrapping an arm around Hanson's shoulders. Wakoa's daughter, Aponi

—whose name meant "butterfly"—sat silently next to her father and smiling coyly in Hanson's direction.

"I have learned much from you, Uncle George. You have showered me with spiritual wisdom. I have also been blessed by Chief Wakoa with a rudimentary knowledge of Indian medicines and ample information on how to survive on the plains," Hanson said with deep appreciation.

"I hear the gold rush is over. Why don't you stay here?" Aponi ventured, unable to hide her desire for Hanson.

"Aponi, though your kindness and beauty tempt me, I must go where I am called," Hanson replied softly, revealing publicly for the first time his feelings for her. "Half a million men have immigrated to California since 'forty-nine. It is their souls, not their gold or my own personal satisfaction I seek."

Uncle George laughed good-naturedly. "Their camps will be easy to locate. Wherever there is gold, men follow."

John Bumgardner, George's son and Hanson's cousin, joined them on the church stairs and called for all to listen to a jaunty new song he'd learned on the flute. Everyone clapped their hands as Cousin John played, while skipping a jig across the porch.

Hanson felt Aponi's eyes still upon him and flashed her a bright smile, knowing in the process that he would taste her lips at least one time before he left.

That winter, they began meeting secretly and kept the secret well hidden. Having also seduced several of the settler's daughters during that same time, Hanson told each woman to keep the relationship confidential, explaining that, as he was seeking ordination, any hint of misadventure could prove fatal.

As the spring of 1858 neared, Rev. George announced a revival to raise money to help Hanson obtain supplies for his impending expedition. Within a few days, word had spread through several Iowa counties and across the river to Illinois about the upcoming camp meeting.

Hanson finished his sermon: "...'if anyone would come after me, he must deny himself and take up his cross and follow me. For whosoever wants to save his life will lose it, but whosoever loses his life for me and the gospel will save it. What good is it for a man to gain the whole world yet forfeit his soul?' Thus sayeth our Lord Jesus Christ, in the Bible at Mark 8:34. In like manner, I hereby foreswear the gains of the world in order to preserve my everlasting soul. 'Whosoever' means anyone; I am that 'anyone', taking up the cross after Him! I will enter the bawdy gold towns unafraid. I will call these lost flocks back to Him in His name! I need only your kind assistance to get there!"

Hearty cheers and "amens" resounded loudly throughout the tent. Chief Wakoa stood in the *de facto* "Indian section" of the tent surrounded by a couple of dozen converts, including his beautiful daughter.

"I give this man a wagon and a mule. Pastor Hanson save me from swift waters," the chief pledged. Louder cheers and "amens" greeted the chief's announcement. Hanson smiled his winning sweepstakes smile and bowed formally from the waist towards the chief.

"And here," the chief lifted high above him a beaded hatband with a silver cross in the center. "This from my daughter. Wear it to show you are minister to our people." The cheers, especially among the settler's daughters, were more constrained this time, as Hanson gratefully accepted and Aponi came forward to tie it onto Hanson's hat.

"The plate is going around as I speak," added Rev. George. "We don't ask for much, and certainly don't give if you cannot afford it. But with God's grace, we will raise enough to send this man of God off with enough supplies to make the gold fields of Californy!" George quickly solicited volunteers to pass additional plates through the crowd.

A few days later, Hanson, Uncle George, Chief Wakoa and Aponi packed the small but stout wagon Wakoa had provided. The chief took a moment to stroke the neck of the harnessed dark brown mule lovingly. "This mule have good spirit and strong back. Also pleasant most of the time," Wakoa informed Hanson.

"What is his name?"

"'Mule'. He is mule; has no name," Wakoa shrugged.

"Then I will call him…Banjo," Hanson replied, smoothing the neck of the mule as Wakoa had done. The mule nodded his head and brayed as if pleased with both his name and master.

When all was ready, Hanson stood in the front of the wagon and spoke his final farewell to the crowd of relatives and female admirers who gathered in front of the church.

"I lay my life in God's hands and proceed into the great unknown."

Several female sighs drifted from the crowd.

"Whatever happens to me, I know without a doubt it is the Lord's plan. Thank you, Uncle George and Aunt Sarah, for all your kindnesses. John, keep practicing on your flute; someday you will play in front of hundreds! Chief Wakoa, thank you for your insights into Indian culture and lore; moreover, thank you for the lessons on how to survive on the plains. Aponi, thank you for believing in me. Uncle

George, those long hours tutoring me in the scriptures and the ministry will never be forgotten. I promise. Farewell till we meet again on the other side."

Hanson sat, adjusted his hat and cracked the whip above Banjo's ears. The wagon jerked to a rumbling start on the trail west. Hanson turned and waved to the onlookers. With sad eyes, Aponi stood next to her father in front of several other teary-eyed young women, all of whom Hanson had deflowered during his stay.

John Bumgardner played a cheerful tune on the flute as the wagon rattled slowly into the distance. Hanson smiled, listening to the merry music diminishing behind him, as Banjo pulled the laden wagon forward. Hanson, alone again, was already missing them all.

# Chapter Nine

Hanson followed the California Trail across Nebraska, evidence of the tens of thousands who'd trudged the trail before him lying discarded on either side the trail. Sun-bleached oxen, horse and mule skulls, and every manner of personal item lay strewn across the Great Plains. Occasionally, a make-shift wooden cross appeared in stark reminder of the human toll.

Banjo was a reliable mule and ate far less than a horse or an ox. He acted cantankerous at times, but Hanson quickly grew to like and respect the steadfast animal.

At one point, Hanson came upon some wagons stopped at a low-water crossing. The animals were drinking their fill, their masters refilling water barrels. The six wagons were separate from a larger commissioned wagon train about a mile ahead. "Followers" like these were typically kept far away, but the wagonmaster of the train ahead was more tolerant.

"Good day and God's blessing upon you. Do you mind if I join your company?" Hanson asked, displaying his warmest smile.

"We could use a minister to bless our meals," Mrs. Clayton, a passenger in the first wagon, observed, returning Hanson's smile.

"And another rifle in case of Indian attack," grumbled the more cautious and disagreeable Mr. Clayton.

"I have never fired a gun," warned Hanson. "I do not think it to be the act of a man of God."

Mr. Clayton spat at the ground in response to Hanson's comment while several other drivers chuckled.

Hanson joined the group following the wagon train. At a watering spot a few days later, Clayton called out to Hanson, "We are on schedule to arrive at Independence Rock, our halfway point, on Independence Day." As Banjo joined the other animals and drank greedily, Clayton continued. "I do not desire to winter over in Nevada or Utah." His comment was met with a chorus of "Hear, hear" from the other travelers.

One afternoon in late May, huge threatening clouds appeared on the western horizon. They looked like the ones Chief Wakoa had warned him about, menacing clouds that produced terrible storms that only arose on the plains.

Standing to survey the approaching storm, Mr. Clayton shouted above the growing whine of the wind, "We need to seek shelter from the storm that's acomin'. There's a protected area about a half-mile back where we can ride out the storm."

Clayton turned his wagon and led the others to a low rocky cutout. Wagon wheel ruts leading into the arroyo revealed that others had taken shelter there. Remains of campfires were scattered about. The group made their way into the shelter, lining up side-by-side along the solid stone inner wall under the overhanging rock. Hanson was left outside in the open; Banjo had picked this moment to make another of his statements of defiance and wouldn't budge.

In the distance ahead, he could see the two dozen or so wagons in the commissioned train circling together for protection. Several of his fellow travelers shouted from the shelter beckoning him, but Banjo refused to move. Hanson slapped the leather reins sharply against the stubborn mule's back, for he could smell the oncoming rain and hear booming claps of thunder. Banjo continued to ignore him.

The wagon train ahead disappeared into an opaque wall of rain. The dry heat of the day suddenly became unbearably heavy and humid. Concerned, Hanson cracked his whip over Banjo's ear, but to no avail.

Hanson grabbed the brim of his hat, barely saving it from a sudden hurricane-like gust of wind. In the sweltering heat, the back of his black suit darkened further with sweat. Shoving the hat under a bundle inside the wagon, he roundly whipped the mule's back. The mule brayed and stamped its feet, but would not join the other wagons. The sky turned an odd green-gray color, a sinister shade that Hanson intuitively recognized as dangerous. Hanson heard an eerie roar and looking west saw a huge black funnel cloud drop from the darkening sky. Whirling winds howled, scrubbing clean the plateau as the sun backlit the grinding black winds and magnified their appearance. Huge widely-dispersed drops of wind-driven rain began pelting him. The roar turned to a rumbling he could feel coursing up from the ground and rocking his wagon. Captivated, he watched the half-mile-wide tornado suck up the circled wagons. Men, women and children, trying to run away, were lifted into the air and disappeared.

Pieces of debris whirled about in the roaring winds, as the white of the wagon tarps flashed here and there, swirling in the dark grip of the cyclone. Then the funnel suddenly lifted from the ground and receded into the clouds, tossing people, animals, and bits of destruction about, discarded, dead.

Hanson's stomach roiled at the thought of the hundred or so

deaths he had just witnessed, and he pushed hard on the brake with his foot as he leaned out to vomit. Bending over the wagon wheel, he felt a different rumble course up from the ground and rattle his bones. Hanson couldn't identify the source, but it was continuously gathering in strength, implying it was drawing near. It felt like the rumble of a waterfall. Suddenly, he recalled Chief Wakoa's warning to stay away from cutouts, hollers and dry creek beds in a prairie storm, because sudden floods could happen. Hanson jumped down, ran towards the cutout and shouted, "Get out! Hurry! Come up here!"

Curious about the commotion, Mr. Clayton pushed his head out of the back of his wagon the same moment a wall of water twelve feet high came crashing down the arroyo. The water sucked wagons, animals and people into its brown muddy slurry, dislodging and hurtling them down the riverbed. Screams of drowning people and braying animals mixed with the roar of the water, only to be silenced seconds later by the flash flood that swept them away.

It was all over in an instant. Not one of his fellow travelers or the wagon train they followed survived.

Hanson Bumgardner sank to his knees and prayed. "Lord, have mercy on their souls. Give me, your humble servant, the strength to continue on..." The rest of his prayer mixed unintelligibly with uncontrolled sobs. The sole survivor, Hanson regarded his situation as a final proof of the importance and sanctity of his calling.

# Chapter Ten

Hanson made his way alone to Fort Laramie, Wyoming, reported the deaths, refreshed his provisions and continued westward. Ten days later he arrived at Independence Rock, well ahead of schedule. There, he joined several other "independent" wagons for the last leg of the arduous crossing.

Traveling westward, the families, one by one, dropped off the path to California—one with a broken axle, a second who's infant died, another simply too exhausted to continue. Each had its reasons for stopping or turning back. The harsh trail constantly drained the strength and resolve of all who travelled it. Hanson soon found himself proceeding west alone; a sole wagon on the vast American plains.

As Banjo plodded along, Hanson practiced sleight-of-hand and card tricks, perfecting his "magic" skills, although his only audience was an indifferent Banjo.

One day, the trail came to a split; one set of wheel ruts headed north, the other continued west. Hanson selected the westward trail, unaware that it led across Shoshone lands. When he noticed no evidence of recent wagon trains along this rutted trail, he slowly became concerned. Although there was good grazing for Banjo, he had encountered no streams to fill his dwindling water barrels. Despite his growing misgivings, he knew nothing better than to keep moving.

The next morning he walked alongside Banjo through the shoulder-high grass, enjoying the morning sun, when suddenly the animal stopped. He encouraged the mule to continue, but Banjo remained steadfast, his nose twitching from side to side. The mule brayed loudly and pulled to his left, away from the trail. Recalling Chief Wakoa's advice about listening to animals, Hanson released his grip on the bridle, allowing Banjo to follow a previously indiscernible path to the left. A hundred yards along the rough path, Banjo stopped before a pond. Although the surface area wasn't large, its cerulean blue color suggested great depth.

Hanson inspected the pond for mineral deposits. Finding none, he leaned close to the water and sniffed. Detecting no malodor, he touched the clear surface and brought his wetted finger to his tongue. Satisfied it was safe, he allowed Banjo access to the pond. The grateful mule quaffed deeply.

Knowing he could not lift a full barrel without help, Hanson used a deep pan to scoop water from pond and carry it to the barrels. He was working on filling the second when he heard an unusual bird call. Pausing, he listened intently. When he heard it again, it had changed to a clucking whistle. Banjo snorted, stamped, backed away from the pond a few paces, tossed his head and brayed loudly, stamping his feet again. Hanson looked about, knowing the mule was signaling something wasn't right.

As if on signal, a half-dozen Shoshone warriors charged from their hiding places in the tall grass. Yelling and shouting, they encircled Hanson and his little wagon.

"Eeeiiii," shouted one warrior who smacked the mule and then Hanson smartly with a stout stick.

"Eeeiiii!" the others shrieked, jumping into his wagon and tearing into his possessions. Item after item arced out the back and thunked onto the ground. A ripped bag of flour followed, creating a thick white cloud when it hit. A crate of Bibles flew out and crashed open upon the ground.

A brave snatched the preacher's hat and, grinning, placed it upon his own head, while the apparent leader growled as if disappointed by the dearth of objects littering the ground. Hanson locked gaze with the leader, trying not to let the fear churning in his gut show in his eyes. The Indian regarded Hanson for a moment, then suddenly struck him soundly on the forehead with his stick. Hanson crumpled to the ground unconsciousness.

A splash of water in the face reawakened him. His hands were tied together in front, and a coarse leather lanyard tied snugly around his neck hung loosely behind.

The Indian who had stolen Hanson's hat jerked up on the lanyard, forcing Hanson to his feet, whereupon another kicked him in the rear and motioned him to move along. Hanson walked barefoot; the second Indian tramped alongside him proudly wearing the prisoner's boots. They walked for less than an hour to their village.

As Hanson entered the village, buckskin-dressed women came out from their tepees to whistle, scream, spit and kick dirt at him. From their utterances and the designs on their clothes, Hanson determined the Indians were the Goshutes of the Western Shoshone tribe that Wakoa had warned about. They were protectors of sweet-water holes and were the only tribe to claim this barren western part of Utah where salts and minerals commonly poisoned much of the water.

His captors directed him into a tepee, pounded a stake in the center ground, and tied the leash to it. His jail apparently also served as storage area, holding blankets, quilts, animal hides and the like.

Once a day, a young but homely Indian woman, perhaps twenty years of age, opened the tepee flap and placed a bowl of tepid stew barely within Hanson's reach. Sometimes, she would squat and watch him eat the mush with his fingers.

"Do you speak English?" Hanson asked repeatedly, always with no sign of recognition. Despite this, he began talking to her daily in a calm reassuring manner, smiling continuously, trying to gain her confidence. A few days later, having established some sense of rapport, he motioned as though he were putting more food in the bowl, and was pleased when, the following day, the bowl contained a more generous serving.

One late evening, as the lights of campfires tinged the sides of the teepee red, the flap was suddenly pulled back and two braves rushed in with sticks and began beating him. After several blows, Hanson, dazed and confused, was untied and dragged from the tent.

The medicine man approached and spoke loudly in broken English. "They think you medicine man," he said, pointing at the hatband in his hand that Aponi had made for him, "But you not!" He raised the hatband in the air for all to see and slapped it down across Hanson's face. Then, turning to the women, he said in Shoshone, "There is nothing to fear! He is not a medicine man no matter what symbols are on his hatband!"

"Please, I am a man of God," Hanson pled aloud. At this the men pounced on him and beat him until he passed out.

# Chapter Eleven

Time passed slowly, until one day the Indian woman who fed him pulled back the flap, entered the tepee and, to his surprise, closed the flap. She looked somehow different.

She pointed at him then herself. Hanson raised his eyebrows, cocked his head to the side, and turned his palms upward to signify he didn't understand. She pointed more emphatically, this time clearly at his crotch. Hanson mimicked the motion and she nodded and smiled.

Kneeling in front of him, she directed his bound hands to her breasts, then reached down and softly grasped Hanson's privates. Aroused, Hanson speculated this must surely be God's way of providing for his release. Leaning forward, he kissed her gently. The next thing he knew, he was untied, and they made love until both were satisfied.

The pattern became an almost daily encounter. One afternoon, she arrived with a sister and together they shared Hanson. Completely exhausted by the time they retied him back to the stake, he was nonetheless hopeful that his salvation might be at hand. It was just a matter of time before his caretaker became careless.

It was raining one afternoon when the two women entered and the three began lovemaking. Hanson moved back and forth from one woman to the other. After several hours, the three were exhausted. They reposed in the afterglow, a woman on each side of him resting her head on his chest. The rain continued drumming hypnotically on the hide walls, lulling them to sleep. Clinging to consciousness, Hanson lay perfectly still until he heard the sound of rhythmic breathing from both sides. Today, he thought, was the day to make his escape. He slowly slipped from underneath the two women. Carefully and quietly, he unraveled his dirt-crusted clothes from the several buffalo hides tossed in passion to the side.

Without warning, the tent flap jerked back and three Indian braves rushed into the tent shouting and whipping the three. A confusing melee ensued. Hanson dove under a buffalo hide to hide his nakedness and keep from being beaten. The three Indians immediately dragged a naked Hanson outside into the cold rain, and using sticks, feet and fists, pummeled him into the mud. Coughing, trying to protect both his privates and head, he curled into fetal position.

A loud whoop startled his tormentors. A war club knocked one brave savagely to the ground; the second and third fell victim to the same club. Hanson cringed in the mud and the other Shoshones who'd been gathering about him turned to face the interloper.

The men were about to rush the warrior with the club when a gun shot rang out. The intruder moved astride Hanson, club in one raised hand, revolver in the other, then pointed the Colt at the angered, but motionless Shoshone braves. "Stop beating man of God!" Chief Wakoa demanded. "Stop or his God strike you all dead!"

Hanson looked up startled.

One brave removed a hot iron poker from the fire and shook it at the chief, shouting in Shoshone, "You do not belong here. He is our slave. We caught him naked with our daughters. He must pay for this!"

"He is my slave," the chief asserted in formal Paiute, Shoshone being a Paiute dialect. Paiute was also the language used for trading between prairie tribes. "He escaped from me. I thank you for catching him. I will pay you for his keep. The Muscatine are not involved in your dispute with your women. I claim the right of killing this slave if I desire," Wakoa said.

Hanson was still curled on the ground, hoping the Shoshone would not simply kill them both, when he observed the Shoshone braves lower their weapons. All, that is, except the one holding the hot poker. He raised it higher, steam puffing wherever rain drops hit the red-hot metal. The old warrior rushed forward, waving the poker overhead, intending to leave a mark on Hanson's face as was custom for the Shoshone in cases of rape.

*Crack!*

A blue-white bolt of lightning streaked down from the black churning clouds and hit the upraised poker, killing the brave. A thunderous concussion followed knocking everyone about him off their feet.

Sprawled in the mud, the acrid smell of burned flesh filling his nostrils, Hanson struggled to regain his vision and hearing. The quiet sound of rain drops striking the mud about him was the first thing Hanson noticed. His eyesight returned more slowly, at first, only in sepia. Slowly, color began to return.

Chief Wakoa, who had been standing to the side and in back of Hanson, recovered his eyesight and senses more quickly, and jumped to his feet. "You see!" he cried, again in Paiute. "He is a man beloved of the white-eyes' God! His God has killed your brave. Help me put this slave in my wagon. I have medicine even greater than yours or his to keep him my slave! Watch out for his evil eye! I will offer you a fine pony for him, if you want payment."

The leader of the Shoshone pushed up from the ground onto one elbow. Coughing and spitting blood, he said in Paiute, "Take him. He is nothing but trouble. I do not want your pony in trade. Go now!"

Wakoa helped Hanson to stand, placed his arm around Hanson's shivering body and led him to the back of a wagon. Hanson climbed in and was shocked to see Aponi sitting quietly, wide-eyed at his condition. He collapsed next to her and she covered him with a blanket. As she cradled his head in her lap and lovingly stroked his face, he realized, just before passing out, she was with child.

# Chapter Twelve

When he opened his eyes, the rocking wagon canopy above him glowed brightly like the inside of a lightbulb. Remembering where he was, he sat up, noting his black wide-brimmed hat with the beaded hatband jostling about on top of a water barrel fastened to the wooden sideboard of the crowded wagon. On the floor next to the barrel and within arm's reach was a clean shirt and pants. Hanson stood with difficulty and dressed as the wagon rattled on. Finished, he climbed out into brilliant morning sunlight.

"Good morning, Chief. Good morning, Aponi. God's grace be with you," Hanson greeted.

Chief Wakoa cast a stern glance in his direction.

"Thank you for rescuing me from the Shoshone. How is it you found me in the wilderness?" asked Hanson more contritely.

"Met Shoshone brave on trail wearing black hat with hatband Aponi give you. Made him tell where to find owner. He hard to convince, but told me just before he died."

"Why?" inquired Hanson. "Why did you come looking for me?"

Wakoa nodded towards Aponi, and said, "She with child. Your child, she says. This true?"

Looking down, Hanson replied, "Yes, I suppose the child could be mine. But I have been gone a long time. Five months."

"She five months, Hanson. Child yours. We find you, so you can..."

Hanson nodded in agreement. "Yes, we will marry. It is the right thing to do."

"The right thing to do," repeated the chief, continuing, "It late in season. We hurry back or have to face winter here."

The chief paused as if searching for the right words. "I not know why they beat you. I not know why you and maidens naked. I not want to think bad of you, Hanson."

Hanson nodded, neither denying nor confirming the chief's suspicions. Instead he smiled, placing his hand on Wakoa's shoulder, and said, "God works in mysterious ways, Chief. Praise God he sent you to save me when you did. I owe you my life."

"You save my life from the waters of river. My debt to you paid. We even, Hanson Bumgardner," declared Wakoa with finality.

Hanson looked at Aponi, sitting quietly next to her father, silhouetted against the bright yellow rays of the sun, and acknowledged that she would be both a beautiful mother and fine wife. "No, sir, I will forever be in your debt," he replied, flashing a winning smile at Aponi.

The chief smiled and nodded his agreement, "She could have anyone. Glad she choose you."

"No more than I, sir. No more than I," replied Hanson, realizing fully for the first time the true beauty of his *de facto* wife.

That afternoon, rumbling eastward, Hanson and Aponi sitting next to each other on the tailgate of the wagon, Aponi pointed toward a cloud of dust rising in the distance.

"Rider coming! Running hard!" Hanson shouted forward to

Wakoa.

Wakoa looked westward and saw the dust cloud being blown to the side by the strong steady prairie breeze and decided to stop. While they waited, Wakoa reloaded his revolver. They watched as the cloud drew closer. It was Aponi who broke the silence. "There is no rider!"

Squinting, Hanson suddenly recognized the charging beast. It was Banjo! As the mule approached, he slowed to a walk, and finally a dead stop directly in front of Hanson.

"They let him go," Hanson said with disbelief.

"They think he bad spirit like you," Chief Wakoa surmised.

Hanson climbed down to examine the exhausted animal. Panting, snorting, stamping, white foam about his mouth, Banjo nuzzled him lovingly on the arm. Hanson retrieved the drinking ladle and offered the beast some water. Banjo extended and flexed his head, braying loudly in thanks. They all laughed. As Hanson gently stroked the mule's flanks, Chief Wakoa noted, "I tell you, that one loyal mule!"

Late one evening several weeks after their escape from the Shoshone, they stopped to camp. The prairie turf was hard and the grass sparse. While Wakoa tended the animals, Aponi began gathering grasses for the animals and sun-dried buffalo droppings for a fire. She was close to six months pregnant and showing. As she bent over to cut a clump of prairie grass, she heard the familiar sound of a rattlesnake's warning. She froze, swiftly scanning the ground and looking for the well-camouflaged creature. A burning stab pierced the back of her calf, and a second strike hit before she could react to the first. Panicked, she dropped the basket and ran towards the wagon. "Hanson! Father!" she cried, the running pumping the poison throughout her system. "Help me! I've been bitten by a snake!"

Chief Wakoa dropped the horse brush and ran to her. Lifting and carrying her to the back of the wagon, he rested her on the tailgate. Wakoa immediately pulled his knife and sliced open her calf. "The blood must run," he explained to Hanson who stood helplessly watching events unfold.

Aponi was sweating profusely and barely breathing. "Father, the snake's spirit has me…"

"Be calm, daughter. Lie still. Bleed out his poison. You will…" Wakoa assured, holding her closely as she began shaking.

"Father…Hanson…" the two words issued from her parted lips like a soft summer breeze. Aponi ceased breathing, and her beautiful eyes glazed.

Hanson decided not to return to Muscatine, Iowa, with Chief Wakoa. Distraught at having re-experienced love, only to have Aponi and his child wrenched from him by the henchman of the devil, he felt compelled to conclude he'd misinterpreted his calling. This time he would get it right: He would return to Virginia and study medicine. In deference to the generous man who had saved his life and to the time they had shared, Hanson gave the wide-brimmed hat and hatband to Wakoa before departing for the familiar Virginia mountains.

# Chapter Thirteen

Standing on the gallows, Hanson looked down at his feet, momentarily lost in the memory of Aponi, recalling their youth and her beauty, but when he tried to picture her face, he found her features had blurred with time. He reflected for a moment on how the years dissolve the memories of even the most momentous events.

The city clock bonged once, signifying the passage of a half-hour of time. Hanson drew a cautious breath, and looked anxiously at Sheriff Hicks, who nodded permission to continue.

"I came back to Pocahontas County, Virginia, where I met my present wife..."

Late in the autumn of 1858, Hanson heard of a Dr. Thomas Brown, who was looking for an apprentice. Dr. Brown would best be described as a combination herbalist, pharmacist, healer and midwife. Having lived and practiced in Highland County, Virginia, for many years, he had earned his title the hard way, by successfully serving the residents and garnering their respect in the process.

At the appointed time, Hanson sat on the doctor's wide porch next to a dozen other men, all desiring to understudy the renowned practitioner. Hanson noted, not without satisfaction, that he was the best dressed and presumed, by what he heard of the small talk among those assembled, to be the most articulate. As he waited, he carefully contemplated how to best present himself and secure the position.

As another rejected candidate exited the house and departed, Cynthia Brown, the doctor's wife and helper, called out Hanson's name. Welcoming him into their home, she directed him to the parlor and Dr. Brown.

Brown, sitting behind an ornately hand-carved desk buried in books and journals, was busy penciling notes on a piece of paper and absently waved him to come sit next to him. Hanson walked to him, but instead of sitting, broke right into conversation: "Sir, you need not waste your time recording information from the previous interviews, for you have, this moment, found your apprentice. I have read the great authors, Hippocrates, Homer, Shakespeare. I have crossed the Great Plains and fought Shoshone Indians with my bare hands! Yet, look at me, sir. Do I appear just another bumpkin? Do I dress as a farmer or frontiersman? No sir. I dress as a physician. The men waiting on your porch may make fine lumberjacks or teamsters. I cannot do those things, sir. But, I have been called by the Great Healer to lessen the pain of the afflicted, and need only your mentoring to begin."

Hanson showed the palm of his right hand, pointing at it with his left index finger. He turned his right hand over to show the back of the hand. Swiftly circling his hand twice, he made his calling card appear between his fingers. Bowing slightly, he handed the card to Brown.

Dr. Thomas Brown was impressed. His thick lips were curled in a wry smile at Hanson's *braggadocio*. The doctor looked at his wife, and, receiving her nodded assent, said, "Send the others away, Cynthia. I will mentor this one in the profession."

While his wife cleared the porch, Dr. Brown laid out his conditions of apprenticeship. "You understand that my apprentice must live here, in this house, with me and my family. You have met my wife, Cynthia. Soon you will meet my daughter, Elizabeth, who is about your age, as well as Amanda and Martha, our two younger teenage daughters. They will tutor you in basic nursing. I will personally mentor you in herbalism and pharmacy. As you can see, my farm is an orchard. You will assist with the harvest and in the greenhouse, where I grow my herbs."

Hanson nodded his agreement to each condition.

"You will also assist in the general upkeep of the house and in the seeing of my patients, for as you can see, I am advancing in age. Your compensation will be room and board plus ten dollars a month."

"I am as familiar with the hammer and saw as with the classics," Hanson replied, avoiding any comment regarding the doctor's young girls, recognizing that living with several beautiful young women could prove to be difficult given his past experiences. Instead, he made a silent solemn vow not to cross the line with any of this generous man's daughters. Hanson concluded the deal, saying, "Sir, I am happy with the arrangements."

Hanson spent the next two years living with the knowledgeable herbalist, honoring his vow of celibacy, concentrating all of his attention on his studies. Hanson watched and assisted as people from all over the state came to receive the healing potions Dr. Brown concocted.

In his instruction, Brown particularly emphasized the careful choice and measurement of each ingredient, warning, "Be very cautious, Hanson, as mistakes of this kind can prove fatal. Proper grinding and mixing are also essential to the efficacy of a potion."

Before continuing, Dr. Brown winked. "But truly, sir, in confidence, my potions and tonics are mostly alcohol, and the best alcohol to use is Bumgardner's brand of rye whiskey." Brown lifted a canvas tarp to reveal a barrel of the rye, bearing the familiar trademark branded in the oak. "Many people simply need a little whiskey to ease their normal aches and pains, and to sleep the night through. Unfortunately, many live in dry counties or have religious objections to alcohol consumption. My potions and tonic permit them a means to imbibe without guilt. Others simply believe alcohol works differently in a medicine bottle. Selling effective potions and tonics is the underpinning of a good pharmacist these days."

Hanson had heard this lecture before and knew that the carrier liquid selected was, in many cases, just as important as the ingredients, and waited patiently for his mentor to continue.

"We have many patients," the doctor said, replacing the tarp, "with cancer, the deadly wasting disease only recently described in the European medical journals. I am unsure how to treat it, but anything that takes away the pain is a blessing. When potions and tonics are no longer effective, I have taken to compounding a special elixir of morphine," Brown revealed. "You excel in potions and tonics; it's time for me to teach you how to create these powerful and dangerous pain-relievers."

Under Thomas Brown's guidance, Hanson quickly mastered this final phase of his pharmacological training, and began seeing and treating patients by himself. Soon everyone began to call Hanson "Doctor Hanson." He tried with great frustration to garner the more proper, "Doctor Bumgardner," but the more familiar name stuck. Slowly, he began to understand and accept the moniker as a sign of high respect from these mountain folks who were his patients.

"Many doctors these days are taking to the roads," observed Brown, cigar smoke circling around his head as they relaxed in the parlor together one mild evening. Brown let the observation hang in the air between them for a while before continuing. "They drive wagons filled with their medicines and travel about, bringing their practice to their patients instead of the other way around. Given your penchant for travel, Hanson, perhaps this approach could benefit the both of us. I propose to build and provide an apothecary wagon for your use. If you accept, you will pay me twenty-five percent of the profits from your travels. You will need to develop a strong signature elixir to establish your name. People love such elixirs, and, as you know, become rapidly accustomed to daily dosages. You'll need a good tonic recipe, and enough ingredients to compound the various potions during your travels, returning here whenever you need to restock."

"I agree without hesitation," Hanson answered excitedly. "Shouldn't we patent the signature elixir?"

"A good suggestion, but let's see how sales go first. So long as we keep secret the ingredients, there is no pressing need to submit a patent application. I have a trusted source of reasonably-priced liquid morphine in Kidville. I will introduce you to him, so you have direct access to my source, and do not have to return here quite so often."

"Thank you, sir. No man could have a better mentor," Hanson said, standing and shaking Thomas' hand vigorously.

Less than a month later, Hanson perfected his recipe for his signature elixir. For his tonic, he blended rye whiskey with honey, cinnamon and several other herbs in minute amounts. Finally, he created a potion base of watered-down rye whiskey to which he added extract of willow bark. The willow would add an analgesic effect to the diluted whiskey, and together, they served as the perfect base to which he could add powdered herbs specific to the patient's problems. He then selected and reviewed with Brown the herbs he would carry with him. They tested the tonic with success on a patient with lumbago, and finally the elixir on a patient with advanced cancer, who reported blessed relief.

Several weeks later, Brown presented Hanson with a fully stocked apothecary wagon. Two doors opened from the back to reveal a built-in chest of drawers for all manner of herbs and supplies along with an all-important mortar and pestle. Forward of the chest was a storage area that carried hundreds of pint bottles of potion base, elixir and tonic. Besides a place to sleep, there was even a removable semi-circular rod, which held a curtain that could be drawn around the rear of the wagon for private examinations.

Hanson was particularly proud of the large stylized letters on the sides of the wagon proudly proclaiming: "Dr. Hanson Bumgardner Apothecary" At the bottom in gilt was painted, "All-Natural Healing from the Wonders of Nature." A waterfall scene set within a circular laurel wreath adorned the center. Below that was a wide step that slid out from under the wagon on either side to serve as a platform from which to address the crowds.

"And the labels turned out wonderfully," Brown said, holding up a bottle of tonic and another of elixir each sporting a black and white miniature woodcut of the scene on the side of the wagon substituting, "Dr. Hanson's Tonic" or "Dr. Hanson's Elixir" for the phrase "Hanson Bumgardner Apothecary" "The bottles are a different size and shape so a patient can find the right one even in the dark." Brown grinned, proud of his foresight.

"Sir, I don't know how to thank you," Hanson replied.

"Sell lots of elixir and return regularly with my cut!" The elder man laughed.

"I shall, sir. Yes, I shall," Hanson declared.

Several days later, he climbed aboard the loaded wagon and struck out. His first stop was Spruce Creek to visit his daughter, Susan, who hardly knew him. Uncle Jimmy had served faithfully as her father with Grandma Riddle acting the mother. Grandma Riddle's own child, Louisa, was the same age as Susan, and Hanson was happy to see the toddlers playing together like twins.

Down the trail at the Bumgardner residence in Ten Mile, his mother, Jane, looked weary and drawn. When her husband, Addison, had finally died, James assumed the role of man of the house, caring for his mother and sisters. Hanson felt sad he hadn't been able to do more than send a few bottles of elixir to his dying father. Their last words had been angry ones between principled men. Hanson stayed but an hour.

Traveling southward through the countryside, Dr. Hanson offered his services and refined his sales presentation. His personal favorite was privately examining people and preparing special herbal potions for them. To his potion base he added different combinations of ingredients learned from Dr. Brown and from Chief Wakoa. Business was good; Dr. Hanson quickly made a name for himself.

One morning, Hanson rolled into the Pocahontas town square, set the brake, and placed a feedbag on Banjo. Pulling out the stage from under his wagon, he stepped up with a megaphone and called out: "Gentlemen, ladies, and children of Pocahontas! Gather 'round! Have you ailments? Afflictions? Cancer? Ulcers? Bleeding gums? Have you other medical concerns? Come one, come all! Dr. Hanson is here to ease your sufferings! Trouble sleeping? Try a pint of Dr. Hanson's Tonic to ease your mind."

A crowd quickly gathered, and Hanson pulled a pack of cards from his pocket. He leaned over and encouraged a young lady to "pick a card, any card." When she shyly complied, he took the card from her, licked the back of the card, and stuck it on his forehead face out displaying the queen of hearts to all but himself.

"I have the unique ability to discern this card through 'thought transfer'. Everyone concentrate on the card." He closed his eyes and feigned concentration. "Yes! Yes! I am getting it! I see a queen. Yes, it's a queen! It is a red queen! And from so pretty a lass, it *must* be the queen of hearts!"

The audience applauded loudly while he removed the card from his forehead and turned it to "confirm." He placed it back in the deck and slipped the deck in his pocket. "Now, you will see…" Hanson began.

A shout interrupted him. "Charlatan! That there deck is a fraud. It's made up of only the queen of hearts," a man in the back of the crowd shouted. "Show us the deck! Show us, if you dare!"

Hanson deftly pulled a second deck of cards he kept in the same pocket and fanned it outward to the audience, displaying the various suits and numbers. More applause. The skeptic, defeated, quietly slipped away.

"As I had begun saying, you will see remarkable improvement in your strength and vitality following the very first taste of my special tonic, but, I'm sorry to say, you will not gain the magical insight just displayed." As a wave of laughter rippled through the crowd, Hanson continued. "Gentle people, step forward. Bring me your aliments! Don't be afraid—there's a woman who knows what she needs! Step right up, Madame."

"Will it ease gout?" an older man in the back asked.

"No, Sir, it will not. But if you will see me after this presentation, I will gladly examine you and create for you a personalized prescription. Just take a number from the hook." He waved the man towards the back of the wagon and continued. "I will see all in need of personal attention in the order of the number drawn. Now, who needs a tonic for hiccups or back pain? Only four bits—a mere one-half dollar —buys a bottle of this fine tonic. Who will be the second? You, sir?"

Hanson sold ten bottles of tonic. Looking to his left, he noted with pleasure the new crowd gathering about the number hook. Stepping down and sliding the platform back underneath the wagon, he pulled a semi-circular rod from the top back area and smoothed the curtain hanging from it. Inside the curtain, he examined his first patient, the old man with gout, who proved to be far from sober.

"Sir, your gout is caused by too much alcohol, eating only red meat, and sitting most of the day. You need to stop drinking, eat only vegetables for a month, and exercise daily." Hanson climbed into the back of the wagon and concocted a powder. "Put this powder in…"

"What's in it?" the old man interrupted.

"Fungi and other plant materials, dried and crushed," Dr. Hanson replied. "Use it in milk, as it has a foul taste. Follow each dose with a spoonful of honey. Do this twice a day, morning and evening. I also recommend a bottle of my rejuvenating tonic to help you sleep better."

The doctor was so sincere in his advice that people rarely ignored his recommendations. When challenged, he could produce mountains of anecdotal evidence confirming the therapeutic effects of his advice, potions, tonic and elixir. In the end, everyone was urged to buy a bottle of tonic; elixir he reserved for only the most severely afflicted.

His second patient of the day stepped inside the curtain and sat on the patient stool.

"Good day, sir. How may I help you?" inquired Dr. Hanson.

"Sir, my urine smells right horrid and it is difficult to pass."

"Have you low back pain?" Dr. Hanson asked, walking behind the stool and tapping the man over the kidneys. The patient jumped in pain.

"Lift your shirt, please," Hanson requested and the man complied. Observing the reddish swelling and warmer temperature of the skin, he concluded the man had a kidney infection.

Dr. Hanson climbed into the back of his wagon and drew open a drawer, removing one of dozens of small bottles of sticky white birch sap. Opening another drawer, he gathered a handful of dried leaves and placed these on the table. He poured the sap onto the leaves, allowing it to soak in, then rolled the leaves together and placed them in a small bag. "Boil these in a quart of water. Drink the liquid from a shot glass four times a day. This bag will make eight days worth of potion, and by the time you finish drinking it, your back will feel better. Your urine will improve as your back problem subsides. That will be a dollar fifty, but I strongly suggest making it two to take with you a bottle of my special tonic, to be used after the potion is consumed."

The man gladly paid Dr. Hanson and hurried out from behind the curtain to begin his treatment.

Hanson drew the curtain aside for the next patient, a lovely well-dressed woman who hobbled in and sat on the stool. "How may I help you today?" he asked with the smile that melted hearts.

"It's here," the woman said, as she lifted her skirt to reveal a foot and ankle wrapped in dirty bandages.

Kneeling before her, he carefully unwrapped the bandages. It proved difficult to avoid wrinkling his nose and turning his face away from the foul smell.

"What happened?" he asked.

"I was cutting firewood for cooking, and..." Hanson's patient began to explain, but Hanson already knew.

"The axe skipped off the wood and hit your foot," he interjected.

"Yes, how did you know?"

"I have seen this before. From the appearance, the wound is about a week old," Hanson explained.

"Yes, you are good."

"I hope so, because I usually have to refer this type of injury to a surgeon," Hanson further explained.

The young woman paled at this news. "I… I had hoped it would heal on its own," she stammered in horror.

Dr. Hanson stood, entered the wagon, pulled open various drawers and took out the needed herbs. Using green moss as a base, he prepared a poultice.

"The moss will draw out the infection, and there are herbs in it to aid in the healing," Dr. Hanson told the woman, packing it around her foot. "I will need to see you every day for a while, Miss..."

"Lewis. Susan Lewis, but you, sir, may call me Sue," she replied, looking up into his eyes with anxious hope.

Hanson looked away and concentrated on wrapping the wound.

Hanson and Sue met each day over the next fortnight. He changed the bandage and poultice at each meeting and was as successful in saving her foot as he was in kindling their budding romance.

# Chapter Fourteen

"And you call yourselves reporters?" Hanson scolded the two newspapermen standing closest to the edge of the gallows, shaking an index finger in their direction. "You reported me to be a bushwhacker, yet you didn't mention what I truly am: a dedicated doctor. You deny me my deserved title, and refer to me only as 'the prisoner'. I saved Susan Lewis' foot from amputation! I saved literally hundreds of lives in Camp Chase during the war, and for others I eased their suffering. Cervantes was correct when he said, 'A man dishonored is worse than dead' for though I die today, the dishonor you heap upon me will live forever."

Hanson stopped his chastisement to take several deep breaths, move away from the edge, regain his composure and continue. "I fell in love with Sue and she with me..."

Susan Lewis was a natural beauty with long brown hair and brilliant green eyes. The infection in her foot healed slowly. Hanson stayed with Dr. Brown during this period to visit, square accounts and to rest, not minding riding the twelve miles to Pocahontas daily to visit the comely Ms. Lewis.

Late one evening, Dr. Brown looked up from the account book and chided, "My, my, Hanson! You must have the devil's tongue! It surprises me how quickly you were able to sell out your inventory."

"The services I carry to the people are well received. They confide to me inside the black curtain what they would not tell their local physician or priest," Hanson observed.

"I *knew* the country was ripe for mobile medical care!" Brown declared, pleased with the outcome of his investment. "One need only see the rapid proliferation of the railroads to discern that we live in an increasingly mobile age, a wonderful age."

"It would be infinitely better, though, if people would put aside their differences," Hanson observed in reference to the growing tensions between North and South being reported daily in newspapers across the nation.

"I agree," Brown confided. "It seems Northerners have not taken the opportunity to travel south before deciding what is best for us here in the South. Despite all our advances, men still seek to impose their will upon others. Rather, they should seek to soothe the ills of others, and comfort them in loss. I only hope this November's election will allow all men to shout and rant what they might so they will feel it possible to join together as a nation once a new president takes office."

"Growing numbers speak of leaving the Union," Hanson reminded Brown. "The Carolinas seem particularly bent towards it."

"'Tis ballyhoo intended to sway the election," asserted Brown.

"There is talk that if Carolina attempts to leave the Union, there will be civil war."

Hanson watched as Brown pursed his lips in thought. "This could benefit you, Hanson. You should continue honing your skills as a physician, and consider joining the army if war comes."

"I want no part of war."

"War is a terrible thing, I agree," said Dr. Brown. He looked thoughtful again for a moment before chuckling. "Perhaps you are correct not to offer your services to the military when, instead, you can charge for healing civilians whose doctors have gone off to war. If civil war breaks out, civilians will be in greater need of your services, potions, tonic and elixir. You are shrewd, Hanson."

"I am not trying to be shrewd, Thomas. I merely have no stomach for slaughter," Hanson reiterated.

A bright June afternoon in 1860 found Hanson still at the Brown farm, compounding new potions. A knock at the door interrupted his concentration. He heard an unfamiliar voice asking questions, and Cynthia Brown reluctantly answering. Hanson stopped his working and walked to the door to find a census taker, marking down her answers. The census taker was asking about the “boarder,” Hanson Bumgardner. When asked his occupation, Mrs. Brown related with a smile, "Hanson is more like family than a boarder. He's a doctor; a cancer doctor, helping the afflicted."

Hanson beamed at her attestation of his profession and watched as the census taker dutifully wrote "cancer doctor" though it was clear from his facial expression he had little idea what it meant.

In the autumn of 1860, Dr. Hanson Bumgardner and Miss Susan Lewis were married in a private ceremony with only family and a few friends attending. Jim and Sam Riddle were there, having brought with them little Susan, much to Hanson's joy.

Despite the women's best efforts, party conversation quickly turned to the election, slavery and the possibility of war.

"I am not so sure all slaves should be immediately set free. Perhaps Gradualism is the best solution. That would allow them to adjust to being a free people," Jim Riddle proffered.

"How can anyone be a partial slave?" James Bumgardner

challenged. "No, slavery is wrong. It must be abolished completely."

"The Bible commands slaves to be loyal to their masters, to obey them and serve them as we all should as slaves of Christ," Hanson gently reminded his younger brother.

"Where exactly does it say that, *Reverend* Hanson?" James snapped.

"Ephesians six, verses five through eight," Hanson replied calmly. "And I did not receive the title of reverend, brother. I was a deacon of the church, no more."

"But you can call him doctor," Thomas Brown interjected.

"Yes, he has earned that title," James admitted, grudgingly proud of his older brother.

"I believe slavery to be wrong; however, like the majority of people, I am not sure how best to lay this institution to rest," Brown said, puffing his cigar and continuing his erudite exposition. "Slave owners say, and rightfully so, that they cannot be deprived of their property without due process. Our Constitution explicitly supports this. To free four million men, women and children without compensation to the owners or slaves would be a disservice to all. Where would they go? How would they live? Might they not, in their desperation, take jobs at wages so low as to be slaves once again? And, in doing so, wouldn't they displace millions of white men from the jobs they currently hold? No, we need a plan to accommodate everyone, one which allows for slaves first to be educated, so they can make appropriate decisions as any citizen might. It will be a long process, not a single event of emancipation."

He puffed his cigar again before continuing.

"The abolitionists reject these arguments, demanding immediate liberty for all slaves, whatever the consequences. Yet I wonder if their new condition might be as bad or even worse than slavery. The Abolitionists do not consider the economic impact of their demands," Brown opined softly, not wanting to incite an argument. "And that is my point. Rushing too quickly into this could cause an economic collapse, rivaling the Panic of '37 when Van Buren fiddled in the White House while our economy collapsed. No, we need not endure more years of depression in order to free the black man. Free them gradually, I say, *and* preserve our economy. But make no mistake about it that, in the end, I am a Unionist. I believe in the Constitution."

Raising his voice, James declared, "The Union and Constitution forever!"

"Hear, hear!" everyone shouted.

"Amen," added Hanson along with several of the women, who seized the opportunity to turn the conversation to lighter subjects.

# Chapter Fifteen

But wishful thinking was not enough to keep the Union together. Secession did happen and, once it began, states quickly aligned themselves on one side or the other. Wanting none of it, Hanson bid Thomas farewell, and he and Sue headed west in the fully-stocked apothecary wagon and another laden with their household goods to Kentucky, one of the few neutral states, to begin their new life together.

One evening along the way, while Banjo grazed alongside their two horses hobbled to a static line, Hanson and Sue discussed ideas on how to support his practice.

"I must especially conserve the elixir, as it is a long way back to my source in Virginia for morphine. I want to locate a closer source in Kentucky. In the meantime, I will substitute laudanum, a tincture of morphine, but it is weak and its potency can vary widely from one brand to another. The tonic I can make from any rye whiskey although I prefer Bumgardner's."

He mentally chuckled, wondering what James Bumgardner's self-appointed thugs would think of his tonic. He typically sold as much Bumgardner whiskey in a month as many taverns.

Sue nodded at each of his points, the flicker of the fire

illuminating her smiling face, although her eyes revealed other concerns.

"What is it?" he coaxed, patting her on the arm.

"We are going to have a baby," she announced, watching Hanson's reaction.

"Hurrah!" Hanson shouted, holding her close. Not wanting to reveal his trepidations, he shouted again, "Hurrah!"

In June 1861, Hanson and Sue occupied a small house in Maysville, Kentucky, situated near the last stop on the Underground Railroad for slaves before the safety of Ohio. The Ohio River ran low here, creating an easy ford. For Hanson the ford was important to establishing a traveling medical practice in southern Ohio as well as Kentucky.

One evening after dinner, Hanson sat reading a newspaper generously provided by a patient from Cincinnati. The paper was only four days old, and he found the news both compelling and disturbing. "Bad news, Sue. The Second Wheeling Convention has voted to reorganize the Virginia Legislature."

"What does that mean?"

"This upstart unionist group has declared itself the 'true' governing body of Virginia. The Yankee Congress will certainly recognize this second legislature in Wheeling. It means they've succeeded in dividing our state." Hanson’s voice revealed his apprehension.

"Where will the dividing line be, Hanson?" Sue asked anxiously.

"Here is a map they have produced," he continued, showing her the newspaper. "It looks like they just drew a straight line north and south cutting right through many counties."

"Hanson, my family farm is in this new state of West Virginia," she observed.

"Yes, as is my mother's farm. But Thomas Brown's place is in Old Virginia," Hanson replied. "To visit and settle accounts, I will have to travel back and forth between the two states."

Discerning Sue's face furrowed in distress, Dr. Hanson assured her, "I need not use major roads, which will likely be bristling with border guards from both camps. I know the forests well."

The nation, in the meantime, continued to plunge into civil war. Throughout the country in both the North and South, men were forming regiments to do their part in the "glorious" struggle. Vicious skirmishes flared up here and there around the nation, including Manassas and Wilson's Creek, where thousands of young men became instant casualties. The Confederate States of America (CSA) was busy celebrating victory after victory.

Dr. Hanson traveled through central Kentucky and south central Ohio to small towns where doctors and medicines were scarce. He provided comfort to those in need. His tonic sold well, particularly in the 'dry' counties of Kentucky. Profits streamed in.

In early September, after their first son was born, Hanson and Sue traveled to unionist West Virginia for a visit. Leaving Sue and infant son George with her family in Pocahontas, Hanson set off to settle accounts with his mentor, as promised.

That night, Hanson slipped silently through the forested mountains into Confederate Virginia on foot. There were several water crossings, however, where he had no choice but to travel the road for a dozen yards or so to cross a bridge.

Hiding in the bushes, Hanson inspected the road in front of one such bridge. Convinced the way was clear, he jumped out of the forest onto the road, and walked as fast as he could across the bridge.

Halfway across, he heard voices. In the far distance ahead, he saw the flickering of dozens of torches, and knew he must make the far end of the bridge before the soldiers arrived. Breaking into a run, he sprinted for the other side, jumping from the end of the wood trestle bridge into the awaiting arms of a narrow tree near the water's edge. He stopped there, panting and peeking around the thin tree as several confederate scouts appeared and began searching the bushes along the road.

A whisper from the tree line startled him. "Hanson, over here!"

Hanson saw the white flash of a lady's handkerchief. Crouching low, he scurried along the riverbank to a grove of larger trees.

"Here!" the same female voice called. A moment later, Hanson joined Elizabeth Brown in the far corner of the grove behind a large tree. Her face was dotted with perspiration and her breasts heaved as she gasped for breath.

"They are searching for me, but do not know it. They are trying to locate the traitor who passed information on their troop strength and movements to the Yankees," Elizabeth explained.

"What? Why?" Hanson whispered in confusion, while the lines of cavalry slowly continued to make their way down the road.

Elizabeth pulled Hanson to her, wrapping her arms tightly around him to disguise their silhouette. Their faces were less than an inch apart. Her blue eyes gazed directly at his chiseled face, alternately lit by the red of waving torches and the blue of the waxing gibbous moon.

"There," shouted one of the soldiers, "behind the tree!"

Elizabeth pulled Hanson to her, pressing her lips hard against his as scouts surrounded them, their rifles, illuminated by torchlight, at the ready.

"Hold!" a private shouted, pointing the muzzle of his gun directly at the two.

"What?" Dr. Hanson asked a sergeant stepping forward, saber drawn. "Can secret lovers have no secrets anymore?"

The sergeant lowered his saber and laughed, turning to the private. "Ah see you have at last found the secret lovers we've been so ardently searching for! Ah am so sorry, Miss Elizabeth. Please excuse us."

Elizabeth squinted against the light. The voice was that of Jonah Wright, a former client of her father's. "Please, kind sir. My dignity. I seek only privacy," she purred sweetly.

"And so you shall have it," the sergeant said. Turning about to address the growing semi-circle of anxious young confederate soldiers, he said, "Put down your arms! Ah know this family well. Their farm lies barely a mile away, men. Let us leave them to their rendezvous. The traitor we seek must surely have crossed the bridge. We must hurry! By your leave, ma'am," he said, touching the brim of his hat. The others followed Sgt. Wright along the embankment and over the bridge.

"Elizabeth, what are you doing?" Hanson asked as the troopers disappeared into the darkness. "Why are you spying for the Yankees?"

"I cannot stand idly by and through inaction support slavery. I want to help the cause of freedom. Even though our farm lies in old Virginia, I support the Union."

They made their way along a path through the trees to the Brown farm where Thomas Brown anxiously awaited his eldest daughter's return.

"Elizabeth! I was so worried," her father gushed as she entered the parlor with Hanson. "And Doctor Hanson, what a great surprise! How did you make it past the guards and patrols on both sides?"

"We pretended to be lovers, Father," Elizabeth interjected,

blushing red. "I only hope it does not damage Hanson's reputation as a chaste and honorable man. Jonah Wright, the son of that horrible gossip, Mary Wright, found us. He is now a sergeant in the CSA. I fear less his saber than his mother's wagging tongue," Elizabeth related with concern.

"I am not surprised…about Wright siding with the Confederacy, I mean. On the matter of you and Hanson as 'lovers,' well, you do what you have to do in war. I am sure his wife, Sue, will understand. It is better than having Hanson locked up, eh?"

"I have no desire to be locked away," Hanson affirmed. "I believe Sue would have similar feelings about this matter."

Everyone had a quiet chuckle.

Later that evening Hanson and Thomas sat together before the fire, enjoying fine cigars while catching each other up on the news. The next day, after they updated their account books, Hanson happily delivered his mentor's portion of the earnings.

On Tuesday, news arrived by a neighbor of the defeat of Gen. Robert E. Lee at the Battle of Cheat Mountain. It was his first offensive as a CSA Commanding General. CSA forces were reportedly scattered and retreating along the roads in the Allegany Mountains.

Hanson decided to use the confusion to return to the Lewis household in West Virginia where Sue was awaiting him.

"I will not go back to Kentucky," she began after hugging him tightly. "It is dangerous here, but this is where my family is, should I need them. I fear Kentucky will soon be overrun by Yankee forces. I can not live and raise a family under continual martial law as the citizens of Missouri now suffer."

"But my darling, I have customers in Kentucky…" Hanson began.

"You will gain new customers here. Old Doc Brown is near retirement and will happily pass on his patients to you. Further, most West Virginia doctors have enrolled in the army. You can service the many patients they have left behind."

A knock at the Lewis household door interrupted their conversation. Sue stepped forward cautiously and opened the door. There stood a wounded corporal, holding his grey kepi hat in hand. "Beggin' your pardon, ma'am, but we was told Doc Hanson could be found hereabouts."

Hanson joined Sue, looking past the corporal into the faces of a half-dozen wounded soldiers standing behind. "Have them sit on the porch, corporal. I will be out to examine them in a moment," Dr. Hanson ordered.

"Yes sir. Thank you, sir," the corporal replied, a look of hope on his grimy face.

Hanson looked at Sue. "Perhaps you're right. Perhaps I am needed here, at least for now, but I will have to eventually return to Kentucky to retrieve our belongings."

Sue smiled and looked to her sisters who nodded their approval. "My sisters and I will prepare bandages. It appears you will need them," Sue said as Hanson headed out to the porch.

Dr. Hanson diligently attended to the wounded soldiers, stragglers from the Battle of Cheat Mountain. It never occurred to him that these wounded men were confederate soldiers, and as he was in West Virginia, a Union state, his caring for these soldiers could be regarded as treason and result in his arrest. Hanson saw only their wounds and suffering, and immediately set to work.

# Chapter Sixteen

The winter of 1861 in the Allegany Mountains was hard with freezing temperatures and heavy snows. Military operations ground to a halt until December thirteenth when Union Gen. Milroy's forces attacked the confederate stronghold at Camp Allegany in Pocahontas County. A vicious daylong battle ensued in a razor-sharp winter wind. The battle was indecisive, but resulted in over three hundred casualties, and once again, survivors found their way to Doctor Hanson's farm for relief.

On this particular day, three Union and four Rebel soldiers waited for treatment in the Hanson parlor while a cold wind whistled outside. Hanson pulled a minié ball from the side of a Union soldier and dropped it on a tin plate with a clank, saying as he bandaged the wound, "You boys should agree to sit down to a game of poker to settle your differences." He chuckled, but did so alone. Glares as sharp as bayonets crossed the tarp-covered floor. Seeing them, he continued, "When this is all said and done, we will all still be Americans."

"'Zat so?" one of the confederates snapped. "They'll still be 'Damned Yankees' and I'll still be a Virginian. I'll still hate them."

Hanson, shocked by the comment, asked, "And who might you be?"

"Gabriel Clem, Thirty-Third Virginia Infantry." Clem walked across the room and shoved a hand towards Hanson. Six foot tall with gray-green eyes, sandy hair, faint freckles, and a gawky gait, he looked more like an oversized adolescent than an adult.

Hanson wiped his bloody hands on a towel, grasped Clem's hand and examined him quickly. Seeing no obvious wound, he shook his hand. "Where is your wound, soldier?" he inquired.

Clem pulled up his trouser leg, revealing a dirty bandage covering his lower calf. Hanson pulled away the soiled bandage and noted a minor slash. The angle, direction, and shallow depth of the wound suggested to him that it might be self-inflicted.

"How did this happen?"

"You didn't ask them Yankees how they was wounded, Doc, so's how come ya askin' me?" the infantryman snapped at Hanson. "I'll tell ya, though: Yankee bayonet—he fell when I kilt him. His bayonet caught my leg."

"I see. Well, the good news is that the wound is slight, so you will be able to rejoin your unit right away," Hanson observed.

Clem harrumphed loudly and looked nervously about the room. "Jus' patch me up, doc, so's I can get outta here." He cast a hateful glance at the Union soldiers. "So's I kin get back to killin' Yankees."

Years later, as Hanson stood rigidly at the edge of the gallows platform, addressing the reporters and relating Clem's ugly sentiments, Hanson raised his hands, palms upturned, emphasizing what he felt was the salient point, his hanging. "That was when I first met Gabriel Clem. He could save me now by just coming forward and telling the truth about this mess involving Woods and Gollier. He has been like an evil shadow following me since that day he entered into my life. Now, on this most fateful day, he is sadly the one man who could confirm the truth about what happened to John Eubanks, the man I stand convicted of killing, and clear my name." There was a distant longing, a searching in his voice. The audience and sheriff watched Dr. Hanson look again over the wall. "Months later," he continued, "in August 1862, I was compelled to return to Kentucky to save our household goods from CSA General Kirby Smith's invasion of Kentucky…"

After packing his household goods into his old covered wagon, Hanson headed east to avoid Smith's men, who, fresh from their victory at Richmond, Kentucky were headed north. Union Cavalry ordered Hanson off the roads as they headed southwest to stop Smith's advance. Hearing sounds of battle a few miles distant, Hanson hid in an abandoned barn. Though it turned out to be only a minor skirmish, he decided to wait awhile longer before continuing his journey, preferring the shelter of the barn to the uncertainty of running into another battle.

Several hours later, he saw four riderless horses walking together along the road. They were Union cavalry horses, three mares following one stallion. Hanson rose cautiously from hiding, placed a finger on either side of his mouth and trilled a two-tone whistle. The stallion responded, coming quickly to him. He led the stallion into the barn, the mares following. Hanson located each animal's feeding bag, filled it with grain, and hung it over the animal's head. Removing the tack from each horse, he noted one saddle streaked with blood.

Bumgardner was contemplating what to do with his newfound herd when a dozen wagons rumbled into view. Looking through the boards of the barn, he saw they were quartermaster wagons flying the confederate flag. A colonel led them on a dark red horse. Hanson walked casually to the fence, waved and flashed his trademark smile.

"A good day to you, sir. What is it that you need of me, sir?" the colonel asked, reining his horse and touching the brim of his hat courteously.

"Good day to you, too, sir. I have four horses for sale," Dr. Hanson replied.

"As you might guess, we have no need for plow horses at this time, my good man." The colonel turned his horse away and back towards the passing wagons.

"I have no plow horses; however, I do have four trained cavalry horses for sale, sir," Hanson replied.

The colonel, intrigued, reined once again and twisted to get a better look at the man. "And how did you acquire these horses?" he asked.

"I whistled and 'poof' they appeared." Hanson snapped his fingers, pulling out of the air the business card he kept up his sleeve.

Laughing at the trick, the colonel inquired further. "And where exactly are these magical horses, Mister...?"

"*Doctor* Hanson Bumgardner, sir, at your service." Hanson gave a grand sweeping bow and handed the colonel his calling card.

The colonel called a rest break and dismounted. Hanson led the colonel and two soldiers to the barn where the horses underwent thorough inspection.

"Three hundred dollars each," Hanson quoted.

"A hundred," replied the colonel.

"Two hundred, sir. A bargain for trained horses."

"One hundred fifty. For stolen war contraband," the colonel countered.

The thought that he was selling war contraband hadn't entered Hanson's mind. Appalled, Hanson reconsidered who he was dealing with and convinced himself he was simply selling 'lost and found' property. Laughing at the thought, he remembered Thomas Brown's comment, "In war we do what we have to do," and he continued negotiations."Two hundred twenty-five," Hanson answered.

"You went up, sir. That is not a very good tactic." The colonel smiled back at the doctor.

"True, colonel, but for that price I will add in the tack for each of the mounts. And fine tack it is, with wool blankets, McClellan saddles, and saddlebags," Hanson explained.

Laughing heartily, the colonel said, "Two hundred each, complete with tack, no more."

"Done," agreed Dr. Hanson and they shook hands on the deal.

Several privates gathered the horses, tied them to one of the wagons and placed their tack in another. To the north could be heard the sounds of another skirmish. Everyone stopped and listened anxiously to the loud booms of artillery, followed, on the breeze, by the pops of hundreds of rifles. The battle was over quickly, but each knew that the suffering inflicted would linger.

The colonel pulled an iron-plated quartermaster chest from the second wagon, and began counting the money into Hanson's hands. "...two hundred fifty...three hundred. And this," he said, "is a Quartermaster's Certificate of Debt owed by the Confederate States of America for five hundred cash dollars or the equivalent in gold. Total payment is eight hundred, as agreed."

Surprised, Hanson asked, "Where do I cash this certificate?"

"At the Paymaster's Office in Birmingham, Richmond or Atlanta, or the one in Staunton, Virginia, if they still have some gold there."

"But, we had a deal. I don't..." Hanson began.

"It is payment in full, as agreed, sir. You did not specify cash. Furthermore, I could not have agreed to payment in full with cash. I will be happy to pay for any other horses, wagons or mules you may be able to obtain, but they must be paid by certificate. You are a civilian. It is a small matter to go to Virginia to get your funds. I must go now. The bugle call you hear calls us to assembly." The colonel replaced the cash box in the wagon, mounted his horse, and ordered the column forward, turning to wave as he rode away. He had purchased four horses with tack for only three hundred dollars. No one was foolish enough to attempt to cross the lines during active battling to seek payment. At least, that's what he thought at that moment.

Hanson watched the wagon train pull away for the assembly point to resupply the confederate troops. He was happy about the three hundred dollars he'd received for pulling in a few strays. It was more than most men made in a year. And another five hundred dollars awaited him in Staunton, Virginia, if he dared to cross the lines. It was then the idea came to him that, as a doctor, he would likely be accorded the courtesy of crossing the line with impunity. Rethinking his situation, he also considered the officer's open offer to purchase contraband of war and became intrigued by the potential profit in it.

Hanson cautiously returned to Ten Mile in West Virginia to his sisters and mother. One evening after supper, Jim Riddle stopped by the Bumgardner home, bringing with him Susan, Hanson's first born. Everyone gathered on the porch while Susan played in the yard.

"I've spent the past year getting my affairs in order so that I may join a regiment and serve the Union," Jim told Hanson. "The Tenth West Virginia Infantry is being formed, and Sam and I are joining. You should join with us and be the regimental doctor, Hanson."

"The only way I will ever wear a military uniform is at the point of a sword," Hanson vowed. "This damned war has split our nation, yea, our very state asunder. I will tend the wounded of both sides. A uniform would only restrict those who I may help." Though the conversation would meander in different directions the rest of the night, it was these words of Hanson's which were prescient.

# Chapter Seventeen

Dr. Hanson had to cross the state line through a steep pass near McDowell Crossroad on his way to Staunton to redeem his Quartermaster Certificate of Debt at the Paymaster Office. Having heard rumors that the army was conscripting everyone who traveled this way, he decided to sneak through on a moonless night.

The pass was well guarded, but Hanson slipped past several sentinels and three guard posts on the uphill side unnoticed. Mounting his horse, he rode downhill. He'd traveled less than a hundred yards before he heard a shout from out the darkness. "Halt! Who goes there?"

"A friend," Hanson called back, surprised. "A doctor."

"Advance and be recognized," the voice commanded, then, "Sergeant of the Guard, post number three!"

Hanson kneed his horse gently as he strained to see who was challenging him.

"Hold there and dismount," the voice commanded.

Hanson grudgingly complied with the order and immediately felt a sharp blow to the back of his head. Everything went black.

Several hours later, he awakened, hands tied at the waist. His captors wore gray uniforms with black cuffs and collars, identifying them as partisan rangers.

Hanson had read about partisan rangers. They received warrants granted by the Confederate Congress allowing them to recruit, train, arm, and command units from companies to regiments for the purpose of seizing military contraband from the enemy. The CSA paid for these purloined goods when turned over to the regular army. The partisans employed guerrilla tactics, preferring hit-and-run midnight raids to the more traditional Napoleonic battle lines where men cut each other down with rifles from hundreds of yards away.

"Well, lookie here, our pigeon is awake," a cavalryman who was cutting an apple with a large knife announced when he noticed Hanson looking about. "Well, *friend*, what do you have to say for yourself?"

"I... I *am* your friend, sir," Hanson reassured his captor while trying to gather his senses. "I am Doctor Hanson Bumgardner. I am...that is, I *was* going to see my mentor, Dr. Thomas Brown in Wilsonville."

"Uh huh," the private responded. "Well, ya ain't goin' nowhere now."

"Kind sir," Hanson pled, "I need only to be on my way. I am a doctor dedicated to helping all, civilians and military alike."

"Actually, you're a prisoner 'til the officer shows up an' tells us what to do with you."

Late in the afternoon, Lieutenant Thomas Reeves finally arrived and introduced himself. Lt. Reeves had long dark hair that stuck out from his slouch hat adorned with a plume from a raven. Heavily bearded, he had dark eyes set in a scowling face that some attributed to his loss of his father and brother at Manassas.

"And who are you?" Reeves demanded in his usual gruff fashion.

"Sir, I am Doctor Hanson Bumgardner of…"

Reeves interrupted. "Yes, I remember your medicine wagon from before the war. You once examined my uncle and made him a potion for his gout. Why are you here?"

"Your men saw fit to arrest me without cause."

"The cause, sir, was trying to sneak past us at night," the private guarding Hanson added.

"The private has a point. Most people do not try to sneak past a picket late at night."

"I was not *sneaking* past, I was riding upon the road. It was late, yes, but I had more than the expected number of patients to attend to before leaving, and my journey home was delayed," Hanson reasoned with the lieutenant.

Reeves stared at Hanson. His uncle had eventually died of his gout, although the tonic the uncle purchased had greatly relieved the man's suffering. "Do you treat Yankees?" Lt. Reeves asked.

"I treat wounded men, not the ideals they fight for," Hanson said defiantly, adding with conviction, "Blood makes all uniforms just dark wet cloth."

"I see. So you admit to treating Yankees? Giving aid and comfort to the enemy?" Reeves pressed.

"I say again, sir: I treat *men*, not Johnny Rebs or Yankees, but bodies of flesh, blood, and bones, shattered by gunfire, cannon or bayonet. I find no flags on the bones of men whom I treat."

Unfortunately, Hanson's defensive comment antagonized Lt. Reeves further, and he began fuming. Calling for a sergeant, the two discussed the matter in low voices for some time. Then, biting off a plug of tobacco, he returned his attentions to Hanson. "As partisan rangers, we don't take prisoners. Instead, we shoot them as we would Yankee spies. I'll let you know when you are to be executed," Reeves snapped, and walked quickly away, his decision made and the sentence pronounced.

"Yeehaw! We's gonna git to execute someone!" the private shouted, pumping his rifle in the air overhead.

"Wait, Lieutenant," Hanson called out, his heart pounding in fear. "I am no spy. I am a humble doctor doing what I can to help the men who suffer this war."

The lieutenant stopped, turned, looked Hanson over carefully and reconsidered his options. Drawing his sword, he pointed the tip at Hanson. "I need an enrollment guard and you have the looks and voice that might aid our recruiting effort. If you will stand as guard for three months, a mere ninety days, I will give you a document attesting to your service to the CSA that will stay this execution and relieve you of having to further serve the confederacy. Do this, or your fate is sealed."

"I'll serve," he agreed without hesitation, shrugging in resignation. He felt some consolation in that he had just agreed to wear a uniform, as he had previously sworn, only at "the point of a sword."

# Chapter Eighteen

Two days later, he accompanied Lt. Reeves and three other guards south on a recruiting drive. The Rangers issued Hanson a poorly-fitting uniform that he wore for a few days until he found a tailor and had the uniform altered. The next day, he caught the lieutenant admiring his "new" uniform. "You know, Lieutenant, if your uniform also looked better, perhaps our recruiting efforts would improve. Just taking a bath, trimming your beard and shining your boots would help, I would wager," Hanson suggested.

"Seeing you in your tailored uniform, I believe now may be the time to test your thesis," he said, whereupon Lt. Reeves ordered his accompanying rangers to the local bathhouse where they each had their clothes laundered and tailored as well. By evening, they were clean and immaculately dressed.

A couple of weeks later, the unit's commanding officer, Col. Billings, sent a company of cavalry to gather the recruits they had gathered for training. "Come over, Doc Hanson, and meet my friend, Captain Harry Jackson," Lt. Reeves said upon receiving the cavalry. Lt. Reeves was actually smiling at the doctor. The three men exchanged greetings. "Dr. Hanson joined up for three months and has been an excellent recruiting guard," Lt. Reeves related to his superior.

"Are you a physician or surgeon?" the captain inquired.

"I am an herbalist, sir. A naturalist physician. I was a cancer doctor before the war," Hanson replied cordially.

"A naturalist physician. Good. Can you treat wounds, and not like the damn surgeon who believes the only answer is amputation?"

It was then that Hanson noticed a mid-thigh bulge on one side of the captain's trousers.

"Sir, may I have your permission to examine your wound?" Hanson inquired discretely.

The captain lifted the split leg of his trousers to reveal a soiled bandage, bloody and black with infection.

"Captain, please sit," Hanson ordered. "I will need to remove the bandage to gain a closer look, but from here, I fear the infection may already be too far gone. Still, I can make a poultice to see if the leg can be saved. After I examine it, I will need to go and procure the needed herbs." Hanson pointed to a camp chair for the captain.

"Sit," Hanson instructed.

"Then, examine and go you shall," proclaimed the captain, sitting, allowing Hanson to kneel alongside and undress the wound.

"Is the bullet still lodged in the wound?" Bumgardner asked, picking away the swaddling.

"It wasn't a bullet. It was a bayonet slash. I killed a Yankee sergeant as he ran towards me, and when he fell, his bayonet caught my leg."

"I see," Hanson said, delicately prodding the wound, and recalled a similar story told him by a confederate private, Gabriel Clem. Clem's wound had been superficial; in the captain's case the bayonet had cut deeply into the thigh. The laceration oozed dark fluid.

"His bayonet has filled you with infection. He may have killed you as well," Hanson informed the captain. Pointing at a private, Hanson said, "Get me hot water and clean bandages. And a good, strong soap, I will need soap, as well."

Over the next half hour, Hanson cleaned, debrided and re-bandaged the wound. "The bandage must be changed and the wound cleaned daily. I need to locate the herbs I require to prepare a poultice to draw out the infection. In short, you will have to come wherever Lieutenant Reeves has me posted so that I can check the wound at least every two or three days."

"I can not take time from my duties to go and find you every two or three days, sir," declared the captain, "so you are now assigned to me. Lieutenant Reeves can find another recruiting guard, right Reeves? You, Doctor Hanson, are now my personal physician and will see to my recovery."

It was in this manner that Hanson began a new life in the saddle as the *de facto* physician for Billing's Partisan Rangers. He was eventually able to send word to Sue that he was serving a mandatory period of service. The company patrolled up and down the West Virginia border, stealing horses, supplies and supply wagons from the Yankees, turning them over to the nearest regular CSA unit for quartermaster payment certificates. Hanson noticed one of the certificates the captain reviewed while changing the man's dressing. It was the same kind of certificate given to him by the quartermaster in Kentucky for the captured Yankee horses.

"Are those any good?" Hanson asked the captain, reflexively touching the one he kept safely hidden in his money belt.

"Good as gold at a Paymaster's Office," Cpt. Jackson replied, flexing the stiff but healing leg. "I refuse to take any payment except gold. They have plenty of currency, but it is of questionable value.

Sometimes, however, they run short of gold," he said, tossing a handful of confederate paper dollars contemptuously on the ground with a scornful laugh.

The captain's assurances as to the validity of the quartermaster payment certificate eased Hanson's mind. He'd been conscripted while traveling to Staunton to redeem his certificate. Noting Hanson staring at the scattered bills lying in the dirt, Captain Jackson said, "You should earn some certificates for yourself, Doc. Accompany us on a mission, and you may take your share of the bounty."

"An interesting proposition, sir," Hanson replied, looking from the bills to the certificate in the captain's hand. He liked the idea of being paid something for his forced servitude. Rethinking his position, he appended, "But only upon the condition that I would not have to kill anyone."

"I believe I could arrange that," laughed Jackson. "Corporal Warren, come here please."

A short rotund corporal came up and saluted. "Yes, sir."

"You will provide guidance to this gentleman on this evening's mission."

"But sir," Hanson interjected, "I haven't yet agreed to…"

"I am ordering you to accompany us on this mission, doctor," Jackson snapped. Then he added more warmly, "It is always best to follow orders."

The corporal smiled and promised with a wink, "I'll see you get back safely." Offering his hand, he added pleasantly, "Jed Warren."

"Doctor Hanson Bumgardner," Hanson replied. Encouraged by the corporal's promise, the two shook hands.

"Fine, we saddle at midnight," Captain Jackson informed them.

# Chapter Nineteen

Following trails known only to Billings' cavalrymen, they crept across the lines and into a Yankee encampment along a creek. Spies had reported the encampment as a supply unit supporting the Indiana infantry that currently occupied the West Virginia side of the lines.

Captain Jackson led the advance team that first killed the watch, then set an explosive diversion. Hanson with Cpl. Jed Warren stood watch, while the rest quietly hitched teams to the several wagons holding much-needed gunpowder as cargo.

"Take this," Corporal Warren whispered, pushing a Colt revolver into Hanson's hands. "Stay here and keep watch. I'll be right back."

"Wait..." Hanson whispered, but Warren had already disappeared into the darkness.

Before him, Hanson watched the silent figures preparing the wagons. The portly shadow of Cpl. Warren appeared directing the men to gather saddle horses as well.

To his side, Hanson heard the rustle of dry leaves and a mumbled curse. He squinted, scanning the darkness until he spotted a Yankee soldier trying to secure a primer on his rifle.

Impulsively, almost instinctively, Hanson quickly closed the distance between them. Slipping from tree to tree he crept up behind the enemy soldier. The infantryman was raising his rifle to his shoulder as Hanson silently drew near from behind. Changing his grip on the Colt to the barrel, he bashed the Yankee on the head with the butt of his revolver. The bluecoat fell to the ground with a loud crash.

The cavalrymen in the distance froze, and after a few tense moments continued their labors with renewed urgency.

Hanson bent over and inspected the unconscious Yankee's head. Searching about, he pulled up some medicinal moss, which he pressed against the wound. At that moment Corporal Warren returned.

"Waste of time," Corporal Warren whispered as he knelt beside the man, pulling his head back by the hair and calmly slitting the unconscious man's throat.

"Wh…" exclaimed Hanson.

Clapping a hand over Hanson's mouth, Warren whispered angrily, "Shhh! You don't want to wake his pals," then, removing his hand from Hanson's mouth, he whispered lower, "The saddle horses are ready. Ride one and lead two more. Got it?"

"Ye…yes," Hanson stammered, dazed by the atrocity he'd just witnessed.

"Good. Now follow me." Warren moved into the darkness with Hanson following. By the time they joined the teamsters, their work was finished and everyone awaited the signal to dash for friendly lines. Warren swung up on a saddle then checked to confirm the others were ready. Satisfied, the corporal hooted twice like an owl, turned to Hanson, and whispered excitedly, "Get ready!"

Three deafening explosions rocked the cool night air, their blinding flashes burning the image of the anxious cavalrymen into Hanson's mind.

"Go!" shouted the corporal, and everyone took off at a wild

gallop for their own lines. With the whips snapping over their backs, the wagon horses took off hard, kicking up dirt and dust as they raced away.

Captain Jackson led a simultaneous cavalry charge directly through the Yankee camp to add to the confusion. Flames reached skyward throwing sparks everywhere, igniting the canvas of the union tents. A few Yankee shots chased the raiders as they disappeared into the darkness along with their valuable cargo.

The following day, Hanson, still disturbed by the actions of Corporal Warren in killing the unconscious soldier, approached Captain Jackson. "I have a grievance, Captain," Hanson announced sanctimoniously.

"In what respects, my good doctor?" Jackson inquired.

"Last night I knocked out a Yankee," Hanson explained.

"Yes, good work. I heard him drop all the way across camp," Jackson quipped.

"Afterwards, Corporal Warren slit his throat," Hanson said. "I find this appalling and want to file a grievance."

"That's it? That's your grievance?" the captain inquired incredulously. He paused a moment to consider his reply before explaining, "You know, Doc, we've been at this a lot longer than you. In the beginning we too would just knock out the enemy soldiers. But later, they would take it out on our men, our farms, our families. Now we simply kill them. No explanation is necessary. This is the nature of war."

Hanson stared at the ground and reluctantly accepted the brutal truth of the captain's statement. "Yes sir," he said, saluted briskly and walked away, still tormented by the event.

Weeks later after participating in a number of additional exciting and quite profitable raids, Hanson mustered out. As promised, he received the discharge papers documenting his honorable service to the Confederate States of America as well as a quartermaster certificate worth one hundred twenty dollars for his share of the bounty. The new certificate was a handsome accompaniment to the crumpled five hundred dollar promissory note hidden in his money belt.

Hanson rode in his cavalry uniform to the quartermaster depot in Staunton, Virginia, to redeem the certificates. Locating the headquarters building for the paymaster proved difficult amidst the bustle of wartime activity, but at last he stood in front of the white-washed building. Armed men loitered outside and in crowded halls, making passage difficult.

Dr. Hanson pushed his way through to the office marked "Paymaster" and stepped in. There were surprisingly few men inside. A sergeant sat at a desk in the center of the room and a few men loitered along the wall.

The sergeant looked up. "Certificate and discharge" he said, mundanely reaching towards Hanson, who handed over the two certificates and his discharge papers.

The sergeant grunted his approval as he read each certificate. "Okay. The colonel pays all certificates on Tuesday."

"Great! Today is Tuesday," responded Hanson.

"But you didn't submit your papers before noon yesterday."

"I acknowledge that. Can you tell me what it means?"

"It means you will have to wait an extra week for payment."

"A week…?" Discouraged, Hanson decided to rationalize with the man. "Sergeant, a week is a long time. With Burnside moving on Fredericksburg, there could be Union cavalry here by then."

"I know. And I also know my orders about when documents must be turned in. If you'd like to discuss this further, the colonel should be back from lunch soon," the sergeant informed him.

As if on cue, a slightly built, white-haired officer marched through the door, not casting a glance to either side as he crossed the floor. The sergeant jumped up from his seat and called out, "Attention!"

Every soldier in the room stood to stiff attention while the sergeant followed the colonel into the next room. After a brief time, the sergeant stepped out and said, "As I call your name, you will report to Colonel Gene Brand, Paymaster, for redemption of your certificates. Anderson, Alan, you're first."

Forty minutes passed while Hanson anxiously waited, wondering if he would have to wait another week for payment. When the final man before him received his pay and left the office, the sergeant came out. "Bumgardner, Hanson. Colonel Brand will speak with you now."

"Ah, Doctor Hanson, Captain Jackson told me that I should expect you. I ran into him along the road yesterday. He says you are the best storyteller he has ever known. So, sir, would you favor me with a tale of one of your adventures?"

Hanson launched into his experience with the tornado in Nebraska, Col. Brand and the sergeant listening with rapt attention.

After the story, the colonel said, "An excellent story, Doctor. The West is one of my favorite subjects. But sir, I have sad news. I cannot pay you in full. I expected to pay you a hundred and twenty dollars, not the six hundred and twenty dollars you clearly deserve."

Hanson intuitively gathered from the way the colonel had phrased his statement that the man had *some* money left in the strongbox. "How much do you have remaining, sir?"

"It is but six hundred; you would be short twenty."

"Twenty dollars is a goodly sum, a month's wages for a corporal," Hanson acknowledged, relieved at what he'd heard. "But as I haven't seen my wife in months. I will forgive that amount if I could be paid the remainder today. In gold coin, sir."

The colonel nodded his agreement.

Hanson placed the money into his money belt, telling Colonel Brand an amusing story. Shaking hands with his new friend, he departed. A bath and shave later, Hanson donned civilian clothes and, seizing the opportunity, rode to Kidville to buy morphine.

Upon seeing his familiar customer, the Kidville pharmacist quickly attended to Hanson's order of morphine. "Here you are," the Kidville pharmacist said, placing a dozen tin flasks on the counter.

Hanson picked up the nearest and examined it, noting its *U.S. Army Hspl. Corps* stamp on the side.

"That's fifty dollars *each*. I want to be clear: six hundred for the dozen."

"Done," Hanson said, stacking twelve fifty-dollar gold coins on the counter. He lifted each flask, opening it and inspecting its contents. Satisfied, he placed all twelve tins in his saddlebags and headed back to Staunton. His plan was to head north, and cross over the pass to Pocahontas.

It was already dark before he left Staunton. He'd heard rumors that the Yankees were not far away, so it was no surprise when he was challenged by two consecutive confederate picket groups. The third group he encountered stopped him. "Where are you headed?" a private asked.

"I am headed home, having done my duty with Billings' Cavalry," Hanson responded.

"I know a Lieutenant Reeves of the cavalry. You know him? And what about Sergeant Lassiter?" the private inquired.

"Well, I know Lieutenant Tom Reeves, having served my duty with him, but I never heard of any Sergeant Lassiter. Where is he from?"

"Good answer, friend. Reeves hails from mah home county, but there ain't no Sergeant Lassiter. So, how come you're headed north? We're the last known CSA troops along the road, and further north it's just Yankees."

"My family name's Bumgardner. We own the Bumgardner Rye Whiskey Distillery. I need to return there to check on business," Hanson lied, embellishing the lie with several fictitious tales about his experiences in providing whiskey to the thirsty confederate troops. After ten minutes, the pickets, chuckling over his stories, allowed him to pass.

Dr. Hanson pushed his mount on through the cold December night. He delighted in the collage of patterns cast by the blue light of the full moon across the valley. At the same time, he was deeply concerned as he'd heard that Lee and Burnside were taking up positions around Fredericksburg for what portended to be a monumental battle. Rounding a sharp bend in the road, a Yankee picket group suddenly confronted him. "Halt! Who goes there?"

"A friend. I am Doctor Hanson Bumgardner, returning from seeing a patient," he lied with a warm smile, hoping to entreat the guard to allow him passage.

"Off the horse, mister," a drained voice ordered, accompanied by the sound of a rifle cocking. Hanson complied, dismounting, holding the reins in one hand while lifting the other in the air. Two grimy soldiers in dirty blues approached him. He could see the fatigue in their eyes and hear the weariness in their voices. One pressed a bayonet against his chest while the second began digging through Hanson's saddlebags.

"And what do we have here? A dandy perchance?" the first Yankee mocked Hanson.

"Sir, I am a physician, a healer, a…"

"A thief!" the second one said, pulling one of the flasks from the saddlebag. "Here, see? 'U.S. Army' stamped in the metal."

The first soldier inspected the flask in the moonlight, squinting and moving it back and forth in his attempt to read it.

"I can explain. I…" Hanson began in defense, reaching for the tin.

"Keep your hands up!" the first one said, motioning with his rifle.

Hanson dropped the reins and held both hands up higher. The Sergeant of the Guard arrived moments later, and, after a short discussion, took Hanson at pistol point to a local post office that had been commandeered for a field headquarters. There two guards watched him while they waited for the Officer of the Day.

Dr. Hanson decided to say that he was attending a wounded Yankee soldier, reasoning that might sway them to release him. He waited until well past eleven, while the wind blew dark cold clouds over nighttime Virginia.

Finally, the officer arrived: a tall gaunt man uninterested in the civilian prisoner. He scoffed when presented the man's saddlebags containing contraband morphine.

"Confiscate the morphine. We will need every drop we can get. The army is moving towards Fredericksburg where a major battle is shaping up. Hold this man as a spy for now. I'll send word on what to do with him after the battle." The officer left as quickly and abruptly as he had arrived, never once speaking to Hanson.

# Chapter Twenty

During the early morning hours, the two Union soldiers assigned to guard Hanson sat at a nearby table playing cards. Hanson sat in a corner watching them play several hands. The larger of the two shuffled and dealt the cards. Placed to the side, face up, were all four queens.

Hanson walked cautiously over to the table. "What game are you boys playing?" he asked in his friendliest manner, leaning forward, and placing his hands on the table in order to palm the queen of hearts.

"Old Maids. You know how?" the beefier private asked, looking up at Hanson.

"Oh sure, but I thought that game was for women. Back home we play Busted Bean."

"That's it; I'm out," said the thinner private, tossing his cards on the table, ignoring Hanson.

"Hey, let me show you a card trick," Hanson said and swept the cards into a stack. After shuffling them quickly, he fanned out the deck before them. "Pick a card, any card," he instructed. "Don't let me see the card, but show it to your buddy."

The skinny private selected the eight of clubs from the deck and showed it to the other guard, who nodded and pursed his lips.

"Good," Hanson said. "Now slide it across the table, face down."

The heavier man snatched the card from his companion and pushed it, face down, to Hanson's side of the table. Dr. Hanson slid the card to the edge of the table. Orienting the deck against the edge and even with the tabletop, he announced, "I'm going to place your card on top of the deck." Placing his index finger on the center of the card, with a sweeping gesture he slid the card from the table onto the deck, deftly substituting the queen of hearts he had palmed.

"Now," he said placing the deck in the center of the table, "I will tell you what your card is, but you must concentrate on it. Concentrate." The privates wrinkled their brows in thought. "Harder. Ah, it's becoming clearer. Keep concentrating. Close your eyes and concentrate harder."

The two closed their eyes. Looking about, Hanson quickly confirmed their rifles braced together against the table were both at half cock, neither with primers on the nipples. He also ascertained that neither guard was carrying a sidearm. To his right, he spotted a log rack with one log about two inches around and two feet long, perfect for his purpose.

"I have it!" Hanson exclaimed. "It is the queen of hearts!"

The two Yankees opened their eyes and laughed heartily, the stockier one saying, "You have it wrong, sir. It was the eight of clubs."

"Well, I could be mistaken, but I think not. Turn over the top card," Hanson replied, flashing a smile.

The private who'd just spoken for the two reached with his grimy fingers and flipped over the top card, "See, it's the…" He was stunned to see the queen of hearts.

"What th'…?" the other private stammered, then they both laughed.

"How about another one?" Hanson purred.

"Wait. Where's the eight of clubs?" the heavyset guard demanded.

"Your friend had it all along. It's under his kepi." Hanson reached over, flicked the man's hat onto the table, and, with a grand motion, produced from inside it the eight of clubs.

"Amazing," the thinner man laughed, picking up his hat and searching inside to see if there were more cards.

"So, how about another one, boys?" Hanson smiled widely.

"Sure!" they replied in unison.

"Okay, this time, take off your hats and place them on the floor so that no cards can jump into them without your knowing."

They tossed their hats on the floor next to each other while Hanson shuffled the deck and fanned it open again, challenging them to pick one.

The two viewed the cards suspiciously; then, the slimmer of the two drew a card.

Hanson turned his back on his guards. "Look at the card, but do not say what it is. Then, place it in the center of the table face down."

The two huddled together to share a look at the card before placing it in the center of the table. "Alright, it's face down," the thin private reported.

Hanson turned around to face them, and slowly circled his right hand over the deck which he held in his other. "This more complex trick will require our combined concentration." Hanson closed his eyes, furrowed his brow and sped up the circling of his hand over the deck. Suddenly, he stopped, opened his eyes and chided them. "You are so suspicious, it is stopping the flow of nature I require. I must therefore ease your suspicions. Each of you place one finger on the card so that I cannot move it without your knowing. Does that help?"

Each reached out and placed an index finger on the card. The thinner guard nodded his assent.

"Now close your eyes again and concentrate on the card so I can see it in my mind."

Each closed his eyes tightly.

"There. Good. Now *concentrate,*" Hanson ordered, continuing to speak while closing the distance to the log rack. Grasping the two-inch log from the rack, he concluded, "I'm getting it...it is coming...here it is!" as he lifted the log high and brought it crashing down on the fat soldier's head. The other guard didn't have time to open his eyes before Hanson walloped him. The two fell from their chairs onto the floor. Hanson kept the log raised for another strike, but found it unnecessary as the two were splayed out on the floor unconscious. Lowering the log, he whispered, "And that's how you play Busted Bean. I bust your bean!"

Hanson dragged the unconscious men behind some field boxes stacked along the back wall. Pulling the sack coat from the skinny infantryman, he tried it on only to discover it was far too small. The overweight soldier's coat was large, but he cinched the man's belt over it and decided it would have do. Retrieving his saddlebags, he confirmed that the morphine was still there. Grabbing a Union kepi, he slipped out the back door.

He couldn't find his horse, so he commandeered a Yankee officer's. He rode away quickly with his body crouched low along the left flank of the horse as he had seen Indians do out west until he cleared the last building. To his surprise, the pickets who were supposed to be standing watch were asleep. Sitting upright in the saddle, he rode pell-mell towards the confederate lines. After a few minutes at full speed, he brought the animal to a trot and nervously looked over his shoulder for Yankee pursuers. To his great relief, he saw none.

Nearing the confederate lines, Hanson spotted three unattended Yankee wagons parked on a side road. Riding around them, he noticed all three were damaged and that each was loaded with gunpowder casks. The first wagon had a broken wheel, the second a shattered tongue. The third had damaged floor slats such that a cask was hanging precariously halfway through it. The Yankees had apparently left them, planning to return later with a repair crew or new wagons.

Hanson rode till near dawn, hoping to find a place to rest and sleep, when he ran into confederate pickets.

"Halt, who goes there?"

Dr. Hanson recognized the voice as that of the picket who had challenged him on his way north.

"Friend, it is I, Dr. Hanson Bumgardner."

"Advance."

Hanson tapped his mount lightly with his heels, encouraging it towards the picket with whom he had shared tales and laughs hardly twelve hours earlier. Men suddenly appeared on both his sides, grabbed the reins from his hands, and pulled him out of the saddle.

"Stop! Please! I am Hanson Bumgardner! I'm a doctor!"

"You're wearing a Yankee uniform. Just yesterday you lied about being one of the Bumgardners who make whiskey!" A hard fist crashed into his face. "Now you're back wearing a Yankee uniform!" Another blow thudded into Hanson's torso.

"Wait," Hanson gasped, holding his ribs and backing away. "They captured me and treated me as a spy!" Hanson cried in his defense.

"You are a spy," were the last words Hanson heard as a blow from behind sent him reeling into unconsciousness.

# Chapter Twenty-One

Dr. Hanson Bumgardner awoke slowly, the pounding in his head accompanied by a sharp pain shooting from behind his eyes to the back of his head. He opened a swollen eye and peered around. He was sitting on the ground chained to a tree not far from a campfire. The light filtering through the heavy gray clouds suggested it was early afternoon. The cold breeze chilled him incessantly, carrying with it smoke from the fire, causing him to choke and cough.

He heard voices, but had trouble distinguishing what was being said. The voices seemed familiar, reverberating as if from down a long tunnel. Shaking his head, a blanket of smoke surrounded him and he tried to call out.

"Gentleme..." he coughed, gagging on the acrid smoke. "Gentlemen. Can you hear me?"

"Hanson Bumgardner? Is that you?" Col. Brand asked through the haze of smoke. "When they said Bumgardner, I didn't believe it."

The winds swirled about Hanson and blew away the smoke. "You were wearing a different uniform last time we met, Doc. It's caused some confusion," Col. Brand observed.

"Yes. I was captured by Yankees. I stole the uniform to make my escape only to be captured by these men. I cannot account for my bad luck."

Turning to the guards, the colonel said, "I will personally vouch for this man. He is no spy. He's a horse thief who served his time in Billings' Cavalry Partisan Rangers. Please, untie him. I have need of such a man."

The moment the privates released him, Hanson stood, leaning shakily against the tree for support while blood filled his legs again. Col. Brand inched next to him and spoke low. "Doc, I came here today to pay these soldiers their wages, only to find that the soldiers are dangerously short of supplies to wage war. I need all the war supplies you can gather, preferably gunpowder, and I need it fast. Any chance you might know where to procure some *ex post haste*?"

"Sir, right now I am uncertain of my ability to continue standing, much less obtain immediate Yankee donations to the cause."

"Perhaps you ran across something—anything—during your travels? I'll pay double the rate per wagon plus ten percent of content value, but I need them right away," Col. Brand tempted.

"Give me six mounted men, four large draught horses and a tool chest, and I'll have two wagons full of powder here tonight," Hanson declared. "Oh, and I will need a change of clothes as well."

That night, Dr. Hanson Bumgardner led his party to the side road where he had seen the abandoned wagons, approaching cautiously to confirm there were no guards.

Hanson and his men scavenged parts from the third wagon to repair the first two. Coupling the second wagon to the first, they divided the cargo of the third between the two repaired wagons and used the draught horses to pull both wagons simultaneously. Three hours after leaving camp, Hanson was accompanying the tandem rig into the confederate camp alongside the wagons.

"Amazing work, Bumgardner!" Brand shouted, eyes wide as he inspected the wagons brimming with casks of gunpowder.

"Well, sir, they must have known we'd need it, and left it there just for us," Hanson replied, proud of his accomplishment.

"Corporal, give me a count of the number of casks of gunpowder," the colonel happily ordered, then turned to Bumgardner to say, "You should consider a commission, Doc. We need men like you."

"As you know, I have finished my duty to Virginia," Hanson retorted." I only ask she pay a fee for these lovely wagons."

"And so she shall! In three hours, you've already accumulated a fine bounty to share with your men, Captain Bumgardner."

"I'm sorry, sir," Hanson reiterated. "I do not desire a field commission, but I will be happy to share the bounty with these brave men without whom I would not have been successful. Any debt I owed Virginia is now doubly paid."

Col. Brand nodded his agreement and led Hanson to the tavern that they were using as a headquarters to celebrate and make the payment.

# Chapter Twenty-Two

Hanson paused on the gallows, pensive again. "In all the time I wore a uniform, I never killed a man. I swear to God in heaven this is true." He looked briefly east, then continued. "The battle that December in Fredericksburg produced many casualties..."

Hanson crossed over into West Virginia carrying his morphine for the elixir. His mother, Jane, had moved from Ten Mile to Pocahontas while the war raged all about them. It was in this manner that Hanson, his pregnant wife and baby George, along with Sue's two sisters, his three sisters, and his mother all came to occupy the larger of the two homestead cabins located within sight of each other. Their nearest neighbor, several miles away, was the respected Galford family.

Finding the smaller cabin also sound, Hanson began repairing it to live in with Sue; however, before he could finish, war casualties from the Fredericksburg battle began arriving, and the cabin became a *de facto* infirmary. Word quickly spread among soldiers that everyone who came to Doc Hanson's infirmary received treatment, regardless of uniform. Many, returning home on foot, stopped in for a change of bandages and a bottle of tonic. Some paid cash, others donated whatever they had in their pockets. Most had no money at all.

One particularly cold December night, Hanson noticed a light flickering inside the "infirmary" cabin. There had been no casualties that day, so he walked out to investigate. As he stepped into the cabin, a saber blade pressed against his chest. "Hold there," the swordsman ordered.

"Who is it, James?" a brawny sergeant asked the man holding the saber.

"Well?" the swordsman asked, sliding the blade to the base of Hanson's throat.

"I am the gentleman of the property, Dr. Hanson Bumgardner."

A murmur of relief passed through the room.

"Doc, I need you to look at a man," the sergeant said, motioning for Hanson to follow.

"And you are?"

"Sergeant George Arbogast, sir. Private James Hamilton you met at the door."

James nodded and flashed a toothy grin as he replaced his saber in its scabbard.

George continued: "In the far corner are Privates John Friel and Morgan Johns. And lying on the table, you may recognize…"

"Thomas Galford!" Hanson interrupted, moving quickly to where the middle-aged neighbor of that name lay.

"Yeah, it's me," coughed Private Thomas Galford, Junior. "Caught one in th' leg. Lost a lot uv blood, see?" He pointed to his blood-soaked left thigh.

"I told 'em about yur wonderful elixir, Doctor Hanson," Galford said, while Hanson raised the compress and looked underneath. Hanson went to the cabinet and got out instruments, alcohol and dressings, then poured alcohol on a pair of forceps.

"The elixir is not for sale at this time. The ingredients are becoming increasingly hard to come by, so I am saving what I have for the most badly injured. However, Thomas, as your wound will require cauterization, you will unfortunately qualify for a dose when I've finished. Did anyone get the bullet out?" Hanson asked, looking around.

They all shook their heads no.

"You there. James Hamilton, right? Hold one of his arms down. And you, John Morgan…"

"Morgan Johns, Doc. Everybody gets it wrong," the twenty-six year old cavalryman interrupted, smiling. "Even Tom got it wrong for a while when we met in the First Virginia Cavalry."

"My apologies, Morgan. Hold down his other arm. Sarge, you and Friel hold his legs."

Hanson poured alcohol directly on Galford's wound, causing him to writhe in pain. Friel turned pale and looked away. Morgan and James gritted their teeth, unconsciously relaxing their grip. Arbogast stiffened and ordered the others to grip Galford tighter.

Hanson cleaned the perimeter of the wound and examined it closely. "Hold him still now, boys," he said as he followed the bullet's course deep into Galford's thigh with the forceps. "Ah, good it didn't get the bone," Hanson said, gripping the lead minié ball with the tool and slowly withdrawing it. Bright red blood began seeping around the wound and Hanson placed a compress on it. "Thomas," he said to his patient. "Hold the compress hard on your leg for a few minutes."

Galford nodded, taking the cloth from Dr. Hanson, who then turned and stroked the bellows, bringing the fire to white hot incandescence. Hanson pushed the tip of a black iron poker deep into the searing heat.

The men tightened their grip as Hanson withdrew the hot poker from the blue-white coals, and quickly shoved the tip into the bullet hole in Galford's leg. Galford bellowed a primeval howl before succumbing to the pain and passing out. The men holding him slowly released his limbs, then the five gently repositioned him more comfortably on the table. Hanson placed a blanket behind his head and another over him.

"He may be out for a few minutes or hours; I can't tell. It depends on many factors. Now, we must wait it out."

Hanson doused the poker in a bucket of water.

"He was adamant about being brought here," Sergeant Arbogast related. "He said we could trust you—that you served in Billings' Cavalry Partisan Rangers. We have been operating like partisan rangers, but on our own. The confederacy still pays for the supplies, but they will no longer issue warrants."

Hanson gazed about the room, recognizing the distinctive uniforms worn by the men. On the table, Thomas Galford Jr., a forty-two-year-old private serving the confederacy in the First Virginia Cavalry, lay barely breathing. Standing at one leg was Private John Friel, a twenty-five-year-old cavalryman from the Seventeenth Virginia Cavalry. Sergeant George Arbogast, the natural leader of the group was barely twenty-three and according to his uniform hailed from Company G of the Thirty-First Virginia Infantry. His friend, forty-one-year-old James Hamilton was also a deserter from the Thirty-First Infantry. Morgan Johns was so dirty it was hard to tell his age but Hanson estimated about twenty-six or seven. His uniform was so tattered and thread-worn it was difficult to tell, but it appeared he was also with the Seventeenth Cavalry.

"Without the warrant, you're just thieves as far as the Yankees are concerned. Yet, it is true, I did serve with Billings' Cavalry, but mostly as a recruiting guard," admitted Doc Hanson.

"Ha, ha! Ask George about recruiting!" Hamilton laughed, changing the subject.

"Sergeant?" Hanson inquired, raising an eyebrow and looking the powerful sergeant directly in the eyes.

"Well, yeah. I had me a bit uv fun for awhile..." the sergeant said, his gray eyes sparkling.

"Go on," Hanson said, drawing him out.

"Well, I was probably the reason they need recruiting guards, because, you see, they pay the enlistment bonus right away in cash," Arbogast confessed.

"So you enlisted in two different units to get the bonus twice?"

"Well, sir, a bit more than that."

"Three?"

"More."

"Four?"

"Go on!"

"What? Five? You enlisted *five* times?" Hanson couldn't believe what he was hearing.

"Five times in two months," Arbogast laughed. "Paid off my debts, put some money away, and decided to stay with the Thirty-First Virginia Infantry because I liked the officers."

"I thought it was because you liked me," interjected John Hamilton.

"It was to protect you," Arbogast said, poking fun at his long-time friend.

Hanson grinned at the young sergeant's admission before changing the subject. "You said you have been operating like Billings' Cavalry. What do you mean exactly?" Hanson inquired, genuinely interested.

"Well, we have been shadowing the Yankees and snagging a wagon or a horse here and there to sell to the confederacy. We trade the wagons for money in Staunton, no questions asked."

"If they discover you are deserters, they'll…"

"They don't ask; they don't want to know because they need the supplies so badly."

"How long have you been operating?" Hanson asked, his curiosity piqued. He'd not heard of any such group operating in this area.

"About a fortnight. We fled Fredericksburg and captured a Yankee wagon, well—found an abandoned one. Then, on the way to Staunton we were able to snag another from a very lost, very lonely Yankee wagoner."

They all laughed at the inside joke,

"After being paid, we successfully seized another wagon. Then, two days ago, when we tried to seize several from a column near Cheat Mountain, we were surprised by Cavalry we didn't know was accompanying the wagons. That's when Tom got shot in the thigh. We rode through the pass at night to get over here. Didn't want to go to a confederate doctor. Too many questions to answer, see?"

"Where's your base of operations?"

"Galford's place…"

Galford moaned loudly and Hanson checked the bandage. It was freshly blood-soaked, so he replaced it with another. Placing his ear against Galford's chest, Hanson listened for the man's heartbeat and nodded his satisfaction at what he heard. Sitting down in a wooden chair and leaning its back against a wall by the fire, he said, "I could've told you not to attack a moving column of wagons. They are always accompanied by cavalry. You need to abscond with the wagons in the early morning darkness while the majority of their forces are asleep, or..."

Sergeant Arbogast took the chair beside him. "Can you help us? Together we could make a lot of money."

Hanson paused, then replied with renewed vigor, "I think we can come to a satisfactory arrangement."

Hanson spent the next several days going over tactics with his new band of raiders. He pointed out that laden wagons were far slower than cavalry, and, drawing on his sleight-of-hand knowledge, suggested they quickly conceal the wagons after taking them while diverting the cavalry elsewhere.

They selected a portion of the road that led around a bend, then down a hill and alongside the river. Just past the bend, they cut tree limbs and bushes, placing them in a pile alongside the road. When they seized one or more wagons, they would divert them off the road, concealing the wagons with the limbs. Friel would ride behind, then past them, dragging a log with his horse to cover their tracks and kick up dust to simulate speeding wagons, leading the Yankee cavalry down to the fast-moving river. There they prepared another pile of bushes to conceal a hiding spot well off the road for Friel.

Hanson would await the Yankees on the other side of the raging river with look-alike wagons, and, upon seeing the pursuers, would charge away from the river as though the wagons had somehow crossed the river. The pursuers would end up searching up and down the river for the ford. Not finding any way across and believing the wagons had gotten away, they would eventually give up their pursuit. Meanwhile, the raiders would have driven the wagons from their hiding place to the Galford barn for concealment until they could get them to the confederates.

Three days later, they executed the plan. Everything went perfectly, resulting in their acquisition of three wagons full of material. The men were elated with their treasure and the prospect of more to come. Later that week, they captured another two wagons using the same tactics.

Realizing the difficulties of moving five wagons through West Virginia and on into Virginia to collect the bounty, Hanson suggested they wear Yankee uniforms over their rebel uniforms while they traveled in West Virginia. When they crossed over the pass, each would doff the Union uniforms in order to pass safely through the rebel pickets. This plan also worked well, and Sergeant Arbogast led a column of five loaded wagons to Staunton for redemption.

After receiving his cut, Hanson temporarily parted company with the group to visit Thomas Brown. When he got there, Hanson found Doctor Brown had aged heavily in two years. Feeling trapped in Old Virginia when his loyalties were with the Union, Brown was left to impotently watch as the war spun on around him. The visit reinvigorated both men.

Hanson returned to West Virginia, ready to once more take on the ills of the citizens and wounds of the soldiers. He had just reined in his horse with his replenished stock of morphine in front of the two cabins when he saw Jane sitting on the porch together with James and Sue. All appeared downcast and forlorn. Sue rose and slowly approached, woe resting heavily upon her face.

"What is it, Sue? What happened? Why is James here in his uniform?" Hanson asked, climbing down from his horse.

James rose and stepped forward, his face reflecting the mournful news. "Hanson, Cousin John Bumgardner…he…" James paused to gather himself before continuing. "Cousin John joined the Iowa infantry, Thirty-Fifth Regiment, while you were away."

"I don't believe it! He has always stood firmly against violence!" Hanson replied, stunned by the news.

"Yes, well, he felt the patriotic call and joined as the Regimental Flutist. They were on the march to Cairo, Illinois, to bolster Grant's Mississippi campaign when he got pneumonia and died." James' voice trailed off to a bitter whisper. "I heard they didn't have winter uniforms…"

Hanson embraced Sue and James, and together they cried for his young cousin. Hanson recalled having foretold that John would play the flute in front of hundreds, never imagining the multitude would be soldiers marching to it.

# Chapter Twenty-Three

One evening several weeks later, while revisiting Dr. Brown to replenish his supplies and square their finances, the two were interrupted by a loud rapping at the door. Elizabeth Brown rose and went to the door. "Who is it?" she asked through the door.

"I'm lookin' for Doctor Hanson," an anxious voice boomed. Immediately recognizing the voice, Hanson signaled to Elizabeth to open the door.

Dallas Galford, the seventeen-year-old son of Thomas Galford Jr., his black hair tangled during his hectic ride, entered the house shaking from the cold. "They've stabbed Private Hamilton and shot Dad again!" he blurted, seizing Hanson by the shoulders. "You've got to come. Hurry! Dad's gutshot!"

Hanson grabbed his hat, pulling on his coat and turned to Thomas Brown. "Sir, I shall owe you forever for teaching me how to serve mankind."

Elizabeth placed a hand on Hanson's chest and stopped him before he could exit the house. "Take the surrey; they are less likely to suspect someone driving a two-seated surrey."

"Agreed," Hanson said, slipping past her and hurried out. He had earned his reputation as a healer on both west and east sides of the new border that split Virginia in two. Union and CSA pickets were familiar with Dr. Hanson and had come to respect his crossing lines to treat civilian and soldier alike.

The moment Hanson arrived at the Galford pioneer house, men jumped to action. Thomas Galford was helped up to show the bullet wound through his left side. Hanson inspected the wound and declared, "The bullet went cleanly through. I need only clean it and treat it to prevent infection."

John Hamilton's wound was more serious. A deep slash to the upper thigh left the wound jagged and shredded. The damaged tissue would need to be cut away. Hanson opened his bag, produced a bottle of elixir, and gave Hamilton a heavy dose. Within minutes, Hamilton was slurring his words and he thereafter quickly passed out.

Hanson trimmed the wound as best he could, then sewed the edges together, pulling the stitches as tight as he dared in order to close the wound. "I need everyone to grab a limb, because I am going to use alcohol to cleanse the wound again. He may wake up." The alcohol, however, elicited only a few brief involuntary muscle spasms.

It was then that Hanson saw a man he'd not noticed previously, sitting on a stool in a corner. The man's face seemed vaguely familiar to the exhausted doctor. Hanson squinted to get a better look.

"It's me, Doc," the phantom answered, remaining in the shadows.

Hanson, his mind still focused on the severity of Thomas Galford and John Hamilton's wounds, didn't recognize the voice.

"Come on, Doc, you remember. From Stonewall's Brigade. Clem, Gabriel Clem. Ya patched me up a few months back." As Clem stood and stepped into the light a shudder ran up Hanson's spine.

"I see," Hanson said, not wanting to reveal his revulsion. He recalled Clem clearly as the vitriolic deserter with the self-inflicted wound.

"Yeah, I gave 'em some information 'bout a of bunch wagons, but they botched the raid bad. You need to train yer bushwhackers better, Doc."

"What happened?" Hanson asked Sgt. Arbogast, ignoring Clem's snide comment.

"Well, we knocked out the two guards Clem said would be there, but as we were harnessing the horses to the wagons, someone started shooting." Arbogast shrugged. "It was a mess, and we had to skedaddle. We were lucky to get away at all."

Hanson nodded. "Let's hold off any further operations for a while. No need to get killed over a war, eh?" After an ironic chuckle, he could no longer hide his fatigue, and he quickly found a bench, curled up on it and fell asleep.

The next morning Sue reluctantly awakened her husband. "I brought a mixed box of bottles of tonic and elixir, as I feared you may need it for Mr. Hamilton."

Yawning, Hanson sat up and admired his wife. "What a delight it is to awaken to you in the morning. I am ashamed that I must present to you so poor an appearance."

"Hanson, you were up much of the night tending the wounded. You needn't worry about appearance," she cooed, combing back his ruffled hair with her fingers. "I barely see you these days what with you running all over the countryside." Sue kissed him on the forehead.

Hanson stood and walked to the bed where Hamilton lay, pulling the bandage from the leg carefully and inspecting the wound before applying a new bandage. Looking back at Sue, who was watching him lovingly as he worked, he smiled and winked. "Your beauty shines, making the path back to you clear for me."

"Why, sir! I do declare!" she said to the amusement of the men in the cabin. Handing Hanson the bottle of elixir, she continued in a more serious voice. "We have sufficient stock for another couple of months, more if we…" Sue dropped the subject, knowing better than to speak of reducing the morphine potency.

"I will not diminish the efficacy of the elixir by reducing the active ingredient," Hanson declared, finishing her sentence. Walking over to the box Sue brought, he opened it and waved Sue to his side. Among the bottles of elixir in the box, he pointed to one without a label, the cork bearing a double "X" carved in the top. Pulling it from its sawdust packing, he whispered in Sue's ear, "This bottle of elixir is special. One dose is sufficient to ensure that the receiver never awakens. You understand?" He stared her in the eye until she nodded, then placed the bottle into her handbag.

Hanson pulled a bottle of tonic from the box and held it up. "Gentlemen, for your amusement! A tonic for the aches and pains of war!" Hanson pulled the cork from the bottle and took a long swig. "Who will join me?"

"I will," Sue cried, surprising everyone by taking the flask from her husband and downing a mouthful. "I don't get to have fun with my husband very often," she said in a raspy voice, coughing from its potency. Everyone laughed.

Clem took the bottle from her and quaffed deeply before passing it to Sgt. Arbogast. Together the men consumed several bottles of tonic that afternoon. Hanson was laughing heartily as he escorted Sue back to the main house to be alone for a couple of hours together. Thomas Galford Sr. stayed with his injured son, Thomas Galford Jr. and his grandson, Dallas Galford, and the others at the "clinic."

The next day, Sue returned to her duties at the family farm. When

Hanson performed Hamilton's mid-morning dressing check, the man was fully awake. "I sure could use some of that elixir, Doc," he said, wincing, as Hanson gently prodded his thigh.

"I know, but I must conserve the elixir. You should be able to put some weight on it in a couple more days, by Friday perhaps."

"Hey! Is this Wednesday?" James Friel said, stopping his whittling.

"Uh, yeah," Sgt. Arbogast confirmed, looking up from his game of checkers with James Hamilton.

"Didn't you say a little bit ago it was the eleventh, Sarge? Eleventh of February? That makes Friday the thirteenth." Friel seemed inordinately concerned.

"I'm not superstitious," Hanson said, motioning for Thomas Galford Jr. to raise his arm. Hanson leaned in to smell and inspect the wound. "Healing good," he pronounced.

"Thanks to you, Doc," the junior Galford said.

"Thank you...Doctor Bumgardner," the senior Galford echoed, coughing repeatedly before catching his breath. He wiped away a long drool of rusty-looking sputum with his handkerchief.

Hanson pulled a fresh bottle of tonic from the case and handed it to the senior Galford. "Here, my friend, use as much as you need. Keep the bottle."

Looking around, Hanson noticed Clem's absence and felt the better for it. Sitting next to Sgt. Arbogast, Hanson asked quietly, "Who brought Clem into the group?"

The sergeant looked mildly surprised. "He showed up one day while you were at the Brown's place. Said the two of you were like brothers."

Hanson raised his eyebrows. "That's not true. He came to me not long ago with a minor flesh wound which I'm almost certain was self-inflicted. He expressed a vitriolic hatred of anyone who in any way sided with or helped Yankees." Leaning against the log wall, Hanson concluded, "Keep an eye on him, George. I don't trust him."

Arbogast nodded his agreement a moment before Clem sauntered back into the cabin, having stepped out, he said, to talk with some soldier buddies passing by. Together, the men spent the rest of the afternoon warming themselves by the fire and talking on that cold day in February, 1863.

# Chapter Twenty-Four

In the early evening, there was a hard pounding at the door. Before anyone could rise to open it, three gunshots tore through the lockset and the door flew open. Yankees streamed in, yelling and pointing their guns in every direction.

James Friel jumped up and grabbed the rifle from the nearest Federal. The soldier wrestled the weapon back, pushed Friel aside and hit him in the face with the butt. Friel flew backwards, slammed against the wall, and tumbled to the floor.

Two Yankees pinned Hanson's arms firmly behind him, while the stalwart Sgt. Arbogast held off a third soldier with his left arm while two more clung to his right. A rifle butt smashed into his stomach taking him to the ground.

"Hold! You are all under arrest!" shouted a lieutenant as he stepped through the door, pistol raised high.

"On what charge?" Hanson demanded, wriggling without success to free himself.

"There are several charges pending against you, *Doctor* Bumgardner," the lieutenant sneered. "The main one is treason. For the rest of your 'gang', well, they are in uniform, so they are prisoners-of-war."

"What about him? He is neither traitor nor threat," Hanson replied, nodding at the elderly Galford. "He's over seventy years old, and his grandson is but seventeen. Surely you do not presume…"

"Surely, I do not take my orders from *you*, Hanson Bumgardner," the self-important lieutenant interrupted. "I do not like this duty, and like it even less when I am required to work with local militia. I need…"

"What do you mean 'local militia'?" Sgt. James Bumgardner declared as he strode through the door, taking his position at the lieutenant's side. "We are the Third West Virginia Cavalry, U. S. Army, we are not militia."

"James, what are you doing here?" Hanson asked in shock.

"My duty to my country, Hanson. You know my feelings," replied James. Sgt. Bumgardner turned to the Union officer temporarily leading his unit. "Can't we let this one go? He's no traitor or bushwhacker; he's a back-hills doctor come here to heal soldiers and civilians alike who suffer from the effects of this war. Look for yourself. He was changing a dressing when we stormed in."

"My information is that he is the leader of this gang of outlaws, and is using his so-called physician status to cross back and forth over the lines with impunity."

"It's not illegal to go in or out of Virginia," James protested.

"It is if you continuously evade the duly-appointed Federal pickets or carry war contraband into Virginia, particularly stolen Federal war materials, wagons and horses. No, sergeant, I can not release any of these men; together, they are a band of horse thieves, bushwhackers, and spies, and *he*," the lieutenant said, pointing at Hanson, "is aiding the rebels by treating their battle wounds."

Hanson felt a knot form in the pit of his stomach. The lieutenant had made it abundantly clear that someone in their midst was a spy, given the detailed information the lieutenant possessed. The elder Galford let out a series of loud, rasping, hoarse coughs. Everyone paused to stare at Galford Senior as he continued coughing and wheezing, trying to catch his breath.

A pair of privates carrying iron shackles entered the cabin, which they placed on each captive's wrists, leading one at a time outside to a waiting wagon.

James looked remorsefully at Hanson, "I'll try to get word to a friend of mine in Wheeling where they'll be taking you. I'll try to secure your release before they transfer you to a prison camp."

"Thanks, James. Let Sue and Mother know of my circumstances; bid them not to worry. Tell them I am unharmed."

James nodded his assent, then took his brother by the arm and led him to the wagon. Hanson studied his brother's stern face and thought, *this war has separated our nation, our state, and now our family.*

"Take care, Hanson," James said, his voice quavering.

"You, too, James, stay out of the way of bullets," Hanson replied, presenting the best smile he could muster.

As the wagon rumbled forth, Hanson tried to recall the name of the lieutenant in charge of his arrest, recalling that the snide officer had recently been a recruiter for a confederate Virginia regiment.

"I was arrested by a Union officer—a scoundrel who raised a rebel company, then turned Union," Hanson related, shifting his weight from one foot to the other on the wet gallows platform. "It is yet another example of how the war bent and altered the lives of all Americans."

Hanson looked down at the men who had come to witness his death. Interest seemed to be waning. The people he was anxiously awaiting might be just over the river, out of sight but on their way. He needed a while longer so they could bring the evidence needed to free him entirely.

"The wagons delivered us to Wheeling, West Virginia where we were held prisoner in the infamous Athenaeum, that many in the South called 'Lincoln's Bastille'. There, Friel comically lived through that Friday the thirteenth, walking backwards, eating with his left hand and such." Hanson shook his head and smiled at the recollection.

"After being held there for two weeks, we were marched to the train station. Along the way, civilians threw rotted vegetables at us. We were taken by train to Camp Chase..." he continued, falling back into the rhythm of his story, watching his audience and their response more closely this time.

A cold wind whipped through the boxcar slats while the train rolled along at twenty miles-per-hour. Hanson saw the hollow look overcoming the men, the destitute empty eyes that replaced the spirited warrior's gaze, as desperation and despair weighed heavily on their souls.

"Give yourselves up to God, men!" Hanson called out in his preacher's voice, catching them by surprise. "Only the Master can soothe your everlasting souls. Give yourselves to Him. Praise the Lord, Amen. Can I hear an Amen?"

Hanson paused but heard no answer. Consternation gripped him until a faint but strong-willed voice called back, "Amen." It was the elderly Galford, struggling to stand. Two men stood and reached to assist him. "Amen," the senior Galford repeated, inspiring the others to join in. Soon their voices formed a single chorus.

"Amen, brothers!" Hanson called out happily. "Give your praises to the Father, sing songs to the Son and be filled with the Holy Spirit.

Amen!"

A loud "Amen!" greeted his call and echoed throughout the boxcar.

"Sing with me, brothers. Fill your lungs with the spirit of Christ! Let your voices rise to His glory! Let us sing *Rock of Ages, Cleft for Me*."

Hanson led them in the well-known hymn, followed by a long and joyous gospel intended to raise their spirits. Afterwards, they sang another hand-clapping gospel, and it spread to the other boxcars. Soon the entire train was singing. The armed guards atop the boxcars heard the captives singing and felt a begrudging admiration for these men who could sing so joyously while heading straight for hell.

Early next morning, the scream of metallic brakes awakened the few who had managed to sleep in the constantly jolting railcar. Men snorted, coughed and wheezed to arouse themselves from the abject boredom of the trip. The metallic squealing increased and the cars banged abruptly together, heaving the men forward despite their best efforts to resist the motion. The car finally came to a complete halt on a sidetrack just south of the National Road west of Columbus, Ohio.

The prisoners could hear the sound of armed men assembling outside the car door: Orders were given and repeated; men quick-marched, responding to the orders, their musketry clamoring. The prisoners peered out between the slats of the cars, trying to make out what was happening in the hazy light of the waning full moon. Suddenly, the sliding door was pulled back and cold pre-dawn air invaded the space heated by their bodies. Slowly, men began to climb down from the car, following the Yankees' orders to assemble in groups. A Union officer conducted roll call to confirm all the prisoners were present before marching them the half mile to the gate of Camp

Chase.

Hanson and Dallas half-supported, half-carried Thomas Galford, Sr. as they struggled to keep up. Confederate soldiers marched in military ranks while civilians walked alongside in disorganized fashion. Yankee soldiers marched alongside the ragged column, carrying rifles with fixed bayonets at port arms.

Camp Chase, named after Ohio governor Salmon P. Chase, who served as Lincoln's Secretary of Treasury, was seven acres of hell. The first indication of their future was the gagging odor of the open latrines that ran the length of the camp into an open cesspool. Thousands of men were packed into three separate areas. The prisoners were housed in one-hundred-feet-long by fifteen-feet-wide barracks. The entire compound was surrounded by wood-plank walls twelve feet high.

Upon entering, military clerks processed them, separating officers, enlisted and civilians. Hanson whispered quietly to Sgt. Arbogast, "George, keep our men safe. We will be back at work within a couple weeks, you'll see."

"I hope you're right, Doc. I can't imagine anything worse than having to stay here," Arbogast said, controlling his rising fears.

A Yankee stepped between them. "You, the boy, and the old man need to move over there." The soldier pushed Hanson gently towards a new group being formed.

Hanson and Dallas interlinked arms around the old man's shoulders and began moving in the indicated direction. "Remember, sergeant. Keep 'em safe," Hanson called over his shoulder.

Officers and civilians were directed to Camp One, the smallest of the three barrack compounds. Civilian political prisoners, upon taking a Loyalty Oath, were free to leave. Most civilians opted to take the oath after spending a few days in the squalid camp. Those more firm in their convictions incrementally increased their period of incarceration and with it, their chance of death.

A single confederate officer accompanied the three towards the wood-plank sliding door separating Camp One from the induction area. Dr. Hanson offered his hand to the lieutenant. "Good sir. Allow me to introduce myself. I am Dr. Hanson Bumgardner, late of Pocahontas County, Virginia."

The officer's eyes widened and his brows uplifted. "*The* Dr. Hanson Bumgardner? The herbalist and magician?"

The second of the two aphorisms took Dr. Hanson aback. "Why…yes, I am Dr. Bumgardner the herbalist. How is it we are acquainted, sir?"

"We've never actually met, sir. I am Lieutenant George E. Shearer of the Fifty-First Virginia Infantry. I was captured at Fredericksburg. Before I was assigned duty in the infantry, I served on General Lee's staff with your distant cousin, Lieutenant James Bumgardner of Bumgardner Rye Whiskey fame. He regaled us with tales of your adventures and exploits as a 'special taster' in order to obtain free whiskey. He extolled your cleverness in staying ahead of the family's loyal, but misguided employees, who believed you deserved punishment for your deeds. He laughed when he told us about how you used his whiskey to make 'tonic' for ailments."

"There is more in the tonic than Bumgardner's Rye Whiskey," retorted Dr. Hanson sternly. "I have seen the therapeutic effects of the additional ingredients with my own eyes!"

"Sir, I meant no disrespect. No doubt there are those whose aches and pains were alleviated by the consumption of whiskey mixed with honey and herbs, and others who just needed rebottled whiskey to be able to drink," laughed the brash lieutenant. "At home, we warmed such concoctions, calling them by the general name, a 'hot toddy', which we happily quaffed whenever embraced by a cold or fever."

"Yes, the tonic can indeed be consumed warm," Dr. Hanson admitted. "I have prescribed it that way for just such purpose, but by no means is it simply whiskey and honey. I studied, under Doctor Thomas Brown of Highland County Virginia, the art of doctoring and intend to offer my services to the resident physician for the time that I am confined here."

"A noble gesture, sir, but take no offense if it is declined. I have heard the surgeon here makes little to no effort to comfort the afflicted."

"Not so, sir," a Yankee corporal, guarding the group which Hanson, Dallas and old man Thomas were joining, interrupted. "We have both sick and hospital barracks. If you have fever, then you go to the sick barracks. Battle wounds go to the hospital to be patched up by our surgeon until the prisoner can return to his own barracks. We are not demons here, whatever you may have heard."

"I trust not, corporal. I am amenable to helping the afflicted in either of the wards," Dr. Hanson replied. "Can you secure me an interview with the Post Surgeon?"

"Yup, sir, I'll do it. We need all the help we can get. By the way, I am Corporal Jimmy Conaway."

"Thank you, Corporal. I am Doctor Hanson Bumgardner. Please convey my compliments to the Post Surgeon," Hanson replied in earnest.

Dr. Hanson quickly fell into the routine of camp life, as it never varied from one long boring day to the next. In the meantime, he anxiously awaited his opportunity to speak with the camp medical doctor about assisting in the wards.

One afternoon, Hanson noticed Corporal Conaway on duty in the guard tower and called out, "Corporal Conaway! Were you able to talk to the Post Surgeon about me?"

"Yeah, sorry, I forgot to tell you, Doc," Conaway called down. "He cannot utilize anyone who is not a loyal Unionist. Take the oath and he can put you to work immediately. Otherwise, you'll have to be satisfied with handling minor ailments in your barracks."

Hanson waved at the guard and shrugged. Disappointed about not securing an interview, he sulked about it the rest of the day.

# Chapter Twenty-Five

A few days later, some men in the camp began suffering diarrhea. In less than two days, the entire camp was sick, including the guards. Seeing a chance to prove himself and make a difference for his comrades, Hanson went to one of several sutler window holes cut in the wall for select vendors with permits to sell items to the thousands of incarcerated men.

"Have you any carrots?" Hanson inquired.

"I do. Have you any money?" the vendor chided.

"I shall have, upon delivery of the carrots. Let's see..." Hanson stroked his chin while calculating the number of men in Camp One. "I'll need about twenty pounds. Can you accommodate my request?"

"Yes, but the cost will be..." the vendor sized up Hanson. "Eight dollars."

"Oh my! I didn't mean carrots made of gold," laughed Hanson. "Thank you, my good man, for the humor. I must pass." He laughed again heartily.

"Six dollars," offered the vendor on the other side of the window hole as Hanson walked away.

"Four!" he yelled back continuing to walk away.

"Five!" the disembodied voice shouted.

"Four-fifty?" Hanson asked, pausing and turning.

"Done."

"I need them immediately. Every hour is precious," Hanson said placing a ten-dollar coin on the windowsill for the vendor to see. "I'll also need a quarter-pound of salt, a half-pound of ginger, a string of garlic cloves and a large iron kettle with a lid. This should be enough to cover the cost and afford you a generous profit."

Two hours later, the vendor sent word to Hanson to pick up the goods. He took the carrots, peeled and sliced them into large sections, and placed half in the kettle. Filling the kettle with water from the camp well, he boiled the carrots along with some salt. When the carrots were well cooked, he mashed them in a bowl and separated the pulp from the juice, while he boiled another pot of clean water. When finished processing all the carrots, he added the carrot broth along with some ginger, diced garlic and more salt to the boiling water. Removing the kettle from the fire after ten minutes, he covered it to let it steep.

"Tell the men in our camp to bring their bowls for fresh soup. Tell them it will help their diarrhea," he instructed young Dallas Galford who hastened through the barracks spreading the news.

Soon a long line of emaciated men moved slowly past Dr. Hanson as he ladled out the carrot soup. For many, the soup was the first nutrition they had consumed during their several days of diarrhea. For those who partook, their diarrhea and the stomach cramps lessened. Encouraged, Hanson prepared a second batch of soup for later in the day.

With their cramps relieved, the men began moving about, praising Doc Hanson. After a second helping of the soup, most were fully cured, unlike the guards who complained to the camp physician that the prisoners were receiving better treatment than they.

Two more days of almost unendurable diarrhea and cramps beset the rest of the camp, while Doc Hanson and the inmates of Camp One continued to recover. It was at this point the chief physician requested a meeting with Hanson.

Bumgardner spent the day cleaning and repairing his clothes in preparation to meeting Maj. Thomas McFadden.

At ten o'clock next morning, Dr. Hanson waited outside the shed serving as medical headquarters. A sergeant emerged and motioned for Hanson to enter. Inside, Hanson found a small table with a bleary-eyed officer seated behind it.

"Doctor McFadden or should I address you as Major McFadden, sir?" Hanson asked, offering his hand.

McFadden stood and shook Bumgardner's hand warmly. "It's doctor over major. I am but a brevet major serving temporarily as Post Surgeon until they appoint another. It is Doctor Hanson Bumgardner, I've been informed."

"Yes sir, but please call me Hanson, sir."

"Hanson it is, then," the surgeon replied, smiling tiredly at Hanson. "I am in your debt already, sir."

"In what respects, sir?" Hanson asked, his eyebrows rising.

"Your diarrhea remedy. I have never seen a remedy work so quickly, and without the usual side effects such as headache, nausea, or temporarily increased stomach cramping. I must have the recipe for the rest of the camp," McFadden related.

"It is but a simple herbal remedy, sir. As an herbal doctor, I have a variety of remedies, for example, against fevers, gout, measles, diarrhea, typhoid fever, malaria, battle wounds and, yes, broken hearts." Hanson smiled his best winning smile.

"If you can relieve our camp of the dysentery and respiratory disease we are currently suffering with the same aplomb with which you conquered the diarrhea in Camp One, you will indeed become a hero to both sides." McFadden said, hands behind his back, as he walked to the window of the small building and gazed out on the camp.

"I thank you for the compliment though it should be directed to my mentor, sir." Hanson gave a quick foreshortened bow that went unnoticed by McFadden.

Turning, the temporary Post Surgeon said, "Nonetheless, I present to you two proposals: The first requires you take the Loyalty Oath, after which I will appoint you an Assistant Surgeon in the United States Army with a rank of second lieutenant. Until you take and pass the strenuous Surgeon's Exam, it is the highest rank I can offer." McFadden paused, clearly hoping Hanson would accept his first offer.

"And the second option, sir?" Hanson inquired.

"Not as pleasant an offer, sir. Should you refuse the oath, you will remain a prisoner, awaiting trial for treason. In the interim, you will work with me in the position of *Acting* Assistant Surgeon, serving without rank as a civilian contract physician under the army's direct command. In either case, you will serve under my command as the Post Surgeon."

"I have never taken an oath, save the Hippocratic oath, and I dare not do so now," Hanson said thoughtfully. "I have no stake in war but to ease the suffering it creates."

"An officer's rank, pay, and prestige would go a long way with both the courts and the Ohio ladies," McFadden offered in temptation.

"What would be the pay for a humble *Acting* Assistant Surgeon, sir?" Hanson asked.

"The usual pay: One hundred twelve dollars per month. But,

since you are a prisoner, and refuse the oath, I would be permitted to offer you only half of that amount."

"Then I accept your offer, sir, to serve as an Acting Assistant Surgeon," Hanson said. "When may I begin? Is a surgeon's apron available that I may protect my clothing?"

"You understand you remain a prisoner, awaiting trial for treason?" McFadden asked, surprised by Hanson's the choice.

Hanson nodded his understanding.

"Well, then, you shall begin this day, in sick barracks which is Barracks Number Five in Camp Two. It holds prisoners with fever and illnesses that might pass on to others. Typhoid and malaria are the most common complaints."

"I see. Am I free to treat the prisoners, or am I but a caretaker?" Hanson asked, seeking to define his responsibilities.

"I hereby order you to treat them with any known and accepted remedies you may know," Maj. McFadden assured Hanson.

Within days, Hanson made a recipe for fever based on garlic. He demanded and received two orderlies to assist in the cleaning of the sick barracks. The number of prisoners in the sick barracks soon began to dwindle in number. The guards of the Union Eighty-Eighth Ohio Volunteer Infantry soon allowed Dr. Hanson to pass unchallenged between the three camps.

One day, walking home to Camp One, Sgt. Arbogast approached alongside, matching Hanson's pace. "Good to see you, Doc."

"And you, George. How is everyone?"

"Senior is getting worse. We may have to send him to the sick barracks," revealed Arbogast.

"Go ahead and send him now. I'll take good care of him," Hanson assured the sergeant.

"I know you will. Listen! Friel says some folks in camp believe they've identified the spy in our group. A band of raiders up in Randolph County was arrested a couple of nights after we were."

"Yes, I remember talking with Myers, Jenny and Warren on the train coming from Wheeling. They were part of that group," acknowledged Hanson.

"Precisely. They say that Clem frequented their meetings as well. Both groups ended up bein' arrested by the same Yankee cavalry."

"As for it being the same arresting cavalry, that was the unit stationed in the area. Besides, Gabriel Clem was in Stonewall's Brigade, the Thirty-Third Virginia. Surely that would suggest he's committed to the southern cause."

Arbogast looked about, then lowered his voice. "Committed or not, they believe it's Clem. Maybe the Yankees are threatenin' him or his family. Whatever the case, it looks like folks here are gonna take matters into their own hands."

"Meaning what?" Hanson asked, slowing his pace.

"The men could call a 'Barracks Court' and if convicted, execute him."

"But wouldn't you be caught?" Hanson asked, correctly assuming Arbogast's intent to be part of the trial.

"Others have been executed before and after we arrived, Doc. They smother a man with a pillow while he's asleep and tell the guards he died of consumption or pneumonia. The Post Surgeon wouldn't find any evidence of force when the body's examined, so it'll simply be sent to City Cemetery for burial."

Hanson was shocked by the simplicity of the brutality in the prison, and the creativeness of the prisoners. "So, why tell me?" he asked. "I can't speak for Clem and get him paroled."

"Don't want him paroled. If he's the rat that turned us in, I might just be the pillow man myself."

Hanson looked at the stalwart sergeant. "Again I ask, 'Why tell me?'"

"Because you may be called to testify in Barracks Court."

"I will have nothing to do with this!"

"Doesn't matter, if they want you to testify, they'll rouse you from bed in the dark of night and drag you to the trial."

"I'll not speak. You tell them that. I'll not speak against another man sharing this hellhole."

The next day, a careworn Dr. McFadden visited the sick barracks. Hanson greeted him warmly. "Doctor McFadden, good to see you. The ranks are thinner than when you last inspected."

"I see, Doctor Bumgardner. The place is much better since you assumed duty here. I am pleased you have followed my orders so well." McFadden gave him a wink.

After the inspection, Hanson walked with McFadden across the yard. Seeing an opportunity, Dr. Hanson decided to broach the topic of Gabriel Clem. "Sir, a prisoner named Gabriel Clem may be in mortal danger from his fellow confederates. I thought him a deserter from the first time he and I met, but they believe him to be a Union spy and may do him harm."

McFadden tapped his lips with his index finger in pensive thought. "Thank you, doctor. I am pleased you have confided in me, sir. I am more and more convinced that you are a Unionist at heart, but will not admit it. Rest assured, we will protect Gabriel Clem from his own."

On Saturday, during the regular prisoner exchange, Hanson was able to send a letter to Sue with one of the exchanged men. In it, he asked her to come to the prison camp in Ohio and bring herbs, tonic, and elixir—as much as the old apothecary wagon could carry.

McFadden made an appearance the next morning and found Hanson pouring steaming water over licorice, creating a thick slurry in the bowl. "Cough medicine," Hanson explained, looking up as the major approached.

McFadden nodded his approval, then called Hanson aside. Speaking softly he revealed, "Gabriel Clem was quietly released yesterday. I moved as fast as I could without arousing suspicion. We didn't want him to have to return to his confederate unit, for, as you suspected, he *is* a deserter, and would, if found out, have been subject to punishment. The rest of the soldiers arrested with Clem–Arbogast, Hamilton and the others–were exchanged in order to alleviate suspicions. You and the other civilians need only take the Oath in order to be released."

"I see," Hanson replied, disheartened at not having had the opportunity to say goodbye to his friends.

# Chapter Twenty-Six

Days passed and another trainload of prisoners arrived, many from the Sixty-Second Virginia Infantry. Two brothers, William and Archibald Matheney, ended up in the hospital, sharing an unusual wound. A frightened Yankee had fired his rifle, forgetting to remove the ramrod from the barrel. The rod flew across the battlefield piercing William's side and coming to rest in Archibald's leg, causing immediate infection. Dr. McFadden deferred them to Hanson to try to save the hapless men. Hanson worked at their bedside for three days and nights, dousing their fever with water and treating the wounds with herbs until he was exhausted. William awakened on the fourth day, his fever broken, overjoyed to be alive and, with tears in his eyes, pledged his undying devotion forever to Doc Hanson. Soon after, Archibald's fever broke, and within the week, the two were well enough to join the other prisoners in anticipation of exchange.

An older man, branded a "bushwhacker" by Unionists, joined the camp several days later. Abe Rhinehart, fifty-five years old with a cantankerous attitude that Hanson admired, claimed the bunk below Hanson, and volunteered as his orderly. Abe admitted privately to Hanson to having led a gang of outlaws, stealing horses and selling them to the confederates. He laughed at Hanson's use of a river to befuddle pursuers, and said he would try it if and when he was released.

Another prisoner, Michael O'Day, Sixth Virginia Cavalry, became Rhinehart's attendant.

Several weeks later O'Day tapped Hanson on the shoulder in the sick barracks. "Sir. Doctor McFadden desires you join him at medical headquarters."

Hanson headed immediately for the new, larger headquarters building. Upon entering, he was surprised to find Sue waiting impatiently. Her excitement was infectious and intoxicating.

"Sweetheart!" Hanson exclaimed, stretching his arms out to her.

"Darling!" she replied, charging into his embrace.

"It is always pleasant to see a couple reunited," McFadden said, smiling jovially.

"There would be no need to reunite but for you Yankees taking my husband, the doctor, prisoner when he was only seeking to tend to the wounded and infirm. The prisoner exchange agreement notes that Regimental Surgeons and their assistants are not considered prisoners-of-war." Sue's words were sharp and biting.

"I see your lovely wife is well informed on the Dix-Hill Exchange Agreement," commented Maj. McFadden, still smiling.

"I would not be, but for …" Sue began, but was interrupted.

"Doctor McFadden is not the cause of my unjust incarceration. Rather he has been a steadfast benefactor," Hanson softly interjected, calming Sue, stroking her hair and breathing deeply the smell of her perfume lingering in the air. Turning from Sue to the officer, he said, "Sue knows I am here because of my refusal to take an unnecessary oath. I should not be regarded a prisoner as I, too, am a doctor, *Major* McFadden." Hanson stressed his colleague's military title to drive his point deeper.

"Sir, the exchange agreement requires you be *in uniform* for immediate parole. I have several times offered you..."

"What offer?" Sue interrupted.

"To become a Yankee medical officer..."

"Oh, Hanson, did you not take his offer?" Sue asked with concern.

"I could not in good conscience swear allegiance to..."

"Husband, you must take the oath," Sue insisted.

"Listen to your wife, Doctor. The offer stands," Doctor McFadden added.

"I'm deeply moved, but I can't in good conscience swear before man and God that which I don't fully believe in my heart," Hanson declared, ending their entreaties. Sue, knowing her husband, gave up.

Over the next month, Hanson suffered with the rest of the prisoners in Camp Chase, attending to their ills, while Sue, following his instructions, convinced Doctor McFadden to designate the apothecary wagon an alternate sutler's wagon. In this way Hanson was able to purchase from Sue necessary herbs, bandages, and liniments for his charges. In addition, Sue made available Dr. Hanson's Tonic and Elixir to the citizens of Columbus.

By now, of the original group, only Hanson and Thomas Galford, Sr. remained. Each knew he need only affirm his loyalty to the United States to be released. Senior refused to take the oath saying it was enough that he was born an American. Hanson realized that, at seventy-one years of age, it was unlikely the man would change his mind. Furthermore, his rapidly deteriorating health would have made travel of any distance difficult if not fatal. Hanson made his decision to stay with Senior, whom he now viewed as a second father.

The war dragged on, the evidence being the swelling and shrinking of the ranks of confederate prisoners. Most had no interest or desire to escape, as it was common knowledge that, in time, a prisoner exchange would inevitably take place. Luckily for the couple, Doctor McFadden allowed the Bumgardners private visitation rights in the old medical headquarters, the building having been relegated to storage.

On June 19, 1863, Thomas Galford Senior passed away in the dark just before dawn. Hanson had been at the old man's bedside counting his slowing breaths and weakening pulse to the end. The elixir made the final days comfortable for the gentle grandfather, whose alleged crime resulting in his death was listed in the Yankee records as "Bushwhacker."

Hanson purchased a coffin for the elder Galford, and assisted with placing the body in the casket and nailing it shut. Several volunteers placed the casket on a cart, and an escort of twelve men accompanied it to the gate while the rest of the prisoners stood in respectful silence. Galford was neither the first nor would he be the last death at camp, but for each of the deceased, all the prisoners would line up and salute as the body passed by. Sue Bumgardner met the cart on the other side to escort it to City Cemetery for interment. The coffin, Hanson noted, passed through the gate uninspected.

Sue was dressed in black and walked alone behind the casket as townspeople watched, morbidly fascinated by the individual burial. These same townspeople seemed immune to the toll of thousands of deaths in battle, or the horrid suffering inside the walls of the camp.

Several days after the passing of the elder Galford, Doctor McFadden called Hanson into his office. "Now that your elderly friend has gone to meet his maker, will you reconsider my offer? It would be much easier if you and Sue could restart your life together outside of here."

"I suppose you're right," Hanson reluctantly agreed. "I will take the Oath."

"Good! I must inform you, however, that the regulations have recently changed; now it requires that you admit your crime. It is a new requirement from Washington. There are many such bad regulations. You will have to agree to having been a bushwhacker," McFadden informed Hanson.

"I will not admit to 'ambushing innocent men,' so I guess I will have to stay after all," Hanson replied glumly.

"Also, Hanson, be aware that a new Post Surgeon is soon to be named. I will then become an Assistant Surgeon. The next Post Surgeon may not be as generous."

"I will accept whatever the Lord sends my way. He gives no man a burden that he can not bear," Hanson affirmed, repeating the oft-used phrase, secretly worrying about the arrival of a new Post Surgeon.

Several nights later, a new group of prisoners arrived at the compound, including two wounded civilians who were sent to Camp One. Hanson found them severely wounded, but not yet dead.

The first passed out from the pain and Hanson, with the assistance of two orderlies, amputated the man's leg to save his life. The second, awake, in severe pain, and terrified at seeing his companion's leg cut off, began screaming. Hanson slipped the man sufficient elixir to cause the man to fall into unconsciousness, allowing Hanson to clean, debride, and dress the man's mangled arm, hoping to save it and his life.

The next day, the arm wound was considerably better. The man, grasping Hanson by his good arm, pulled him face-to-face and promised through gritted teeth, "I have gold hidden in my belt. You can have it all for some more of that elixir, Doc."

Hanson let the man sip until his eyes slowly rolled upward and he passed into blissful oblivion. Hanson, looking cautiously to his left and then right, slipped the money belt from the prisoner and placed it around his own waist. Then, he examined the first of the two who remained passed out. In the man's vest pocket, he found a wallet with a photo and several bills. He took the bills as payment and slipped the purse back into the man's vest.

Hanson was awakened the next day by one of his orderlies stating that the civilian whose leg was amputated was no longer breathing. Hanson confirmed the death. Attendants wrapped the body in a dirty sheet and respectfully carried him to the gate while the rest of the prisoners again stood at attention and saluted his passing in memorial. At the gate, the attendants laid the body on the ground. Hanson watched as two Yankee guards opened the sheet and searched the man's pockets. A Union sergeant seeing them shouted and waved them away. The body lay untouched and unattended until a wagon arrived to take it to City Cemetery.

# Chapter Twenty-Seven

On Tuesday, February 12, 1867, three days before Hanson stood on the gallows, Sue and James Bumgardner were continuing their search for Gabriel Clem. Sue was certain that had Gabriel Clem appeared at the trial to back up Hanson's story, the jury would have acquitted her husband. Now, it was up to them to locate Clem to bring him back to testify in order to stop Hanson's impending execution on Friday.

They arrived at a crossroads in southern Virginia known simply by the name of the tavern, Powderhorn Tavern Crossing, that occupied the southwest corner of the intersection. It was rumored that a man fitting Clem's description, riding a black and white spotted Appaloosa, had been spotted there recently.

"There's only two ways out I can see, the front door and a side door," James said, scouring the building from afar.

"He's in there, James. I'm sure of it. That's his Appaloosa at the rail," Sue said excitedly. "It's unlikely he'll just give up, and, since he is a coward, equally unlikely that he'll shoot it out. He'll head out the side door," she confidently predicted as she pulled her .32 caliber Colt revolver from her purse.

"I'll cover the side door then," replied James, knowing Sue could identify Clem but he couldn't.

Sue entered the front door of the tavern. Two men sitting idly at the bar, looked over their shoulders, surprised to see a woman. Three men sat at a table along the far wall playing cards while a fourth snored face down on the table. Engrossed in the strategy of the game, the card players hardly noticed her entering. A dozen other unoccupied tables were scattered about against the walls.

Then Sue spotted Clem, sitting alone on a chair not ten feet away, flipping cards at an upturned hat. He tossed a lazy glance towards the open saloon door, the sudden bright sunlight backlighting the person standing there in silhouette. The moment the door shut, he recognized Sue Bumgardner moving quickly in his direction.

He jumped up, and showing his open palms to indicate he was unarmed, said, "Sue, it is good to see you," as he minced around the table to keep it between him and the angry woman pointing a revolver at him.

"Take your lover's quarrel elsewhere, lady," shouted the bartender, who ducked quickly behind the bar when Sue swung the pistol, first his direction, then back at her quarry.

"Oh, we will," Sue said. Clem upturned the table and crouched behind it as she took aim. "Won't we, Gabriel Clem? On your feet, you bastard. You've some fast traveling to do!" She motioned him up with the gun and he slowly rose, hands held high.

Suddenly, he heaved the table at Sue, and crouching low, dashed for the side door to make an escape. Sue dodged the table and, aiming low to wound rather than kill, fired one shot, then another. The men at the poker table leaped out of the way, pulling tables and chairs down around them for protection while the men at the bar hastily splayed flat on the floor to present as little a target as possible.

Sue fired a third and fourth round as Clem leaped over another empty table and stumbled into the door. Turning the handle, he pushed, but the door didn't move. Hurriedly, he tried a second push, but the door steadfastly refused to budge. As he prepared to put his shoulder to the door, it suddenly flew open and Clem saw the butt end of a rifle just as it made contact squarely between his eyes.

Gabriel Clem awakened several hours later, hands and feet bound as he bounced in the back of James Bumgardner's lightweight buckboard wagon pulled by Hanson's stalwart, graying mule, Banjo. Clem moaned with pain as he attempted to find a comfortable position.

"So, you're finally awake. Good. I was afraid James hit you hard enough to put you in a coma," Sue Bumgardner said.

"No matter," Gabriel snarled. "I won't testify. Let 'em hang Hanson; I don't care."

"No, Clem, you've got that wrong. We're taking you back, and you *will* testify. You will tell them the truth: that Hanson did not kill Eubanks. You will tell them that he had nothing to do with Eubanks' murder," Sue demanded.

"An' how exactly do I know that?" growled their prisoner.

"Because you know who killed Eubanks. I think you ran because you're involved in the murder. You've proven you're jealous of Hanson. You hate him, so you wanted him to take the fall," Sue stated, staring Clem right in the eye.

"Zat so? An' what if I did? I hate everythin' Hanson is—smart, handsome, good with the ladies. I hate him and I don't care a whit if that sonuvabitch..."

"Because he is everything you could never be?" snapped James. "It's true, Gabriel. You are neither smart nor handsome nor good with the ladies."

"But I ain't the one facing the gallows, am I?" Clem caustically retorted, sitting up and facing his captors. "Now you two can join him for kidnapping me. Ha, ha!"

"James, stop the wagon," Sue directed. James obeyed, Banjo braying his objections. "It's like this, Clem: You have a choice and you may as well make it here and now." She searched the woods on either side of the pike. "You see that boulder over there?"

Clem didn't respond, looking instead at his feet, which angered Sue so much she snatched the buggy whip and struck him across the face. "You see that boulder over there?" she growled again, pointing with the whip. He glanced up and nodded.

"That is where Jim and I will bury you if you continue to persist. The patrons at the Powderhorn were told you're an escaped horse thief, which is the truth, damn you! If you won't back up Hanson's story, then you are of no further use to us and I'll end this here and now!" Her voice rose as she angrily pulled the pistol from her purse and aimed it between Gabriel's eyes.

James reached out and took the gun from Sue's hand. Then he cocked it and aimed it at Clem's head. "Well, Clem?" he prodded impassively. "We've been searching for you since September when Hanson was arrested. We've only a few days left to get you to Marietta to stop the hanging. If you are not going to cooperate, then we might as well end this now. I was a sergeant in the Third West Virginia Cavalry and I have no qualms about killing one last rebel."

James' bland expression said more than his words, and struck fear in Clem's heart.

"Alright, I'll talk. Jus' tell me what ya want me to say," Clem said, already scheming in his mind how he might incriminate them with witness tampering.

"I want you to tell the truth," Sue said. "Hanson isn't guilty and you know it."

Clem looked at Sue, wondering exactly how much she really knew and worried that she had somehow uncovered the whole dark truth. "I'm sick and can't travel," he protested. A round of raspy coughing seized him.

Sue took the weapon from Jim, uncocked it and replaced it in her purse. "I'm sick, too, Gabriel. Of you. Of your 'friends'. Of everything you say and stand for. And, sick or not, you *will* travel," Sue stated.

Clem nodded his reluctant acceptance of the situation, and the wagon jerked to a start and continued following the deep-cut ruts in the road on to Ohio.

# Chapter Twenty-Eight

The rain began falling on him again, and Hanson stretched tall, searching above the gallows walls, praying James and Sue had somehow had found Woods or Gollier or Clem and were just over the horizon on their way to save him. Hanson swallowed hard as the men watching him from below shifted uneasily in the slow steady rain.

A second bong sounded from the clock on the square indicating the passage of a full hour since Hanson had begun speaking. The time was now one o'clock.

"I was treated quite unfairly in Yankee captivity," Hanson continued edgily, "yet felt rewarded in that I was easing the suffering of the incarcerated. Upon Galford's passing, McFadden's offer became viable but for the new confession requirement. I nevertheless continued to assist Doctor McFadden..."

On Tuesday, June 30, 1863, McFadden greeted Hanson in the yard of Camp One. "I bring good news. General Headquarters rescinded the requirement to confess in order to be released; you need only swear allegiance to the Union and promise not to take up arms or cross the state line. The Provost has agreed to change the charge against you to 'aiding rebels,' a charge normally reserved for doctors who treat the wounds of enemy soldiers, or for other non-violent acts of rebellion."

"I will agree to that. I can spend Independence Day with my wife," observed Hanson, relieved his day of release had finally arrived.

"As part of the release agreement, because you are a Virginian, you must swear allegiance to the Virginia government created in Wheeling in 1861."

Hanson nodded his understanding.

"As a civilian you will be required to report to the Atheneum for additional orders. I will contact Lieutenant Colonel Darr, the commandant there, and advise him you are working for me. However, *you cannot cross the state line*," McFadden emphatically reminded Hanson.

Hanson again nodded his agreement to all of the conditions as they walked together towards the administration building to sign the papers.

The battles taking place at the time of Independence Day in 1863 gripped both sides of the nation. Lee's second invasion of the North collapsed. CSA General George E. Picket led the disastrous "Picket's Charge" at Gettysburg, Pennsylvania. CSA Major General Sterling Price failed in a futile attempt to take the fortifications at Helena, Arkansas, to relieve the besieged CSA forces in Vicksburg, and Vicksburg fell to Grant, its defenders and citizens having been starved into submission. "The Gray Ghost," John S. Mosby, led his Mosby's Rangers into Ohio to capture arms, supplies and the attention of the nation as Lee retreated from Gettysburg.

Hanson sat in the kitchen of the small apartment Sue had rented in Columbus. He put down The Ohio State Journal, a notoriously Republican-leaning daily, and rubbed his eyes. Looking at Sue percolating the coffee on the stove as the early morning sunlight softly outlined her form, he offered, "We can't believe a word this rag says about the war. Men at the camp say Mosby is raiding all over eastern Ohio and into Pennsylvania. This paper says they have him trapped along the Ohio River. The river, it says, is high from the rains and he can't cross into Pennsylvania or Virginia."

"Can we have one conversation that doesn't involve the war?" Sue asked testily. Hanson stood, crossed the kitchen, and rubbed her shoulders as she poured a cup of coffee.

"It's hard, Sue. The war touches everyone more each day. It is like an unwanted relative, always there, demanding attention." He nuzzled her neck and she turned to face him. "It won't let go of us," he finished as they embraced.

"Let's go to California. Let's go out there ..."

"No, Sue, good or bad, I know my fate is here in Ohio, not out there. Here, I can make a difference, do some healing."

Sitting down at the table with the paper and a freshly-poured cup of coffee, Hanson scanned the headlines again, and expressed his thoughts: "Mosby may end Camp Chase. I am hearing about numbers in the thousands captured in Lee's failed offensive in Pennsylvania. If Mosby is cut off and his corps captured, Camp Chase will be completely overrun by prisoners."

"But it will be short lived, won't it?" Sue responded. "Surely, they will continue the exchange. It is the only humane thing to do."

"Sue, there is nothing humane about this war," Hanson declared, sipping at the hot black liquid and recalling days in the camp when three-day-old coffee was considered a luxury. Hanson put down the paper and stood to go. "I am working today in the hospital with Dr. McFadden. I don't know what time I will return, but rest assured, I will return as quickly as possible."

# Chapter Twenty-Nine

At the camp, the guards warily awaited news of the thousands of prisoners-of-war they knew were on the way from Gettysburg, Vicksburg, and Helena; Mosby's men were still evading the Yankees, but their capture seemed imminent. Designed to hold two thousand prisoners, the camp already exceeded capacity by over a thousand.

Anticipating a sudden massive influx of wounded, Dr. McFadden had the entire hospital re-cleaned. Hanson directed the reorganization of the beds into 'V' configurations so the bunks would occupy less space, thereby increasing the hospital's capacity. The wounded were always the last to be exchanged, and the medical staff anticipated caring for the men much longer than the average prisoner.

Soon, boxcars full of prisoners-of-war began arriving hourly, adding thousands of prisoners to the already over-burdened camp. The overcrowding in camp was so horrific that hundreds had to sleep outside on the ground with little more than a worn blanket. The look of defeat in the eyes of most told Hanson that the war was nearly over, though some of the hateful stares incited fear within him of a never-ending conflict.

In the hospital, Dr. Hanson saw carnage as he had never seen it before. He had previously been assigned to treat the walking wounded who generally had superficial or at least non-lethal wounds. Now, he and Dr. McFadden debrided charred and ravaged skin, amputating as many limbs as medically required, and dressing the rest. The odor of burnt and rotting flesh cut deeply into Hanson's psyche. He had seen men die before, but not so many so quickly.

As he became lost in the confusion and commotion, a young corporal grabbed his arm. Hanson saw his begging eyes. "Doc! Doc! Ya'll gotta take a look at me. My left leg hurts so bad!"

When Hanson bent over to examine the leg, he was not shocked to discover the leg was gone, lost to the saw-blade of a battlefield surgeon. The crooked stitches barely holding the stump together oozed black blood.

"Orderly! Scissors and catgut! Now! This man needs immediate attention!" Turning back to the corporal, he said, "I'll see what I can do about the pain, soldier," and pulled a bottle of elixir from his inside breast pocket. "Here, take a sip of…" Hanson stopped mid-sentence as he examined the corporal who was slack-jawed, motionless, his eyes glazed in a fixed stare. Placing an ear to the man's chest, he confirmed the obvious. With a quick sleight-of-hand motion, he lifted the dead soldier's wallet, pocket watch and jack-knife, and slipped them quickly into his vest, waving away the orderly who had returned with the tray of requested items.

"He won't need those after all," Hanson informed the orderly who nodded and hurried away to locate the burial detail.

Knowing the Yankee guards would search him upon leaving the camp, Hanson headed to the storeroom in the southwest corner of the medical building. Stepping behind several neat rows of boxes, he located a particular corner wall slat two rows from the floor. Prying it loose, he slipped the purloined goods inside the wall. In the hiding place were a stack of cash, several gold pocket watches, and a cigar box containing assorted jewelry and gold rings—mostly wedding bands, the vow "till death do us part" having been completed in Hanson's war-corrupted logic. *The dead do not need the money, and the Yankees would rob the bodies at City Cemetery anyway. The guards don't give a damn for a man alive and shouldn't benefit just because they were selected to carry the body to the grave. Rather he, as the soldier's physician, should be reimbursed for the care he had provided.* It was with this false reasoning that he justified his behavior.

That evening at home, Hanson decided it was time to breech the subject with Sue. "As you know, dear, I have, from time to time, reluctantly agreed to accept the payment in various forms from those offering it out of gratitude for my services. I have secreted it in wall stash in the storage area of the medical building. The stash is fast filling up, and the new wounded from Gettysburg seem to be dying as quickly as I treat them. I am concerned about getting caught with the goods before I can determine a means by which to remove it from within the stockade."

He was surprised to hear Sue's pragmatic reply: "They don't check your shoes, do they? Just pat you down, right? Put the cash in your shoes and we can benefit from it right away."

"There is quite a bit, dear."

"Then make a cash transfer every few days. As for the rest, I'm sure you will find a way if you put your mind to it."

Kissing her, he declared, "Perfect. A worthy challenge," and set himself to the task.

The next day, he measured and sketched several accurate drawings of the corner. Several days later, he built a corner shelf in the barracks, stacking boxes of supplies upon it. Prying a board loose at the side of the shelf gave quicker and more discrete access to the cache. That night, he removed a large stack of bills and layered them into his shoes.

Sue laughed at Hanson when he walked in the door, saying, "Your work is making you a great man. You are a full inch taller coming home than going to work."

Hanson sat on a kitchen chair and shook the bills from his shoes. "I brought the large bills first, figuring if I got caught it would be for a more worthy amount," he laughed.

"Don't leave the small bills behind, husband," Sue chided.

"No, I will simply wait 'till the risk is less for the lesser reward." They laughed together until their laughter trailed off into silence and Sue sat next to him.

"You need to know, husband, that I saw that horrid man in the market again today," she related anxiously.

"Which horrid man, dear? There are so many." Hanson chuckled.

"I am not joking, Hanson. I saw Gabriel Clem lurking at the market today." Sue shuddered at the memory.

"Lurking? How is it one lurks at the market?" Hanson forced a smile, trying to hide his uneasiness about Gabriel being in the vicinity. The man should have been exchanged back to the Thirty-Third Virginia Infantry instead of simply being released, Hanson fumed.

"He's trouble," Sue said simply. "I knew it in Virginia, but said nothing. I don't trust that man," she declared. "I don't know if he recognized me, as I pulled my large blue hat down over my eyes."

"I believe it is time for me to buy you a pistol, perhaps a thirty-two caliber you can keep in your purse. These are dangerous times and there are many dangerous men about, not just Clem. I don't like that man and don't trust him, either. The men in the camp planned a

Barracks Court trial for him. When I mentioned it to McFadden, bingo, the next day he's released and the men proposing the Barracks Court trial are all exchanged. I'm guessing I saved his life that day."

"I'm not sure why," Sue said and shook her head in disbelief.

"Nor I, darling. Nor I," whispered Hanson, drawing her closer.

On Sunday, July 26, 1863, Cincinnati transferred eight hundred ninety prisoners to Camp Chase. These were the captured rebels from Morgan's Raiders. The hospital overflowed into the adjacent barracks. Hanson and Rhinehart were assigned to greet the wounded and performing triage, selecting those the surgeon would see and those with less dangerous wounds which could be treated later.

Five men carried a wounded man on a makeshift three-by-six-foot wooden stretcher several inches thick. The wounded man was young, his shivering, sweating, and paleness suggesting a heavy loss of blood. As Hanson examined him, the four men who had carried the young man crowded tightly about Hanson. Looking left and right, Hanson asked, "Could I have some room, please?"

The four, after looking at each other as if to gain a group okay, leaned back. The moment Hanson proceeded, the crowd closed in about him again.

"How is he, Doc?" the oldest of the gathered men asked, concern apparent on his baleful, filthy face.

Looking around the circle, Hanson noted the men shared the same warrior features, and surmised they were of the same family, perhaps brothers or cousins. All save two: A black man and another soldier who stood behind were definitely not related.

Looking at the black man, Hanson said, "You are free to go. There are no slaves here. Take the Loyalty Oath and be on your way."

"Like hell he will!" the man standing beside him snorted angrily.

"Like hell I will!" the black man repeated even more emphatically.

Wanting to lighten the sudden heaviness permeating the room, Hanson put on his disarming smile, asking, "What unit are you boys from?" to put the men at ease.

"Seventh Kentucky Cavalry," snapped the old man, his fierce eyes flashing.

"Yet yours is not a Kentucky accent, private," Hanson pointed out congenially as he continued to examine the young man on the table.

"We were recruited in Grapevine, Texas, as cavalry. We called ourselves Gano's Guards. When we got to Tennessee, the rebel commanders folded us into the Seventh Kentucky. We were captured along with General Mosby's Corps."

"I see. Are you the leader of the family, then?" Hanson offered the man his bloodied hand, keeping his tone gentle, but insistent.

"John M. Woods," the old man said, shaking Hanson's hand vigorously. "This here's James Woods, and Samuel Woods. Just behind them, that's Polk Wade, and our former servant is Hardin Battle. Your patient is John Woods. 'Junior' we call him. And, yes, we all come from the same family in Texas. Polk was a field hand come to us along with Hardin before the war. Hardin picked his own name when he enlisted...Hardin Battle, see?"

"I like it very much," Hardin smiled, his eyes shining. "It was my first act as a free man. My second was to enlist in the cavalry with my family here." His rich robust voice sounded refreshingly melodious as he wrapped his arms around James and Sam's shoulders.

"I like it, too, then," Hanson offered with an even broader smile. Not wanting to engage further, Hanson returned his attention to the young man, resuming his inspection of the younger Woods' wound.

"This wound is deep and ripe for infection. It needs to be watched closely," Hanson said. "He's also lost a lot of blood, and could greatly benefit from some tonic, if you have any money. The Yankees won't pay for it."

"Okay, I'll pay. But it better work good," the eldest, John M. Woods, warned.

"It will," Hanson assured. "Abe, escort our newest inductees to a sutler's window where they may purchase some tonic, please." Abe Rhinehart nodded and waved his hand, beckoning the other Woods to follow. Polk and Hardin stayed.

Hanson dressed Junior's wound after packing it with herbs. Junior, Hanson concluded, was like a brother to Hardin and Polk, as they were all near the same age and most likely had grown up together. Despite the wound, Junior kidded with his comrades before surrendering to sleep. Luckily, his young body responded well to treatment and he began to heal quickly.

Two days later, medical attendant Abe Rhinehart approached Hanson. "The litter they carried Junior in on is a shipping box, you know."

"Yes, but he won't leave it. I suggested to him he would be more comfortable on a…"

"James Woods let slip that it's full of cash, and Hardin confirmed it not five minutes ago," Abe said excitedly. "It's mostly paper money along with some gold and silver coins taken in Morgan's Raid."

"Surely not! They smuggled it all this way?" was Hanson's surprised response.

"Yes, by carrying Junior wounded on top of the box like a haphazard litter. It's absurd, but it worked. Only thing is, now they're concerned about getting it out of here. The ruse won't hold long with

Junior getting better so fast. I hinted you had a secret stash back in the storeroom, and that, maybe, for a fee…"

"What are you talking about?" protested Hanson.

"Listen. I can read you like a book, Hanson. I'm not sure where it is exactly, but I seen you and all the other doctors purloin the valuables of the dead. It's common knowledge. What nobody knows is how you can get it past the guards. We all assumed you had bribed several guards…"

"I never saw any of the doctors take from the dead."

"Right, and they and nobody else ever saw you, either," Rhinehart retorted.

"Well, remember from now on that you have *never* seen me or any other doctor taking from the dead," Hanson emphasized. He paused a few moments. "You mentioned a fee?" he asked quietly after recouping his composure.

"Ah, yes! The monetary motive triumphs once more. They will pay ten per cent to protect it while they're here in camp."

"How much do they have?"

"Over five thousand dollars," Abe replied.

"I will be discharging Junior Woods to the general prison population soon. When I do, lean the pallet up against the far storeroom wall."

Two days later, Hanson declared Junior fit to join the rest of the prisoner population, and late that night broke open the box, secretly moving the money to his hiding place under the corner shelf.

# Chapter Thirty

Dr. Albert Longwell received his appointment as the new Post Surgeon at the end of July, 1863. Brevet Major McFadden became Assistant Post Surgeon, returning to his permanent rank of lieutenant. Despite the rapidly deteriorating conditions, Hanson found Maj. Longwell a source of continual delight. Even when they had to begin billeting hospital and sick barracks overflow in the yard, Maj. Longwell remained optimistic and jovial. The Major met with his staff in an effort to lighten their spirits and prepare them for the next onslaught.

He started this day's meeting in his usual inimitable fashion.

"I know you all love a good play on words, but can you really stand the *pun*ishment?" He waited for the groans to die down before continuing. "I must make an admission to you, boys. I have a fear of needles because they really *get under my skin*. And, how about the forty-niner whose career didn't *pan out*? Aha, ha, ha!" Longwell laughed, unable to contain himself, joining in with "his boys."

When the laughs quieted, Longwell's face became serious. "It's going to get worse, men. Supplies are dwindling and Lincoln no longer recognizes the Dix-Hill prisoner-of-war exchange agreement. When we bring men into camp now, they will remain here until war's end. It is not at all a pleasant prospect..." his voice trailed away, leaving each to his own thoughts.

"As of today, we'll start having the orderlies boil all the used bandages and dry them in the sun." The meeting continued with order after order regarding the careful conservation and, wherever possible, re-use of all medical supplies.

By mid-August, everyone in the overcrowded camp was sweltering in the summer heat. The stench of the cesspool permeated the entire grounds, and James Woods and Hardin Battle contracted diarrhea. Hanson had to feed the two heavily-diluted carrot soup by hand, conserving every drop, as vegetables had become hard to come by. Slowly, the two responded.

One late August morning, John M. Woods angrily approached Hanson. "Doc! I just got word we are to be transferred to another camp, not exchanged. What the devil is this? We had a deal!"

Hanson raised and eyebrow and spoke softly. "What deal are you talking about, John?" he asked, not having heard about any transfers.

"I heard they are transferring us to Camp Douglas," Woods growled, his eyes flashing.

Relieved to hear it was not about knowing about the end of prisoner exchanges, Hanson replied, "Transfer? I haven't heard about this."

"They might as well kill us right here," Woods replied. "Everyone knows that no one who goes there ever lives to return home. And what about our money?"

"It will be safe here," Doc Hanson tried to assure Woods.

"I don't want it here! You were supposed to get it *out* of here," Woods growled.

"There's been no way to get it out yet, but I'm working on it.

Leave the money here where it's safe…"

"No way! The money comes with us, dammit!" Woods yelled and stomped off in a flurry of angry arm waving.

Hanson went to Maj. Longwell that morning. "Major, I am concerned about the condition of several prisoners slated to be transferred to Camp Douglas. I would be happy to check them for you…"

"You needn't worry, Doctor Hanson. I just finished going through the hospital and sick barracks and certifying those not able to travel. Thank you for the offer, however. Have you finished your own rounds yet?" Longwell's tired eyes commanded respect.

"No sir. I'll see to it immediately, sir." Hanson pivoted and headed out the door, thwarted in his attempt to keep Woods and his kin in camp. As he walked ruefully across the compound, he was met by Abe Rhinehart, who confided more bad news.

"I am slated for release, Hanson."

Swallowing his disappointment at losing such an able orderly and friend, he replied, "Abe, that is great news! It's time for you to leave this place of misery and return home to family." Hanson continued his walk across the compound and Abe matched pace.

"No, sir. You don't understand. I want to stay here with you. I want to continue helping you. That no longer being possible, I want to introduce you to someone I met here who I think might be able to take my place. He bunks next to the Woods. He was with the Thirty-Third Infantry and captured at Gettysburg. He's not been here long but is already close as kin to the Woods boys. I overhead them trading stories about stealing horses and gold."

"Was the new man a Partisan Ranger?"

"I suspect such, though I don't recall having heard him actually say that, really." Abe saw John M. Woods in the crowd nearby, grabbed Hanson's arm and stopped him. "John! Over here!"

John Woods strode confidently across the compound towards Abe, constantly looking over his shoulder as though expecting someone to follow. As he made his way through the crowd, Hanson saw Gabriel Clem taking several jogging steps to catch up with Woods.

"That's the man I was talking about, Doc. He served with Stonewall's Brigade!" Abe said, pointing at Clem.

*Gabriel sure pitches that line often,* Hanson observed in his mind, wondering where this was all going.

"Doc Hanson, we meet again!" the six-footer said, shuffling up to Hanson.

"You know each other?" Abe asked, caught off guard.

"Yep. Doc here patched me up once. We was arrested together once, too," Gabriel Clem bragged.

"Is that so?" John Woods asked, squinting one eye and raising the brow of the other.

"Well, yes. I did patch him up. A minor wound. And, yes, we were arrested together along with several others in a house where I was attending a patient," Hanson agreed, calmly siphoning off the steam from Clem's story.

"Well, then, this is good," John M. Woods declared. "Gabriel has a way out of our jam."

"And how is that?" Hanson questioned.

"Sharing prison with a man helps to build trust. I haven't known Gabriel long, but I know I can trust him. He says he can take the oath, get out, and hang around Columbus. That way he can keep watch on you. This war can't last much longer and, if we survive, Gabriel will make sure we come back to our money; if we don't survive, Gabriel has promised to return it to our family in Texas. He'll keep track of you, Hanson. Meanwhile you, Abe, will keep track of Gabriel, and Hanson will keep our money safe." John pointed his finger one-by-one at Gabriel Clem, Abe Rhinehart, and Hanson Bumgardner.

"I don't know. This vastly complicates things…" Hanson replied.

"No arguments, Doc," Woods said menacingly. "Unless you get my money to me in Camp Douglas, this is the plan. I hear now they're planning to take us in the morning by train."

Hanson thought quickly. "Alright, Gabriel can watch me, Abe can watch him, and I will watch the money until we can get it to you. But if the Yankees find it, we all lose."

"Yeah, we lose our money, Gabriel and Abe lose their percentage, and you lose your life. Keep the Yankees from finding the cache or that's the penalty. I can be quite creative about having people killed." John M. Woods, normally fierce-appearing, now looked truly malevolent.

"I will keep track of Gabriel and the doc," Abe said fiercely. "I suggest that instead of leaving, Gabriel become an orderly here. That way he'll have a better eye on the doc. I can watch from outside…"

"I like that even better. See to it, Doc," John ordered. Looking each man in the eyes, he spit in his hand and put it out towards them to finalize the agreement. "Then, it's done."

"Done." Abe and Gabriel both spit in their palms and the three clasped hands. Hanson paused, then reluctantly put his hand on top, saying, "Done."

Hanson put in a request for Gabriel Clem as his orderly, but after Rhinehart was discharged, Clem was once again abruptly and surreptitiously released from the prison, much to Hanson's surprise.

# Chapter Thirty-One

November proved formidable. Pneumonia ran rampant in the camp, as the soldiers captured during the summer had no winter coats. Hanson, increasingly exhausted, lost track of the number of dead. Maj. Longwell continually searched for creative means to maintain staff health and morale, seeking and accepting humanitarian assistance from the local community to provide desperately needed food, clothes, bandages and medicines.

Hanson, for his part, prepared a tonic of spring water, honey and lemon to relieve the constant coughing. Despite the medical staff's best efforts many died. So many, in fact, a new cemetery had to be opened closer to the prison.

When Hanson arrived home one late November evening, he could immediately tell something was bothering Sue. "What is it, dear?" he inquired, despite his own fatigue.

"Today, while I was preparing to take the button necklaces to the Garden Club tea, I saw Gabriel Clem on the sidewalk, looking in."

"Surely you must be mistaken, dear," he said, trying to calm her fear.

"I am not mistaken, husband. When I went out the back door, I could see him hiding behind the chestnut tree out front. I was able to get the drop on him by coming up around the bushes."

"Whatever would you do that for, Sue?"

"I stuck my Colt in his ribs and told him to be gone. I told him I would kill him on sight if he ever threatened you or me again. He professed admiration for me and respect for you, and claimed he just happened to be passing by, but I had watched him for quite a while before going outside. He left quickly after I confronted him."

"You were brave to confront him, darling, though I would have preferred you called the police."

"I have worse news, dear, so please sit." She led Hanson to the fainting couch, clutching a worn envelope to her chest. Sue looked at him with melancholy eyes. They sat and he took the letter from her shaking hands, unfolded it and began to read.

"No! Not Sammy!" he cried as he read. "Not Sammy and…oh, my God, Jim, too!" The letter related the battle death of Sam Riddle and the severe wounding of Jim Riddle while serving in the Tenth West Virginia Infantry at the Second Battle of Rappahannock Station. "Jim is back home in Spruce Creek, but not expected to survive, and I cannot cross the state line to be with him! Oh, Merciful Heavens!" Hanson and Sue cried together, mourning Sam's death and praying for Jim's recovery. It seemed the darkest of times.

Two days later, Hanson received word a new sutler wanted to meet him. When he arrived at the sutler's window, he watched Gabriel Clem finish a transaction, charging six dollars for a worn-out blanket.

"Still cheating every living soul, I see," Hanson said as he stepped up and the soldier walked away wrapping himself in the blanket against the cold.

"Better than robbing the dead," Gabriel snapped back, unintimidated, cocking his head to one side.

"Touché," replied Hanson. "But if I rob the dead, then you should be careful you're not my next victim. Show up at my house again…"

"I don't frighten easily," Gabriel Clem snarled.

"And I do not threaten lightly," Hanson retorted through gritted teeth. "I warn you, Gabriel Clem: My wife is armed and is a crack shot. Come around my house again and you *will* be the next dead man I rob."

Hanson walked away, ignoring Clem's arrogant reply.

In late February, 1864, Sue received another letter relating that James Riddle had died of his wounds in January. Once more, they mourned, Hanson recalling Jim Riddle's promise to take care of his mother, Jane, and his daughter, Susan, which had proved a comfort to him during his own time of need.

Spring heralded warmer weather. One afternoon, after Dr. McFadden and Dr. Hanson finished the rounds and were heading back together to medical headquarters, McFadden sadly informed him, "My health is failing; I can't go on like this, Hanson. I fear telling Dr. Longwell, but I must end my service."

"You've done more than anyone I know, Doctor. I'm proud to have served with you," Hanson said to him with earnestness. "I will always be appreciative of the kindness you showed me, and the time we've worked together."

Dr. McFadden left just before an outbreak of smallpox swept through the camp in May, 1864. There was little the medical staff could do other than make the suffering thousands comfortable.

The war continued to drag on. Word of the privations of the Union prisoners at Andersonville reached the North, and the Yankee newspapers made the rebel camp seem worse than Camp Chase. The Camp Chase guards responded by treating their rebel prisoners even harsher. Conditions continued to deteriorate throughout the summer as more confederate prisoners flowed into camp. Repatriated confederates who enlisted in the Union Army replaced the regular Union camp guards, and inflicted terrible retribution on prisoners with whom they were previously confined. Eventually, army command had to transfer the repatriated rebels to Indian duty along the western frontier to alleviate the oppression.

One particularly hot summer day, as another group lined up for the march to the train station for transfer, Hanson heard a familiar voice in the crowd.

"Doc! Doc Hanson," a man shouted from the line.

Looking up and down the line Hanson spotted someone waving at him and headed over to a wasted sergeant in a barely recognizable CSA uniform standing in the line.

"Hey Doc! Remember me? I'm a sergeant now. I was a corporal when you last saw me," the gaunt man related.

Hanson stared at the man's face, and, though the man's eyes did seem familiar, he could not recall the man's name.

"Warren. Jed Warren, remember?" the thin man continued.

Hanson was shocked. The formerly rotund corporal had become a walking skeleton.

"Yes, I remember, Jed," Hanson reassured him. "How long have you been at the camp? Why didn't you ask for me? I could've at least gotten you more rations…"

Loud orders were shouted and the line reluctantly reacted by marching in place. Warren kept step as he spoke. "I got my fair share of rations—what there was of them. I didn't want any special treatment. I just hope those horror stories about Camp Douglas aren't true."

"I am sure they are not," Hanson replied, trying to reassure his former comrade. "How did you get captured?"

"Billings Cavalry was attached to Lee's command when he invaded the North. We were retreating from Gettysburg when we were ambushed. Our dear Captain Jackson and Lieutenant Reeves were killed. I was knocked out cold in the skirmish and woke up a prisoner."

"Corporal Conaway!" Hanson shouted to the guard. "This one can't travel."

"Sorry doc," the corporal replied. "I have to make sure they all get on the train. No exceptions."

"Thanks for trying, doc," the emaciated sergeant replied, resigned to his fate. "Don't worry about me. I'll be fine."

Another shouted order started the line marching forward, out the front gate towards the train depot. Corporal Conaway called out the cadence, as swirling dust arose from the hundreds of marching feet. As Hanson watched the line tramp out the gate, he considered the irony of Jed Warren being taken captive while unconscious.

In late October, Drs. Hanson and Longwell walked across camp, stopping just short of the kill line before the gate where the Yankees typically patted them down before leaving for the day. "We must find a way, Hanson, to convince the general staff that starving these men won't force the Johnny Reb's to feed their Union prisoners," Maj. Longwell stated.

"Sir, I don't think the rebels *have* any food to feed the men in Andersonville. I hear their CSA guards and staff are starving there as well," Hanson observed. "And Grant has brought siege warfare and civilian starvation to this war. I don't think he will relent on behalf of rebel prisoners-of-war."

"I agree. Perhaps we can begin addressing this difficult issue by inspiring the local citizens here to favor us with a food drive. We need something to garner public attention. Perhaps a cake auction…" Maj. Longwell said, drifting into a combination of exhaustion and reverie. "Oh, that reminds me. The definition of an auctioneer is someone who *looks for bidding*. Ha, ha!" The major chuckled at his obtuse joke, then gripped Hanson by the arm excitedly. "Here's some good news from Army Command. They have decided to turn the hospital into a barracks, and build a new hospital. There will be some tearing out and rebuilding necessary to accomplish this, but in the end we will get a new, larger hospital."

Hanson's heart skipped at the thought of the possible discovery of his cache, and smiled broadly to conceal his concern. "That's great news, doctor. How soon?"

"Very soon, I am told. Hopefully before Christmas. It would be a welcome gift."

Hanson knew he must act quickly to move the cache. The next day, during his rounds, Dr. Hanson selected a deceased soldier, a Private Curtis Hooks, and commanded an orderly to have the sutler Gabriel procure a casket and deliver it to the hospital. Several hours later, Hanson and Gabriel placed Hooks in the casket, then pushed it together to the storeroom. There, under Gabriel's watchful eyes, Hanson packed the coffin with all of the spoils—over nine thousand dollars of gold, silver, paper money and jewelry. After nailing the coffin shut, Hanson sought six volunteers as pallbearers to move the coffin to Rebel Cemetery at the south end of camp for burial.

As usual, prisoners lined the way to offer a final salute while the pallbearers marched with the coffin on their shoulders to the entrance in a slow, solemn pace. There, the guards loaded it onto a wagon for its final journey to the cemetery. "Smallpox," Hanson warned the guards, knowing that would be sufficient cause to not open the casket. Clem watched from his sutler wagon and Hanson spied from the compound, noting the exact spot where the Yankee soldiers buried Hooks.

That night Hanson took a pick, shovel and lantern and headed for the Rebel Cemetery. The cold November night air sank into his bones as he comically balanced the pick, shovel and lantern while creeping through the cemetery to disinter Private Hooks and retrieve their valuables. The sound of digging along with several voices startled him. Dousing the lantern and crouching, he approached stealthily. Peering around the trunk of a craggy tree, he saw several men standing about Hooks' grave, grumbling about the cold and the work. Hanson watched, his anger increasing, as two men awkwardly transferred the casket from inside the grave to three colleagues standing above. It was too dark to make out their faces. He thought momentarily of surprising them, but he had no weapon. Outnumbered five to one and without a weapon, Hanson remained hidden and watched. The five men placed Hooks' casket on the wagon and began refilling the grave. Knowing he could not retrieve the money, Hanson silently backed away, returning to his house angry, frustrated, and frightened.

"That damned Gabriel! He purloined the purse before we could divide it! I'll wager he, his men, the loot and the wagon will be long gone by tomorrow. In fact, *we* should be gone tomorrow, dear, to put distance between us and this camp in the event that Gabriel runs off with the money and the Woods gang comes here looking for it."

"Relax, dear," Sue reassured. "You'll figure a way around this. You are so intelligent, you'll find a solution." Hanson, sitting next to her at the kitchen table, slumped forward, his face in his hands as he pondered some way out of the mess.

The next day, he went to camp and was surprised to find Gabriel at his usual spot. Hanson quickly approached. "What have you done with the money, you…"

"What're ya talking 'bout?"

"You know damned well what I am talking about! I saw you and your men dig him up last night," barked Hanson.

"Hanson, this charade is unconvincing," Gabriel growled back, then he paused and a moment later turned the accusation around. "You took the money for *yourself*, didn't you? You went to the cemetery last night, took the money and now you're trying keep it all and blame me! Hogwash!"

"No, Gabriel. I saw five men dig up the coffin and carry it away on a wagon…" Hanson studied Gabriel Clem and was certain he saw genuine confusion in the man's eyes. It was clear Gabriel suspected him as much as he suspected Gabriel. "Where were you last night?" Hanson interrupted himself.

"Played cards 'till midnight waitin' for word from ya." Gabriel, seeing Hanson's anger subsiding, calmed, too. "Hanson, I did *not* dig up anybody last night," he offered with sincerity.

"Well, someone did, and we better figure out who or Woods will kill us both. That man's crazy," Hanson retorted.

"On that, we both agree," replied Gabriel.

That evening, Hanson walked through the cemetery and confirmed Hooks' coffin was gone. Hanson noticed that several other graves were also dug open, making Gabriel's protests of innocence plausible.

Returning home, he ordered Sue to begin gathering their things. "Sue, we need to get out of here and fast. Go down to Addison where our old landlord from Maysville, Kentucky, now lives. I hear he has several small places to rent. See if one is available. If so, rent it. I will resign and we'll move there."

The Bumgardners moved to the tiny town of Addison in Gallia County, Ohio, just as the news broke about Dr. Joab R. Flowers, a medical doctor from Columbus, who was caught selling confederate bodies he and his associates had dug up from the Rebel Cemetery to the Cleveland Medical College for dissection. Hooks was apparently one of the dozen that Flowers had disinterred. Hanson was not surprised to learn that at Dr. Flowers' trial, no mention was made of finding any money in the casket.

# Chapter Thirty-Two

Dr. Hanson Bumgardner walked the gallows to the side table for a drink of water. "I want to thank you for listening so attentively," he said, taking the hood from his shoulder and casually laying it upon the table before taking a long drink. "I suppose it is fitting that I never benefited from the money taken from those poor souls. In fact, it is about to cost me my life, for it eternally linked me to John Woods." Turning to Reverend Mullenix with a soulful look, he asked, "Reverend, who will receive my mortal remains if Sue or James doesn't make it in time?"

The reverend pointed to a man standing below, "Mister Rider has agreed."

"Very well, then," he said, nodding his satisfaction. Then, turning back to his witnesses, he remarked, "I want to thank my attorney, Senator Sam Knowles, a former captain in the Ohio National Guard during the recent conflict. I thank you, sir, for your service to the Union and for steadfastly believing in my innocence."

Returning to his place at the center front of the gallows, he continued, "In Addison, Sue and I..."

The Bumgardners set up house in late 1864 in Addison, Ohio, along the banks of the Ohio River. The money Hanson had originally secreted out in his shoes was considerable, but would be nothing near the amount necessary to satisfy Woods, should he locate them. Accordingly, Hanson and Sue assumed a low profile while they considered how to further proceed.

The ever-present quiet rush of the river filled their days as they wintered over, reminding them constantly that across the watery state line was West Virginia. The war seemed far away without newspapers or neighbors.

Out riding on a warm winter Sunday, Hanson and Sue were surprised to see alongside Pole Cat Road an abandoned Union Army Autenrieth Apothecary Wagon. The forty-inch right rear wheel's spokes were shattered, causing the top-heavy wagon to fall on its side. Sue and Hanson rode over to the wagon to investigate. All its supplies had been pilfered. From the rotting floorboards, it was apparent that the wagon had been in the ditch for some time.

A surrey happened along just then and the driver, seeing Hanson looking over the wagon, said, "It would be a relief if someone would remove that eyesore. Been there since Mosby's raiders overturned it."

"Perhaps I can accommodate the community, sir," Hanson said, smiling and tipping his hat. Later that afternoon, Hanson purchased a new wheel, and he and Sue retrieved the wagon. Over the next several weeks he repaired and repainted it.

"I wish I had the same talent as the artist Thomas Brown hired for my first wagon," lamented Hanson, "but I believe the message is clearly displayed." He stepped back to examine the large yellow letters proclaiming "Dr. Hanson Bumgardner, Tonics and Elixir" on both sides of the otherwise black wagon.

"Yes, Hanson," Sue agreed. "And you have repaired the damage, replaced the floorboards and fixed the drawers. It is a fine wagon."

"When I discovered the fifth wheel was slightly bent I hammered it back proper," he said, laughing and flexing his bicep. "I'm a decent blacksmith it seems." Within a couple of weeks, Hanson had begun making rounds, practicing medicine, selling his potions, tonic and elixir for income.

Hanson and Sue greeted the official end of the war in April, 1865, with the same joy felt by all of the war-weary population. Armies had already begun disassembling and men returned home to reclaim the lives they left behind.

On a rainy afternoon in mid-1865, the Bumgardners had set pots on the tables and floor to catch the water pouring in through the dilapidated, leaky roof. Hanson suddenly cocked his head to the side and listened intently, trying to hear past the rain pounding on the roof and dripping in the pans to the sound he thought he had heard.

"What?" Sue questioned.

"Shhh!" Hanson stepped towards Sue. "Outside, did you hear?"

They both strained to hear, becoming tense, their adrenalin flowing. Suddenly a loud crash on the front door startled them, causing them to bang into each other, each grabbing the other for security. They stumbled a few paces sideways to regain their collective balance when a voice boomed out, "Hanson Bumgardner! You in there, Doc?"

Hanson immediately recognized the voice of his former orderly, Abe Rhinehart, and opened the door. The man stepped quickly into the house, rain sheeting from his oiled-leather poncho onto the entrance rug. "Not fit for man nor beast this day," he said, stamping his feet and pulling the poncho off over his head. "Sir, it is good to see you," he said, embracing Bumgardner in a big bear hug.

"Good to see you, too, Abe," Hanson replied, slapping Abe's back.

"I've been looking for you since Appomattox. I got news. Woods was released in February at Point Lookout just before the war's end. He's been looking for you all over Virginia, and I don't think it will be long before he comes here. My sources say that rat Clem is with him, blaming you instead of that ghoul doctor for stealing his money."

"I don't know who has Wood's money. I surely don't have it," Hanson stated. "It's like I said in the letter I sent you: Dr. Flowers hasn't gone to trial yet and isn't talking."

"Yeah, I figured," Rhinehart replied, raising an eyebrow at the pots and pans collecting water before sitting in a chair offered by Sue. "Even so, Woods blames you for losing it."

"He needs to blame that sorry excuse for a doctor, not me."

"*Doctor* Hanson, need I remind you that you stole from the dead?" Rhinehart gently chided.

"I didn't sell their bodies for profit. That's morbid. Disgusting," asserted Hanson.

"Well, I'm afraid I've got more bad news, Hanson. Your friend, Major Longwell…well…" Rhinehart paused.

"What, Abraham? Go on…" Hanson urged.

"The major died mid-March. There were over nine thousand prisoners in the camp before the war ended. Longwell got the typhoid in March and was gone in three days."

"Oh no! Cordila must be beside herself in grief," sobbed Sue, grasping Hanson's arm.

"No Sue. Sadly, she lies beside him in the grave. She died of the same malady barely three days after they buried the major. They left behind two orphans." He paused while Sue wept openly for the loss of their dear friends.

"I don't know how to break this, Hanson," Rhinehart cautiously continued. "The news moves slowly sometimes, particularly if a name misses the first casualty list from a battle, but I learned that Sergeant George Arbogast was killed in May of '64 at the Battle of Spotsylvania Courthouse. He was killed in Grant's pre-dawn attack on May twelfth, at the Mule Shoe salient. They say he was a hero."

"No doubt, Abe. No doubt. He was a hero to me," admitted Hanson, his voice cracking before breaking into sobs.

# Chapter Thirty-Three

The midday sun arched overhead in a cloudless azure sky while Hanson, sitting on the porch next to Abe, considered all the bad news he had received. A couple of wagons stopped at the furthest in the line of three cabins several hundred yards distant. The landlord, accompanying the wagons on his horse, dismounted and ushered one of the men into the cabin. A few minutes later, the two emerged and shook hands, the renter signaling with a jerk of his thumb over his shoulder for the others to begin carrying in their goods. Several more men appeared from the wagons, formed a line between the cabin and the nearest wagon, and began passing the goods down the line into the cabin.

Hanson watched the activity, eventually calling out, "Sue, come outside and take a look at this." He continued to watch as she joined him on the porch.

"Have you see any women in the group?" she asked.

"No, just men," answered Hanson. "The ladies will probably come at a later time. Or, these could be a traveling group of laborers, or a troupe of entertainers."

Later that afternoon, after the two wagons were emptied and the horses put away, the Bumgardners noticed the men lounging in the shade of their porch and decided this was the time to make acquaintance.

Hanson and Sue approached the cabin carrying a tray with a pitcher of lemonade and glasses for their new neighbors. Abe decided to join them and followed at a considerable distance behind. The men visibly stiffened and began passing anxious glances between one another as the Bumgardners approached.

As they stepped up into the dark shadow of the porch a moment passed before their eyes could adjust. Before either could make out the men's faces clearly, they heard an unwelcome familiar voice.

"Well lookie here! Ha, ha, ha!" John M. Woods' voice reverberated from across the porch. "I don't believe it! We've been looking for you throughout Virginia for weeks, Doc, and now you turn up in Ohio bringing us refreshments!"

Dr. Hanson's heart sunk. He scanned the face of the imposing man and those of the members of his gang. "John Woods, a surprise to be sure. How is it you've come to rent here?"

"Like you, I needed a discrete place to hide, and our mutual landlord came highly recommended. Ha, ha. I can't believe our good fortune." The laugh and smile were out of place on his cruel face.

"Yes, this landlord asks no questions, Woods, but beware. He has a loose tongue. Tell him only that which you care not if the world knows," Hanson cautioned, angry for not heeding his own advice and hoping to deflect Woods' mind from the money.

Woods' face darkened. "So, Doc, where's my money?" he demanded.

"You must have heard about the grave robberies from Gabriel," Abe interjected, stepping onto the porch and joining the group.

"Well how about this? Abe Rhinehart, too! My lucky day! Yeah, well, Gabriel said you would claim the money was lost to some grave robber," John said to Hanson.

"It is the truth. Gabriel helped me nail the coffin shut," Hanson told him.

"That's true," Gabriel Clem said, stepping out of the house eating an apple. "But I don't know who dug him up."

"Well, Hanson?" John M. Woods grumbled menacingly.

"I don't have the money," insisted Hanson. "I could try to obtain the forty five hundred from a benefactor, but I don't have…"

"Forty five hundred? Hell, it's more like eighty one hundred," Woods snarled.

"The amount entrusted to me was five thousand. My ten per cent fee would be five hundred. Thus, I owe you forty five hundred."

"No, you damned snake-oil peddler. You owe eight thousand one hundred, which is nine thousand less your ten percent fee of nine hundred. When you agreed to protect our money, you became a member of my gang. It's time now to split it all equally."

"I never agreed to…" Hanson was interrupted by an elbow from Sue. She nodded towards Hardin Battle, Polk Wade, and Sam Woods who had their hands on their revolvers.

"Oh, I see. Well, okay, then," Hanson backpedaled, realizing that further argument would be futile or even fatal, as he couldn't even pay the lesser of the two amounts.

"Where is the rest of the family? Where's Junior?" Hanson asked, changing the subject and flashing his fabulous smile.

The men's stern faces softened briefly, then hardened again.

"He died just before Christmas last year in Camp Douglas," the grizzled old cavalryman said, Woods' voice uncharacteristically soft in recollection. "Muh brother James's gone, too. Died the month before."

"They were my friends…more like brothers…" added Hardin Battle, shaking his head in disbelief, tears welling in his eyes.

Hanson folded his hands and placed his fingers to his lips, his own eyes stinging with tears. "I saved him from death's clutches. Had I not, he would've died. So why would God…?"

"God ain't got nothin' to do with it, damn it. Pneumonia and starvation killed both of them, plain and simple. And while Lee may have surrendered, I ain't done yet. There's Yankees out there who don't deserve livin'." He spit in disdain, then continued. "Hanson, until you repay me, and repay me in full, you and your wife will serve me like Hardin here. He's almost paid his debt to me for raisin' him. You and your beautiful wife will serve me well, I foresee, or…."

"How so, Woods?" Hanson interrupted, bristling at Woods having included Sue.

"You and the missus are both quite handsome. Wouldn't you say, boys?" The men all laughed. "Not like us. Our faces are twenty miles of bad road. In these hard times, handsome still means trustworthy, so I believe you will have no problems passing these." Woods reached into his vest pocket and pulled out several twenty dollar bills, offering one to Hanson.

Bumgardner took the bill and examined it closely, stepping from the porch to look at it in direct sunlight. "This bill is superb! Flawless! Even a Federal Paymaster would be fooled! Where did you get these counterfeit bills? How much did you have to pay for them?" Hanson asked, impressed with the quality.

"We stole a press and plates during a raid in Tennessee, so technically they're not counterfeit. As for cost, we only paid for paper and ink. We stopped just long enough to print several thousand of these. Yes, Hanson, you and your wife can easily pass these bills where we could not."

"Imagine me trying to pass a ten, much less a twenty," Hardin chuckled to everyone's laughter.

"You have tens as well?" Hanson asked, considering the prospects. Noting Sue's smile of agreement, he realized the plan was perfect. "All right. I will pass forty five hundred worth of these for goods, services, or simply cash, and at that point we call it even."

"Forty five hundred is a good number to start, but your debt is ninety one hundred. But don't look so disappointed. Once you begin passing these and accumulating goods, you'll see it's like eating apple pie. Once you start, it's hard to stop." John M. Woods' lips curled in a wicked smile, and all the men chuckled knowing the truth of what their leader had said.

# Chapter Thirty-Four

The summer of 1865 was a time of cautious restraint for the two former enemies, North and South, each fearful of reigniting the war. Sue and Hanson used their salvaged medicine wagon to travel all over Ohio, Kentucky, parts of West Virginia, and Pennsylvania, passing the bills and selling elixir. Sue would cash a twenty at the dress shop to buy a five-dollar dress that she would then wear into the next town and repeat the process. Hanson took a wad of tens and twenties to the local bank, flashed his winning smile, and exchanged them for large bills, "as they are easier to carry in the cramped apothecary wagon."

Hanson quickly surpassed forty five hundred dollars in cash. They frequently stayed at the best hotels for an outrageous fifty dollars a night. They enjoyed all manner of room service, from hot baths to massages to daily shoe shines. Hanson repeatedly explained to Woods that they should stay a day or two before passing the money elsewhere in order to establish credibility.

It was a glory ride. Hanson and Sue purchased anything they desired. Hanson bought a tailor-made suit for over one hundred fifty dollars and expensive dresses and jewelry for Sue. It was during this time that Hanson bought a dark blue, almost black, Plug hat that he came to love. It soon became his trademark.

The rest of the gang followed from a safe distance, meeting with Hanson and Sue between towns to divide the booty. Between meetings, the gang members would disappear for a few days. It bothered Hanson that Woods and his men were riding to adjacent towns and counties, taking risks by frequenting saloons and prostitutes. In Hanson's mind, if this continued, it would only be a matter of time before one of the gang members inadvertently boasted and got arrested.

One evening, Hardin Battle joined Hanson and Sue at their home base cabin for dinner.

"John wants us to go on another horse raid tonight," said Battle, "but to be truthful, Doc, I am tired of it. He keeps promising we will stop stealing horses when we have enough money, but the way he talks, we'll never have enough. Each raid is more dangerous than the one before. Some day, one or all of us is gonna get caught or killed…"

"I quite agree," Hanson interrupted. "The counterfeiting operation is netting sufficient money without the need to steal horses. Perhaps I should talk to John about this."

"Good luck. You know how stubborn Woods is," Hardin said.

Hanson didn't get the opportunity to speak to Woods that night. The gang had left at dusk, their destination unknown, but their purpose clear.

The next afternoon, Hanson walked from his cabin to the cabin the others shared to confront their leader. "How many horses did you steal last night, John?"

"Ten. One broke his leg so's we got back with nine," he chuckled and coughed simultaneously. "That's another eighteen hundred dollars. A good take by my reckonin'."

"A good take, except for this," Hardin Battle added, holding up his arm. His arm, swathed in bandages, was a bloody mess.

"Oh, Hardin!" Hanson exclaimed as he stepped to the man and examined the wound. A flap of skin was torn free and dangling from his upper arm. "This needs to be cleaned and stitched back together as quickly as possible. How did this happen?"

"Well, Sergeant Finch caught us removing horses from his barn and got me with his shotgun. John killed him before he could get a second shot off."

"Sergeant who?" Hanson asked, confused.

"Finch," John Woods explained. "Sergeant Franklin Finch. The bastard was a guard at Douglas. We should've killed him before we took the horses. Then Hardin wouldn't have been shot."

"Look, we don't have to steal horses. The bills racket is providing more than enough money," Hanson said, sewing the skin flap back on Hardin.

"Hanson, you do your part—keep passin' those bills—an' leave us to our part. We're horse thieves, plain and simple," John explained. "An' remember this: By patchin' up Hardin, you've become an accessory to murder, just like that Dr. Mudd, who patched up John Wilkes Booth. They convicted Dr. Mudd, an' he missed hangin' by only one vote. One vote! Maybe they'll hang you," he chuckled, narrowing his eyes menacingly at Hanson.

"Listen, John. You risked everyone's lives to capture nine horses worth maybe two hundred each, running the risk of capture every time you sell one. If you recall, last month I passed over two thousand worth of bills to one bank in one morning! No risk, no shooting, no chance of injury or being caught. What say you, men?" Hanson looked at the men with pleading eyes.

The men grumbled and talked quietly among themselves until

John said for them, "No, Doc. This here's *my* gang. We began as horse thieves, an' I say we continue as horse thieves. An' what I says goes." Woods cast a threatening glance at the men around him as he gripped his brace of revolvers. The men nodded, though it was apparent that they also saw the reasoning in Hanson's approach.

Late that night, Woods stood outside their hideout, watching the Ohio River pass, thinking about the next heist. He was planning a raid against another former guard at Camp Douglas when Gabriel approached.

"Ya best be cautious, boss," Clem said to Woods. "That Hanson, he's been trouble ever since I first came 'cross him in Virginia. He's smart, sneaky, and he's put a target on your back. He wants to boss the outfit. Ya better watch him."

"He better watch *me*, you mean," snarled Woods. "Soon as I'm done with him, I'm gonna dump him. I've been thinking for some time how best to eliminate him. We don't have to worry anymore about his friend, Abe; he leaves next week to go back to farming. That only leaves Hardin Battle. He listens to Bumgardner. He could be a problem. He's liked the man ever since he patched up Junior's gunshot, and now the man's patched him up, too. We better watch them both." Woods cupped his chin in his hand as he thought.

"Hanson's wife, Sue, could be a problem as well. She pulled a gun on me once," Clem revealed.

"Thank you for the warning. I'll keep her under watch, too," he said with an evil grin.

A month later, Hanson made a trip through central Ohio alone, Sue and their three boys being ill. The trip was successful and he brought back a large amount of money, while John continued leading the other men on raids to seize horses.

Several days after his return, Hanson watched the men ride away into the sunset, wondering why Woods demanded continuing the raids. At first, Hanson thought it pure greed, but it was clear there was something more. Something deadly.

When the group returned several days later, Hanson noticed that Hardin Battle was not with them. "Where's Hardin?" he asked the men as they sat exhausted in the saddle, receiving no answer. "Men, where's Hardin Battle?" he repeated.

Woods gave a grunt as he tied his tired horse to the hitching rail. "Hardin said he'd had enough. We gave him cash an' two horses, an' he headed back to Texas."

"Really? He never said anything about wanting to go back…"

"He paid his debt to me, an' now he's gone back to Texas. That's all there is to say about it. Done. Over with." Woods stomped into the gang's rented cabin and slammed the door.

The other men returned to the cabin together after pasturing the captured horses and bedding down their mounts in the pole barn. They looked wretched as they dragged themselves up onto the porch and took up their usual seats.

"I don't want any more of that," Sam Woods said. "That was too much shooting for my liking."

"Was Hardin killed?" Hanson asked with apprehension.

"No, Hanson. And whatever John says Hardin said, is what Hardin said." Polk Wade cast his eyes down as he spoke the obviously rehearsed line.

"Well, what did *Hardin* say, that John didn't?" Hanson pried.

"Uh, *John* didn't say such. Uh, maybe something about Texas?" Wade looked confused, his eyes flicking from one man to the other. No one volunteered anything more.

"What did Hardin say?" Hanson pressed harder.

"He said he was going to back to Texas. That's it…" Woods' gruff voice wafted back out the door.

"Over with. Done. Yes, I know," Hanson finished the line as Woods stepped back through the door and onto the porch.

"Right. So no more talk of Hardin," Woods said easing into a bentwood chair.

Later Hanson told Sue of the conversation.

"Perhaps he has treated Hardin as a member of the family for so long he feels that Hardin has 'run away from home' so to speak," Sue offered.

"No, it was more nefarious. Wood's expressed no concern or love for Hardin," Hanson assessed.

Sue considered her husband's uneasiness, then delivered some important news: "Dear, we received several letters by mail today. The men you kept track of from Camp Chase and wrote are more than willing to participate in our business venture."

"Excellent, we can move the printing press here from Kentucky to the middle house and set them up there. I will coach them about passing bills. It's perfect, Sue. Our new men can scatter these across Virginia, Ohio, Kentucky, and Tennessee. They can pay us fifteen cents on the dollar for the bills, and keep the rest." Sue nodded her approval. This new approach would be far safer. "It won't take long for us to have enough money to retire. We can pass the business on to the best of the lot, for a price, of course." They grinned at each other at the thought of being independently wealthy.

The following morning, Hanson awakened early to the sounds in the pole barn. Investigating, he found Samuel Woods leading out a saddled horse.

"'Morning, Sam," Hanson said, smiling and eyeing the man closely.

"Hanson," Sam nodded.

"Headed to town?"

"Naw. Headed out. Back to Texas. Whaever. I'm surely not staying here," Sam said, avoiding Hanson's prying eyes.

"Then I'll miss you, as will Sue. You should tell her good-bye," Hanson said, shaking Sam's hand for a final time.

"I think it would be better if you told her for me. I gotta get an early start," he said, continuing to avoid eye contact with Hanson.

Sam grasped the saddle horn and prepared to mount, then paused, looking down the road over the saddle. Hanson sensed Sam wrestling with a moral dilemma. Finally, Sam turned and nodded to the gang's cabin. "You have an enemy in that house." Hanson nodded a quiet acknowledgement as Sam mounted his horse. "I don't like the direction this here gang is going, so I am leaving." As he began to leave, he said, "'Going to Texas'. That's what I'd appreciate if you would tell Sue… and John."

"Well, if you see Hardin Battle in Texas, give him my regards."

Sam Woods reined in and leaned down closer to Hanson. "Doc, I loved Hardin like a brother. And I respect you as a doctor, as did he. Hardin compared every doc in Camp Douglas to you. He said many times if James and Junior had continued to have you for their doctor, they would be alive today. You see, he liked you too much, Hanson, and it cost him dearly. I won't be seeing Hardin in Texas, or anywhere else, and if you're as smart as you seem, you'll get out now while you can. Farewell, Doc!" Sam wheeled his horse and spurred it to a gallop.

"Farewell, Sam," Hanson called as the man rode away, never looking back.

# Chapter Thirty-Five

On Wednesday, February 13, 1867, the trio made an uneasy camp next to a spring-fed creek. The drizzle made traveling ponderously slow and difficult. Banjo stood hobbled nearby, wearily crunching on grain in a feedbag.

"Can't ya untie me to eat?" Gabriel Clem complained, eliciting nothing but the rise of an eyebrow from James Bumgardner. Clem coughed as he tried to pick up a piece of meat from the tin plate before him.

"Gabriel, why did Woods frame Hanson?" Susan Bumgardner asked, her curiosity overtaking caution.

"Ya gotta understand: I hate Hanson; I hate him a lot. But Woods, he detested Hanson with every fiber of his being. He blamed Hanson for the loss of their war booty, an' the death of his brother, James, an' his son, Junior," Clem divulged.

"But that was at Camp Douglas, over a year after Hanson *saved* Junior," Sue hastened to point out, unable to believe this was the basis for Woods' intense hatred of her husband.

"Yeah, well, lots of folks have pointed that out to John M., but to him, it just don't matter. He claims Hanson could have kept everyone in the gang safe at Camp Chase jus' by sayin' they were too sick to travel. That was the reason he recruited Hanson into the gang in the first place: To keep 'em safe and from bein' transferred away from their money."

"Hanson did try, but the Post Surgeon had already walked through the hospital and decided who would go and who would stay. It was out of his hands," Sue explained.

"Zat so? Hmm, I didn't know that. At any rate, Woods 'specially hated Hanson for losing their money. I told him that Dr. Joab Flowers and his gang beat us to the money, but it was no use. I even showed him the newspaper accounts of the ghoulish affair, but he still hated Hanson for losin' the money. Woods knew Hardin would back Hanson if push came to shove about who should lead the gang, an' so he took care of Hardin," Clem disclosed.

"How?" James asked, joining the conversation.

"It was quite unpleasant. Woods got lathered into a rage and took it out on Hardin—that's all I'm gonna say. Sam left the next day, and Woods blamed that on Hanson, too. In Woods' mind, everything bad that happened after he was caught on Morgan's Raid in Ohio was Hanson's fault. We all tried to talk him into going back to Texas after the war, but he wanted to come here to 'even the score' with Doc and some other damned Yankees."

James' eyes narrowed, "Other folks keep score, too, Gabriel," he reminded.

"Well, John M. Woods eventually got his. He drowned in the Ohio," Clem said.

"Yes, we recently heard. A ferry accident," Sue said.

"Yeah, a ferry accident," Clem confirmed as he stared into the fire.

In the summer of 1866, the Woods gang continued their crime

spree in post-war Ohio, but their numbers began dwindling. In response, Hanson invited Michael O'Day, formerly of Camp Chase, to join them. O'Day brought with him William Matheney, whom he befriended at Camp Chase. Several days later Matheney left without notice or saying farewell. Over time, several others came and departed in the same manner. Hanson believed them to be threatened enough to leave. Or perhaps worse, John had eliminated them for one reason or another.

It quickly became difficult to keep track of all the new members coming and going. First, there was Moore, then Ryan. Polk Wade met a girl and left the gang. Woods brought in "Guns" Jackson to replace the man. It was Guns who, more than anyone else, aroused Hanson's darker suspicions.

"I am concerned about so many men passing through our secret home base, John. I think we need to find the men separate quarters somewhere else," Hanson told Woods one afternoon.

"An' you're gonna pay for it outta your share?" Woods gruffly challenged.

"I am concerned about security, John. We have to keep the group small. Just like in the war, the more who know, the more that *will* know."

"Don't tell me how to run this gang!" Woods ended the conversation.

Later that evening, Woods pulled Clem aside and said, "I think you're right. Bumgardner is dangerous. He's trying to run my gang, and I'm fed up with him."

"I wondered how long it was gonna take for ya to see through him. You gonna shoot him? If ya call him out, watch out for his wife. I told ya, she pulled…"

"Yeah, yeah. The wench got the drop on you an' stuck a gun in your belly. Naw, I'm not gonna shoot him; An old partner of mine is comin' up from Texas and I've got a plan in mind for the two of them," Woods said chuckling ominously.

It rained throughout September. Hanson drove a wagon to the feed store at nearby Gallipolis for supplies. In the shop, he ran into Woods, talking with a man he'd not seen before.

"Doc Hanson, I want you to meet a an old friend of mine, J. J. Gollier. He runs an oil wagon out of Boiling Springs, West Virginia. It's just like the one you described seeing in Oil Rock some time back. His wagon's for rent, maybe for sale."

"Mister Gollier. A pleasure to meet you, sir, " Hanson said offering a hand before asking, "John, why do we need an oil wagon?"

"I was hopin' you would accompany J.J. to our current site of operations. We need to move somewhere safer, and we've acquired too much to use our regular wagons safely. Especially to move the printing press up from Kentuck'. Your cover will be that you're plannin' to move, and need his heavy-duty wagon to haul your furniture there."

"Why don't we hire some wagoners to do the job?"

"You were the one who said the fewer involved, the better. Besides, you never know when we might need a good, heavy wagon. J.J. says he will rent to us anytime we have need, but he needs a cover story each time in order to maintain a legitimate business and deflect the eyes of the authorities. Your 'move,' which it will turn out has to be done in several hauls, will provide us with cover stories for a while, Hanson. Unless you can talk him out of the wagon. Pay him fair price; he's a friend of mine."

"The wagon's not for sale," Gollier said flatly.

"I am surprised to see someone of your humble size running so heavy a rig. It usually requires a significantly larger man," observed Hanson, sizing up the man.

"Be assured that I am much stronger than I look. I can handle my wagon," Gollier retorted, his feathers ruffled.

"No offense intended, of course. Truly, J.J. you do appear stronger than I," Hanson quickly replied to put Woods' friend back at ease.

Several days later, Woods met Hanson and Sue on their porch and said, "I'm concerned about our landlord. He's been sniffin' around lately."

"John, he's been personally overseeing the repairs to the roofs at my request, not sniffin' around," Hanson laughed.

Ignoring the comment, Woods motioned to Hanson to come closer. "I've decided now's the best time for us to make the move," he said quietly. "We'll use Gollier's wagon to move your family from here to Columbus. If there are any problems with the wagon, we'll find out while moving your household goods, before we haul the press."

"Seems kind of sudden…" Hanson began.

"*I* decide what the gang does an' when an' where it goes. An' if I say…" Woods growled, his anger flaring.

"Fine, fine, John. Whatever you say, " Hanson interrupted to calm him down.

"Gollier is on his way bringing the rig from Boiling Springs. You'll meet him in Belpre. There, you will pick up the rig an' bring it here. We'll load up your goods an' move you up to Columbus where I've rented a new place with several houses and lots more space. Here's the address." Woods handed Hanson a folded piece of paper. Then looking at the rain-heavy clouds he observed, "If…"

"Why don't we…" Hanson began.

"Why don't you shut up? I got my reasons for everything I do," Woods declared. "It's already late, so head up there tomorrow. Meet Gollier at Dye's Stable and Livery tomorrow afternoon. Jim Dye runs the place. Take the sorrel horse and leave it at the livery. While you're traveling with J.J., he can teach you how to handle a multiple horse team."

"More than two horses? I've never driven more than a two-horse team, John," Hanson said, his concern showing. "Most times just a single mule. I don't know…"

"You'll do fine, Doc. Heck two, four, or six don't matter, the technique is the same," chuckled Woods. "Riding with Mosby, we learned to drive any size team an' lead any number of saddle horses, too," he bragged. "Listen to J.J. He's expert at handling the rig. An' remember: We want that rig. I got plans for it. During the trip, if you can't convince him to sell it, we can chloroform him so it looks like a robbery. We can chloroform you as well, so it looks like you were a victim, too. Still, if you can buy the rig, I'll cover whatever you offer."

Hanson hesitated, wishing Woods had never found out about the chloroform in the apothecary wagon. Woods seemed uncommonly generous. "What plans?" Hanson finally asked, curious as to the overall operation.

"I'll fill you in on the details when you get back here with the wagon," assured Woods. "If you can't buy the wagon, we'll take it. Either way, I've got to have that rig."

# Chapter Thirty-Six

On Thursday, September 13, 1866, Hanson left for Belpre wrapped in a poncho and wearing his now familiar Plug hat. The gray overcast skies yielded neither rain nor sunshine. The roads were muddy and made for slow traveling, but Hanson arrived, as scheduled, in mid-afternoon, and made his way directly to Dye's Livery, where he hoped to find J. J. Gollier waiting.

When Gollier was not to be found in the stables, the livery owner, Jim Dye, suggested that the man Hanson was looking for might best be found across the street at the saloon. Hanson went to the saloon and returned within minutes with Gollier. Together, they hitched the team to the large converted army munitions wagon fitted with an around-the-perimeter iron rack designed to hold barrels of oil. There were five horses: four bays and a single gray stallion. The gray was tied to the back of the wagon. Worse, the animal appeared to be ill.

"The gray is normally a sound and spirited horse. I think he ate some bad oats. Perhaps we can find him a halter-mate along the way," Gollier said, climbing aboard and taking the reins.

Hanson sat beside him. "Let's hope the others don't get sick. I agree about finding him a halter-mate…"

"Doc Hanson! Hey there, Doc!" a high-pitched voice called out from across the street. "'That's not your usual apothecary wagon. Wouldn't have recognized you but for the hat."

"A good day to you, Mister Miller," Hanson said, smiling and doffing the hat. "What think you of this rig? It's a beauty, isn't it? You wouldn't know where we could find a halter-mate for the gray, would you?"

"Doc, it's a fine wagon, indeed, and it appears this team has worked together for some time. Sadly, I don't know of anyone at this time with a good lead halter mate for the gray, but I shall keep you in mind. Good to see you again. Cheers!"

"Cheers to you, sir," replied Hanson. As they pulled away he felt the wagon shudder and looked back at the right rear wheel. It was wobbling. "Stop the wagon," he said to Gollier, and they spent the better part of an hour jacking up the wagon and resetting the wheel. Apparently the nut had somehow worked loose.

As they resumed their departure, they came across another acquaintance of Dr. Hanson, riding up next to them on a black horse.

"Bumgardner," A. J. Snyder said, "It's kind of late to start a journey, don't you think? Perhaps you and your friend should stay overnight at the hotel?"

"No, sir. I thank you for your concern, but we must be getting on," Hanson replied, waved his hat at Snyder as the wagon bumped its way through another rut.

"Suit yourself, man," Snyder replied with a shrug, and galloped ahead.

"The man's right, Hanson. We'll not be able to make much distance before nightfall," lamented Gollier. "Perhaps we should overnight at Hill's Landing? It's cheaper than a hotel, and there's but a small charge for the horses and wagon."

"That would be fine by me. I am tired from my ride to Belpre and the preparations," agreed Hanson.

The trip along the river south was no less taxing, the heavy wagon repeatedly side-slipping in the wet slimy mud. As they made their way away from the town, Hanson asked, "So, J.J. or Gollier, which do you prefer?"

"Gollier," the driver replied.

"As you wish, Gollier. Have you reconsidered Woods' offer to purchase this rig?" Hanson asked as they suddenly lurched left to right in unison.

"Yes. I have. Hauling oil is hard work. I would prefer city hauling. You know, like hauling vegetables from the train yard to the market."

"That is a much preferable duty, I'll admit. Have you a price in mind?" Hanson asked.

"Fifteen hundred dollars would take everything: the rig with canvas cover, tack, chains, racks, leathers, plus the team. These four as you can see are used to pulling together," Gollier replied.

"This is a solid rig and a fine team. I think I could justify a thousand dollars. The gray is, after all, sick, and the left inside bay seems unsure. The canvas cover requires cleaning…"

"Alright, twelve hundred, then."

"Eleven hundred, no more."

"Done," they said simultaneously, then laughed. Hanson felt satisfied knowing that he had not just acquired the wagon and team, but was helping Gollier move on to what he really wanted to do. At the same time, he knew Woods would regard eleven hundred dollars as a bargain.

Hanson pulled out his wallet and dug through it. "I have eight hundred in twenties and some smaller bills. I propose to pay you eight hundred dollars and this mortgage on a property in Virginia. Though the mortgagee has missed a couple of payments, it is certainly worth four hundred dollars," Hanson offered.

Gollier grunted at the suggestion.

"Or, how about I pay you eight hundred now and the remainder when we get to Addison?" Hanson asked.

"That will work just fine. Congratulations, Hanson. You are now the new owner of this fine rig!" Gollier said, slapping Hanson on the back.

After a while, a smaller wagon approached from behind. As was the custom, the driver called out, "Passing on the left!" to alert the two he was overtaking them. When the wagon was even with them, the driver looked over and saw Gollier driving and Hanson sitting beside him eating a melon. "Evening, gentlemen. How's your journey been?"

"Wet," laughed Hanson, "and my new rig needs a mate for the lead gray to make it a six-horse team. I would happily give a couple hundred dollars for a good mate for my lead."

"Ah'm sorry, sir. Ah don't have one for sale, but ya'll should check at the livery in Gallipolis. They carry good stock."

"I thank you, sir, and to whom should the merchant in Gallipolis be grateful?"

"Dugan Noland of Danham, sir. Mah apologies for not introducing mahself sooner."

"Well Mister Noland, we are planning to stop for the night near Lewis's store at Hill's Landing. Would it suit you to join us?" Hanson happily offered.

"Thanks for the invitation, but, no, sir. Ah'm behind schedule, and more time on the road tonight will bring me closer to catching up. It's this cussed rain."

"Good evening to you, then," Hanson replied as the swifter wagon pulled ahead. Recognizing a house on their left he said to Gollier, "Pull over here," and jumped down from the rig. Walking to the side of the wagon, he opened the built-in tool box and pulled out a halter. "Wait here a minute, Gollier. I know the fellow who lives here, and I think we can buy some hay from him at a particularly good price." Looking towards the horizon, Hanson spotted Sam Stone approaching the pike.

"Hey Doc, how're you doing? That's quite the rig ya have there!" Stone said, scanning it quickly from front to back.

"It's bigger than my usual apothecary wagon, that's for sure. Say, Sam. I'd like to buy some hay for my new team." Hanson held up the halter and the two headed together towards Sam's barn. Hanson intended to use the halter as a measure, and to carry the hay back.

"A hundred pounds, ya think?" Sam asked, filling the halter.

They carried it to the wagon where Hanson asked Gollier to heft the hay-filled halter and guess the weight; he estimated a hundred pounds as well.

"Fair enough," Hanson pulled his wallet and took out a dollar.

Sam looked at the dollar and said, "I'll havta go up to the house to get your change."

"Never mind," said Hanson, and began counting out change with one hand, hefting the hay over his shoulder with the other. "Oh, that's short forty cents," Hanson said, then looking up to Gollier, "have you forty cents for the hay?"

Gollier dug in his pocket, then handed down the coins to finish the transaction. Hanson tossed the hay in the back and they moved on.

Dusk was fast approaching when they pulled into Hill's Landing.

Hanson immediately went to the house and paid Mrs. Hill for the night. From there, they walked to Lewis Dry Goods and Sundries a quarter-mile up the road. A small brass bell announced their entrance into the shop. Mr. Parker Lewis, the slightly-built proprietor, knew Hanson from the doctor having stopped by on his many trips.

"Good eve' to ya, Doc. What kin I do for you and yur friend this fine evenin'? Didja park the medicine wagon at the Landin' for the night?"

"Well, yes and no, Parker. I am staying at Hill's Landing, but it's not my apothecary wagon I am parking there for the night. I am taking a wagon down to Addison to move the family," Hanson explained, looking from one goods display to another. "Would you happen to have a pint of your famous wine waiting for me?" Hanson asked.

"Yes, the moment I see'd you walkin' up and I got it ready," smiled Parker.

"Thank you ever so much. It's been a long trying day," Hanson replied, accepting the bottle and breaking the seal. Pulling out the cork, he took a long draught directly from the bottle, then offered the bottle to Gollier. Gollier took the bottle, took a taste, then as long a draw as Hanson. Smiling, Hanson nodded at Gollier and the pint bottle, encouraging him to take another swig.

"Very good," Gollier said, wiping his mouth with his sleeve. "*Very* good, indeed!"

"Then we shall have another, Parker. Your wine tastes particularly good on a cool autumn evening," Hanson said.

"Where ya movin', Doc? Shoot, I hope you'll still make yur usual rounds hereabouts," Lewis said, handing Hanson another pint. "Folks have come to depend on yur famous tonic."

"Just moving to be more centrally located. You can be sure you haven't heard the last of me. Have you any eggs, Parker? If so, I will take two dozen for I have craved eggs since I began the day and I would have them for supper and breakfast as well."

The shopkeeper reached under the counter and began retrieving the requested number of eggs while Gollier placed a bottle of horse liniment on the counter and motioned to Hanson for another drink of wine. Hanson handed the bottle over after taking another drink, all the while keeping strict count as Parker placed the eggs in a paper bag stuffed with another crushed bag in the bottom to act as a nest.

"Two bits a dozen and two dollars fur the wine," Lewis said. Hanson handed him three paper dollars. Lewis turned to Gollier. "Liniment's a dollar." Gollier opened his wallet that was stuffed full of the money. Unable find a single dollar, he handed Lewis a twenty.

"Sorry," Gollier muttered, but Parker Lewis just shrugged and made change.

Back at camp, Gollier tended to the horses while Hanson returned to the Hill's house.

"Evening, Roger. How are you?" Hanson began.

"Well. And you, Doc?" Roger Hill replied.

"Quite so, thank you. I was wondering if Missus Hill has a pan I may borrow to cook our supper and breakfast in."

"Sure," the man replied, turning and calling into the house, "Mother, please bring a big fry pan for the doc here."

"I need to wash some clothes. Is that for hire?" Hanson said, pointing at a flat bottom skiff.

"Sure, two bits for the rent." He held his hand out and Hanson paid.

Mrs. Hill appeared at the door and pushed her husband aside. She handed Hanson a pan, and he tipped his hat. "Could you please make me a pot of your famous coffee in the morning?" Mrs. Hill, flattered, smiled broadly and nodded in agreement as he dropped payment in her hand.

Hanson smiled his signature smile and once again tipped his hat. "Thank you, good folk."

Back at camp, Hanson set about making dinner. As Hanson was about to serve it, Gollier, sitting near the fire, rolled up his sleeves and Hanson noticed "J. J. Gollier" tattooed on his left forearm.

"What is that?" Hanson asked, nodding at the tattoo, having never seen one before.

"It's my name, written under my skin. I got it in Louisiana during the war. I figured if I was to get my head blown off, they could still identify my body, see? It's called a tattoo and it's permanent," Gollier explained.

"Well, I'll be. I never saw such a thing before," Hanson replied, setting down the pan of cooked eggs and looking closely at the mark.

"Usually, it's sailors get them done on islands in the South Seas."

Hanson, his back to the road, heard hoof beats and turned to see a familiar face.

"Why if it ain't Hanson Bumgardner," Gabriel Clem said, as he slipped down from his saddle. A moment later John M. Woods and "Guns" Jackson pulled up and dismounted as well.

"What's for supper, Hanson? Smells awful good," Jackson asked.

"We don't have time for that, Guns. We need to get to get across the river to the dance. Come with us, Gollier; there'll be ladies. We kin all have some fun," Woods said, winking enticingly at Gollier.

"Just to let you know, Woods, we bought the wagon today for eleven hundred. I gave him eight hundred in advance," Hanson informed his boss.

"Great! Then we've something to celebrate! But, wait. Someone has to stay here to watch the horses and wagon. That'll have to be you, Hanson, but don't worry, we'll be back, soon." Woods leaned in closer and behind his hand spoke low so that only Hanson could hear. "We'll get him drunk, steal the money back, and tell him tomorrow the prostitutes stole all his money." Then, speaking louder, "Hanson's kindly agreed to stay here with the rig while we all party. He'll make sure a passing riverboat doesn't scare away the team."

Hanson nodded his agreement, despite his tacit disappointment about being "disinvited" to the dance.

"We'll need a way to cross the river," Woods said looking directly at the skiff.

"I've rented the skiff to do some laundry, but…"

"It'll do just fine," grunted Woods.

Gollier sauntered over to Hanson and asked, "Hanson, I'd feel better if I could hold that mortgage deed until you pay me the rest of the money."

Hanson dug in his leather satchel and obligingly handed the deed to the wagoner.

Satisfied, Gollier joined the other three men in the skiff and, winking, shouted to a dispirited Hanson, "If the whores are pretty and I don't make it back tonight, I'll meet you at Point Pleasant. If the whores are ugly, then I'll see you here in the morning!"

Everyone laughed.

# Chapter Thirty-Seven

Hours later, Hanson heard the sound of oars splashing in the water as the skiff returned minus Gollier.

Hanson looked questioningly at Woods, who ignored him, then at Jackson, who merely grunted.

"Woods chloroformed him, but he kept wakin' up. Woods gave him more chloroform, and he stopped breathin' after that. Bumgardner, I believe we killed the man," Gabriel Clem nervously revealed.

"Wha...?" Hanson barked at Woods.

Woods pulled his revolver, and pushed it into Hanson's ribs. "What's done's done. Take the wagon and git on to Addison. We're for sure moving operations now. Come on boys, we gotta git out of here. Now!" They walked their horses quietly away from the landing so as to not awaken the Hill family, and once clear, galloped off into the night.

Dawn was gray, cloudy and wet, and found Hanson deeply concerned, alone in his wagon. He'd rolled a pair of worn cavalry boots he found in the wagon into something resembling a pillow and used the tarp as a blanket. He hardly slept, worrying all night about Gollier. Perhaps Gollier wasn't dead, he reasoned, only so thoroughly knocked-out from the combination of alcohol and chloroform that he'd appeared dead. He convinced himself that that was what had happened and Gollier was alive, stranded on the other side of the Ohio River. He stretched and headed up to Hill house where Mr. Hill's wife had a pot of coffee ready. "Thank you, Missus Hill. Your coffee is famous along the Ohio," Hanson said. He took the pot to the campfire where he began preparing the remaining eggs for breakfast.

After eating and returning the pot and pan to Mrs. Hill, he harnessed the horses, recalling as best he could how Gollier had bucked the back strap, hip strap and trace carrier together. A sprinkle fell as he drove the massive wagon onto the roadway from Hill's Landing. The rig began to slide. Hanson frantically whipped the reins and the wagon suddenly lunged forward onto the roadway.

From his front porch, Roger Hill called out with a chuckle, "Hey, where's your partner? The guy that knows how to drive that rig?"

"I had hoped he would show me again the tricks of this rig, but he's gone," lamented Hanson, pressing his thumb against his lips and tipping his head back as though drinking from a bottle. They both laughed.

"That gray of yours is looking pretty sick," Hill pointed out as the team continued slowly on the pike.

"Yeah. I'm gonna have to do something about that," Hanson replied. "'Gotta take care of the horse so he can take care of you'," he said, quoting a well-worn truism.

As Hanson drove on the sprinkle changed into a slow but steady rain, making the roads even muddier and more difficult to travel. After an hour, he came upon David McLaughlin walking his fence line.

"Top o' the mornin' to ye, Doc. Begorra, that is one sickly horse, sir. What have ye done for him?" McLaughlin said, greeting Hanson.

"I hoped he would walk it off, but I think he has the colic. I didn't want to bleed him, given the inclement weather," Dr. Hanson bemoaned.

"Gonna hav'ta, Doc. T'would be even better if you made up a tonic or potion to go along with the bloodletting."

"Yes, I can do that. Does your wife have red pepper? I could make a good colic remedy with some red pepper," Hanson replied, pulling the wagon to a stop.

McLaughlin returned after a few minutes with some red pepper. Standing at the back of the wagon, Hanson opened his jack-knife, selected a small vein on the gray horse's neck, and made a small incision. Hanson was applying his thumb over the wound to control the amount of blood loss when suddenly the horse reared, splattering blood on Hanson's face, shirt and sleeves. Before he could regain control, there was blood all over the back of the wagon. Hanson eventually stemmed the flow, then applied a bandage.

Hanson prepared a red pepper tea enema and administered it to the gray. Within an hour, the horse had a huge bowel movement and it began to move about more freely, loud flatulence accompanying the cure. After waiting out a heavy shower with McLaughlin in the back of the wagon, Hanson bid him adieu with thanks for his assistance in curing the horse.

As Hanson continued on the road to Addison, the rain came in earnest, slowing his progress. It was almost an hour before he could again urge the team to a sloppy trot. After making some progress, he came to a skidding stop next to a wagon parked half on and half off the roadway, partially blocking it.

"Good day, sir," Hanson called out. "Is all okay?"

"All is fine, sir," the man standing at the side of the rig replied. "I'm merely awaiting the recession of the Hocking River in order to proceed. I see you are leading one of your horses," he said motioning with his head to the rear of the wagon. The man began walking towards the back of Hanson's rig where the gray stomped and snorted. Hanson set the brake and jumped down to join the man.

"I bled him this morning. It was a mess with the animal spraying blood everywhere," Hanson said, stretching.

"Yes. I can see that. It appears older, though," the driver said, pointing at some older bloodstains on the canvas side.

"It was a war wagon, sir; I was referring to this blood here on the back. The horse is for sale, sir. I also administered a cathartic this morning and he *is* recovering well," Hanson related.

"I see. How much for the horse?" The man asked.

"One hundred fifty dollars," Hanson replied.

"For a sick horse?" the man questioned.

"Because he is a recovering horse. He would be worth more otherwise," Hanson calmly related.

"No, sir, but thank you for the offer," the man said, declining the offer but still eyeing the wagon and team.

"Then the entire rig and team for two thousand," Hanson suddenly said.

"Why?" The man's curiosity was piqued.

"I'm tired of smelling oil," Hanson replied, telling the truth as the oil-soaked boards of the rig constantly stank of sulfur. "Tired of hauling oil," he corrected, to back up the story.

"A high but not unreasonable price. Still, I will pass on buying the rig," the man said. "I already have an occupation to keep my hands busy," he said.

"Doctor Hanson Bumgardner," Hanson ventured.

"Ed Fuller, Doctor Bumgardner. Looks like we may be here for a couple of hours, at least until the Hocking River drops below the bridge."

"Only if it stops raining...and even then, it will be a while," Hanson replied, beginning a conversation that lasted through several on and off showers.

Near four o'clock, unwilling to wait any longer, Hanson directed his wagon around Fuller's and splashed across the bridge. Once safely across, he waved good-bye to Fuller and slogged his way on through Coolville traveling south.

Just north of Tupper Plains, the rain began pounding again. Hanson urged the team faster and the team pressed forward to a trot. They were moving quickly along this hard-packed section of road. Too late, he saw a sharp turn in the road and realized the speeding rig could not make the turn. He pulled the reins forcefully to slow the team while he pushed hard with his foot on the brake. It was slow to grab, being wet and slippery with mud. The team slowed into the turn, but momentum carried the rear wheel off the road, leaving the wagon teetering on the roadway by only three wheels. Hanson whipped the horses to pull harder before the wagon slipped backwards and was completely lost. The team responded by lurching hard into their heavy leather collars and pulled the wagon forward onto the road again. A furlong down the road, Bumgardner slowed the team to a stop, his heart pounding in his ears, and gasped for breath. The team gasped as well, tossing their heads, snorting loudly, and stamping their hooves as if knowing how close to calamity they had come. The rain slowed again to a steady drizzle, and Hanson, his courage recovered, flipped the reins lightly to restart the journey.

Coming across a high and level spot, Hanson stopped to set up camp for the night. While darkness fell, Hanson set up a hobble line for the horses, and crawled into the malodorous wagon, pulling the water-soaked tarp about him.

It rained non-stop through the night with periods of torrential downpours. Hanson, sickened by the sulfurous odor of crude oil soaked into the floorboards, stayed huddled in the wagon the entire next day. Frightened by his experience of running the cumbrous rig off the road he felt he could not safely travel in such heavy storms. Saturday passed slowly, the rain continuing unabated.

Near dusk a man on a horse stopped by the wagon. "Hey! You in the wagon! I am James Miller. Do you know you are on my father's property?"

"The poem or the song?" Hanson replied testily, poking his head from inside the canvas top. Looking at the wet man on the horse, he could tell the rider didn't get his joke. "The answer is 'no'. I don't know whose property I am on. I am a traveler seeking emergency shelter in this storm. Does your father charge rent? I will gladly pay for a night's stay," Hanson offered.

"No need. Just clean up after yourself. Yankee soldiers always left a mess."

"Got it. Clean up. Say, one can make good money with this rig. Twelve dollars a day. I'll sell it to you, and you could start a new career," Hanson offered the humorless but sincere James Miller.

"No, thanks," Miller deadpanned. "And who should I tell my father is camping on his property?" he asked, as the rain began to hammer straight down, drumming on the canvas top.

"Bumgardner! Doctor Hanson Bumgardner!" Hanson yelled, the loud heavy rains dampening his voice.

"Who? Yaruer?" the man called back, holding his hat on his head with one hand as the wind began swirling the heavy rain about.

"BUM-GARD-NER!" Hanson shouted as a crack of thunder sounded, scaring the horses, who whinnied loudly as he called out his name.

"Silent letter, you say? 'A-RU-ER', then? Okay!" The man spun his horse and headed quickly up a trail.

Hanson smiled and shrugged, settling back into the wagon out of the rain.

On Sunday morning the rains stopped and blue sky began peeking through clefts in the clouds, promising sunshine. Hanson prepared the rig and continued his journey southbound. As he left, he spotted James Miller riding along the road and waved. Miller waved back.

At about midday, Hanson pulled into Pomeroy, Ohio. Spotting several men gathered together, he stopped and led the gray horse over to the men. "Gentlemen, could any of you help a war veteran out? I need to sell this horse in order to make my way home."

The men looked at the horse, but none seemed interested. One finally spoke up. "How much are you asking, friend?"

"Bumgardner's the name, friend, merely a hundred fifty dollars for this fine animal," Hanson offered.

"Name's Hibbard. George Hibbard, Mister Bumgardner." They shook hands, and Hibbard inspected the horse. "The animal looks as though it's recovering from an illness. I will nonetheless offer a hundred dollars for it," Hibbard said, adding, "To help you in your plight."

"Thank you, sir, for your offer, but for one hundred dollars I will continue to trail the horse behind," Hanson said. "Help a fellow veteran of the Ohio volunteers, by meeting the fair price of one hundred fifty."

"One hundred twenty five," Hibbard counteroffered.

"I apologize for my insisting, but it must be one fifty if I am to return home with anything to show to my family for my time away," Bumgardner replied, standing firm.

"Then I'm afraid I must pass. Good day to you, sir." Hibbard tipped his hat and moved on.

Continuing, Hanson arrived in Addison that evening to Sue and his boys' fervent embraces. Hanson kissed Sue, then his three sons, George, William and James, each in turn. After putting the boys to bed that night, he said to Sue, "I marvel how blessed we are, Sue. I have everything a man could want: a beautiful devoted wife, three fine sons, money in the mattress, and loyal friends."

"I'll agree with everything up to money in the mattress and loyal friends," Sue began with a weak smile. "Woods came by while you were away, saying he needed money and you had agreed to make him a loan. I gave him all but about three hundred dollars. Oh, Hanson! I didn't know what was going on, and I feared for you and our family! There was always a lot of activity at the Woods place, but recently, nothing."

"I paid eight hundred out of pocket for the rig Woods asked me to purchase for him," Hanson said. "When I saw him at Hill's Landing, I told him such, but he didn't pay it back as promised. I'm worried that we'll never see him or our money again." Hanson again thought about Gollier, and prayed he was merely unconscious when Woods left him for dead.

The next morning, Hanson's landlord, Dr. James Barton, stopped by the Bumgardner residence. "Doctor Hanson, good to see you're back."

"Thank you, Doctor Barton. I know why you are here, and I am sorry to have to tell you I don't have the money. Once my accounts receivable are satisfied, yours will be as well, of that, I assure you," Hanson said, flashing his trademark smile.

"Thank you for your honesty, doctor. Landlords need payment, you know," he smiled back, adding with a chuckle, "By the way, doctor, I would also appreciate your settling the matter of the ten dollars owed my wife for pawning a watch, as it appears as if you are moving." Dr. Barton waved a hand towards the two empty cabins and the large wagon parked in front of the porch.

"Rest assured the debt *will* be satisfied. And, yes, I'm thinking of relocating to Parkersburg or some other more convenient location," Hanson replied, not wanting to reveal their real destination was Columbus.

"Seriously, Hanson, where will you be headed?" the doctor asked, renewing his question.

"No telling, really. Maybe Greenbrier, Virginia. Maybe somewhere in Illinois. I haven't decided yet," he replied, evading the question.

"Then I'll be back to settle accounts tomorrow," Dr. Barton promised.

"I'll be here, then again, maybe not," Hanson said jokingly. "But either way, I will make certain all accounts are settled before I leave."

# Chapter Thirty-Eight

Later that morning, Hanson took the gray to Gallipolis in another effort to sell the animal, but was yet again unsuccessful. Hanson used the last of his personal money to settle rent and store accounts. While at the store, he visited the lumberyard and bought several new boards to replace the oil-and-blood-soaked ones in the wagon. Seeing Ed Ramsey, he asked him if he could help repair the wagon, and together they spent the remainder of the morning repairing the floor and the tail boards, as well as the small feeding trough on one side. When finished, Ramsey wished Hanson a good journey, declaring the rig solid, safe, and dependable given its new boards and heavy, cast-iron munitions-wagon-style suspension.

That afternoon, the Bumgardners loaded the wagon with their belongings.

"Do you suppose Woods has stood by his promise to rent housing for us in Columbus?" Sue worried.

"He gave me an address to go to, Sue," Hanson assured her as he hefted the last box onto the wagon.

Sue looked toward the silent unoccupied Woods' house. "I wonder where they are right now," she mused, her eyes revealing deep-felt misgivings.

"I don't know, Sue. There is no telling with John M. Woods. We have very little money left after paying Doctor Barton, and I still need to hire a driver with some of what we have left, for I have proven that I am no heavy wagoner."

The following morning, they left Addison headed south to Gallipolis where they sought out a teamster and engaged the services of Bob Woolley. Woolley carefully inspected the wagon and team, nodding his approval and admiring its good condition.

"If you like, I could make you a deal on it, and you won't have to take us anywhere. You could easily make twelve instead of four dollars a day if you owned a rig like this one," Hanson offered.

"I don't have near enough saved up, Doctor Bumgardner. This job will do me just fine for now," Bob replied.

The rains returned as they passed through Burning Springs, and once again hindered their travel. Bumgardner and family stayed the night at a bed-and-breakfast in Thurman; Woolley spent the night in a hammock under the rig.

The breakfast next morning at the inn was so wonderful Hanson invited Woolley to join them and paid for the teamster's meal. After breakfast, they continued along the rutted and muddy pike. They barely made Richmond Dale before a full-fledged storm cut loose. Choosing caution over speed, they made camp even though it was still mid-morning.

Friday morning's sky was clear with red streaks of light radiating from the horizon as the sun brought forth a new day. After a cold breakfast, they continued on their journey. The gray horse, still trailing, appeared fully recovered. Stopping briefly in Chillicothe, Hanson was able at last to sell it. They continued their journey until about halfway to Frankfort, when unexpectedly Gabriel Clem, riding an Appaloosa, pulled up from a full gallop alongside the wagon with disturbing news.

"I've been looking everywhere for you, Hanson!" he shouted, coming to a halt along with the wagon. "I've important news. Woods sent me to..."

"Just tell me the news," Hanson interrupted harshly. His instincts told him the news wouldn't be good.

"There's a warrant on you for murder," Clem grimly revealed.

"What?" Sue screamed. "You and Woods' gang have gone too far this time, Gabriel! Curse you all to hell!"

"Hey, I'm just the messenger sent by Woods to warn you, but if you want my opinion, you oughtta dump this wagon and your family, find a horse and ride west as fast as you can. Sue and the family can join you later," Clem suggested.

"I have done nothing wrong!" Hanson declared. "They can not convict a man for a murder he didn't commit! Although I have broken many of God's commandments, I have *never* killed anyone!"

"That said, I'd still take one of the team horses and ride as fast and far away as I could. We'll take care of Sue and let you know when it's clear to return. Woods promised that."

"Well, tell Woods to get me out of jail instead, because I am not running. That would be sure to make me look guilty. I'll not run. I'll not abandon my family alongside the road." Hanson was adamant.

"I'll tell him, but you should run while you can. Listen, I gotta get outta here. I don't want to git caught with you." Clem spurred his leopard-spotted Appaloosa and disappeared past the next curve.

"Hanson, maybe you had better do as Gabriel suggests. If it is a frame up, as it sounds, you're better off out of jail," she said.

"I need to think," Hanson stated as they continued rattling over ruts and bumps in the clay roadway.

Knowing a murder warrant was out for him, Hanson held the fear inside and controlled the trembling in his hands. He caught himself breathing in short quick gasps as he tried to think. They *did* kill Gollier that night at the dance, he concluded, but he couldn't figure out how he'd been implicated. *Even if Sue is right*, he thought, *it's a poor frame up,at best*.

A few miles outside of Frankfort, four deputies caught up to the wagon. "You Hanson Bumgardner?" an overweight deputy with a large moustache asked, eyeing Hanson closely.

"I am Dr. Hanson Bumgardner," Hanson said rising from the seat, placing a hand on Sue's shoulder, and bracing his foot against the kickboard.

"I have a warrant for your arrest for the murder of John T. Eubanks," the deputy said.

"Who?" Sue and Hanson asked in unison, their startled eyes wide open in bewilderment.

"John Thomas Eubanks," the deputy said gravely.

Hanson looked at Sue, "I have no idea what this is about." Turning back to the deputy, he asked, "Who is John Eubanks?"

# Chapter Thirty-Nine

The rain continued as James and Sue Bumgardner headed towards Marietta, Ohio, with their prisoner, Gabriel Clem. Although permitted to ride on the seat beside Sue, his hands remained tied to his waist and his legs hobbled.

"This is taking too long, I fear," worried Sue, as she looked up at the dark sky.

"We'll get there; we have 'till tomorrow at noon and the roads are getting better," James said. "Once we deliver Gabriel, they'll have to stop everything."

"How could you, Clem? How could you frame Hanson?" she asked, furious in her frustration.

"Like I said, it was easy. Woods planned it all." He coughed harshly before continuing. "Woods told Hanson that Gollier was the mark, and to negotiate and pay a "fair" price for the wagon using his counterfeit cash, which Woods promised to reimburse later. Woods told Gollier that Hanson was the mark. Gollier was to pick up the old ammo wagon the gang had stolen from Eubanks and left at Dye's Livery in Belpre. He was told to get Hanson to buy this wagon with all the cash Hanson had. Gollier thought they were framing Hanson for the stolen wagon, and that we would get Gollier out of camp that night before the deputies arrested Hanson for theft. Gollier didn't realize he was marked for death. Hell, Woods probably planned to kill me, too, but he needed me to make the ruse work. He wanted to see Hanson in total despair. 'Make him suffer a trial and wait hopelessly for certain execution'. Those were his words to me."

"I still don't see how this implicated Hanson," Sue confessed.

"That's the beauty of this frame up. He has no defense because he never met the victim. It's a perfect plan." Clem coughed heavily again. "Hanson just had to follow the predetermined route Woods set out for him and everything would happen on its own." Clem coughed again, this time producing blood-streaked milky sputum that he spit away. "I may not make it to Marietta," he said as another coughing fit seized him. Sue dug in her purse, pulled out a bottle of Dr. Hanson's Tonic and poured a double dose for Clem, who gratefully accepted it.

Back at the gallows, Dr. Hanson stared down from the platform at the crowd awaiting his death. "You proved nothing," he said, pointing at the prosecutor, Col. David Alban, "other than I traveled a particular route that ultimately brought me here to the gallows. I am condemned to die by the thinnest of circumstantial evidence simply because I traveled those particular pikes."

He turned slowly and walked the length of the gallows. The sun peeked momentarily through the gray overcast and then hid again. Looking into the ray of sunlight, Hanson's face appeared tense. It was plain to see that he was composing himself.

"I recall the trial—that hasty affair designed to take my life. I remember the gallery, loud and abusive, their minds made up regarding my guilt before a single word was spoken..."

"Motion to dismiss is denied," Judge Erastus A. Guthrie rapped the gavel on the routine dismissal motion filed by Dr. Hanson's attorneys, William Loomis and Senator Sam S. Knowles, both of whom had agreed to handle the case *pro bono*—for free. Hanson was certain that Knowles believed in his innocence. Loomis, he felt, was less enthusiastic about defending the only murderer to go on trial in Washington County, Ohio, in living memory.

Col. David Alban, the District Attorney, nodded and smiled at his assistant, Thomas Ewart, who had written the brief opposing the motion. Although older than Alban, Ewart was the junior in terms of legal experience, and Alban had agreed to let him share duties throughout the high-profile trial. The December 1866 murder trial generated huge interest, and the courtroom overflowed with spectators.

"Jury selection will now begin," Judge Guthrie directed. "Bailiff, read the names of the potential jurors. If your name is called, please rise and take a seat in the jury box."

The bailiff read the first twelve names and five men sat in the jury box. He continued reading from the list of male landowners until all twelve seats were filled.

"That's it? They take anyone responding to fill the jury?" Dr. Hanson anxiously asked.

"We will soon have the opportunity to examine them individually to agree on which ones will be kept," Knowles calmly assured him.

Several hours passed while the prosecution and defense examined and cross-examined the potential jurors. The most common reason for dismissal was having already formed an opinion as to the guilt of the prisoner. For example, Mark Green, when asked if he had an opinion stood up and yelled, "An opinion? Hell yes, I've an opinion 'bout this and all them other Johnny Rebs. Hang 'em all, I say! As for this 'un, everybody here knows he's guilty! Hang him on a Sunday so's everyone kin come an' watch!"

Green was promptly dismissed. Another man was dismissed for health reasons, and several others for a variety of reasons. Many simply did not show. Non-appearance for jury duty was unusual in Washington County and most folks believed the high number of no-shows was because no one wanted to serve on this death penalty jury. The jury was only up to ten when the bailiff called the last name on the jury roster. No one came forward.

Looking around the courtroom, Hanson asked, "Now what?"

"I don't know," Loomis said. "I've not had this happen before."

Judge Guthrie called the counsel before the bench. Hanson watched Loomis, Knowles, Alban and Ewart, talking low, faces close.

The attorneys returned to their tables and Judge Guthrie called out, "Are there any other landowning gentlemen in the crowd?"

"What?" Hanson cried in disbelief.

"Don't worry, Hanson, I've agreed to this," Loomis said. "It's better for us than waiting another month to get this trial going. The longer we wait, the more the people seem to be turning against you."

Two men stepped forward, one more slightly built than the other.

"I don't know…" Hanson began.

Ignoring Hanson's remark, Judge Guthrie proceeded. "Your name, sir?" he asked the larger of the two.

"Hollister, your honor, sir. R. D. Hollister. That's my name."

"Mister Hollister, for the record are you a landowner in Washington County?" Judge Guthrie inquired.

"Yes, sir, I am. I…" Hollister replied.

"Have you formed an opinion about the guilt of the prisoner?" Guthrie further inquired.

"Not really, sir. I guess…" An indifferent shrug accompanied the answer.

"Please sit in the jury box." Guthrie motioned toward the eleventh chair. "And you sir, your name?" he asked the remaining man.

"Simeon F. Seeley, your majesty," Seeley answered, raising chuckles from the gallery.

"Your honor," corrected the judge.

"Well thankee, your majesty," the slightly built Seeley replied. Judge Guthrie rolled his eyes.

"*Mister* Seeley, are you a…"

"Landowner? Yes, sir. And, no sir, I haven't an opinion yet about what this here man's done. I come jus' to watch, but now, I gets to be part of the ceremonies!" Seeley's folksy forthright manner endeared him to the rowdy crowd.

"Yes sir. Fine. Please take the final seat over there in the jury box," Judge Guthrie directed.

Hanson looked to his legal team, Loomis and Knowles and raised his eyebrows, "That's my jury?" Hanson asked.

"Yes, Hanson. And they will decide your fate," Senator Knowles replied as he examined the impaneled jury. "Listen. In the front row, are the two drawn from the audience, R. D. Hollister, who looks to be about sixty-five years old. His wedding ring says he's married, and the woman and five kids he left in the audience have to be his family. Simeon F. Seeley, roughly sixty years of age, is not as literate, but he's a retired dry goods dealer, known about these parts for his fair-handedness. He's married, too. That's his wife with their two sons in the audience. Next is William Cole, thirty, single, a farmer, and next to him, Augustus S. Curtis, the forty-one-year-old flour miller, married with five children. Occupying the next juror's chair, Hanson, is farmer Augustine Dyer, thirty-six, married, also with five children. Finally, seated next to him we have C. D. Ford, forty-eight, a farmer who has often spoke out against the war, who has but one child with his wife Edna." Knowles raised his eyebrows and offered Hanson a smile.

"In the back row is Hiram Gard, fifty-six, a married merchant with four children. Sitting next to him is a fifty-one-year-old carpenter, John Henry, married with three kids. David H. Merrill, thirty, another single man who is a merchant occupies the next seat. On his left sits George W. St. John, a forty-year-old farmer and father of five. Two more farmers finish out the row, Cyrenus Stacy, forty-nine, married to Lucy—their five offspring are at home—and finally, James Ward, fifty-four, married with four children." Hanson was impressed with the depth of the Senator's knowledge of each of the jurors.

Hanson surveyed the jury, trying to analyze if they were right for him. Their average age he estimated was older than he was. Half were farmers, who tended to be suspicious of doctors. Most were married, like him, and had children, also like him.

Sen. Knowles whispered, "It seems a good jury. Augustine Dyer serves on the Children's Home Board of Trustees. He loves children and is a careful thinker. All in all, it seems a reasonable miscellany of occupations and a diverse enough group capable of rendering a verdict based on fact rather than predetermination or showmanship," he assured Hanson.

Judge Guthrie rapped the gavel and declared a recess until nine a.m. the next day. Sheriff Hicks motioned for Hanson to stand and handcuffed his prisoner for the trip across Second Street to the jail.

# Chapter Forty

The following morning, Judge Guthrie opened proceedings the moment the clock on the square finished striking nine o'clock. "Colonel Alban, your opening remarks, please," he requested.

Alban stood, gave an exaggerated nod at the judge, and then turned to the jury. "Gentlemen of the jury, we will show that Hanson Bumgardner was the sole cause of the death of John Thomas Eubanks. We will show that he met Mister Eubanks in West Virginia, accompanied him through that state until crossing into Ohio, camping below the township of Belpre at Hill's Landing. There, on the evening of September fourteenth of this year, he murdered John T. Eubanks while Eubanks slept in the munitions wagon that Bumgardner coveted. We will show that the accused then mutilated the body to prevent identification, tossing the beheaded body in the Ohio River. Subsequently, he proceeded to meet his family in Addison. There, he exchanged the damning bloody floorboards in the wagon he stole with new ones. He then fled west with his family, whence he was captured. You jurors must decide on several important points: One, whether the body found is that of John T. Eubanks. Two: Did John T. Eubanks meet a violent death? Three: Is it clear that the person who caused that death is none other than Hanson Bumgardner? You need not fear being asked to pronounce any sentence. Judge Guthrie will do so in accordance with the law. That way, your conscious is clear to vote as you see fit. Watch, listen, and when we're done I believe you will have no doubt that Hanson Bumgardner killed John T. Eubanks. Thank you for your time, gentlemen."

"Well done, counselor," the judge remarked while the crowd whispered their approvals. "Mister Loomis, have you any opening remarks?" Judge Guthrie asked.

Loomis rose and slowly approached the jury. "Gentlemen of the jury, Hanson Bumgardner firmly claims his innocence of the charges the State has brought forth. Keep in mind that the State is required to prove *beyond any reasonable doubt* each of the points stated in order to convict. If any one fails, their case fails. My client is innocent in the eyes of the law, and remains so, until you decide he is guilty. I agree with Colonel Alban: You need to listen very carefully to the evidence and if you do, I believe you will see that it is insufficient to convict a man of murder. This case is a shell, no more, without substance, without one iota of evidence to prove my client's guilt. The prosecution will attempt to weave a circumstantial fantasy. Listen and you will be obliged to agree that Hanson Bumgardner is not guilty."

The courtroom silence was broken only by the sound of Loomis' footfalls as he crossed the room back to the defense table where Hanson and Knowles waited. After he sat, the judge said dryly, "Thank you counselor." Turning to the prosecutor, his voice more cordial, he continued, "Colonel Alban. You may call your first witness, sir."

"George Stone," Col. Alban said loudly. Stone stood and shuffled his way to the single wooden chair next to the judge's desk. The Court Clerk administered the Witness Oath, and Stone sat uncomfortably in the straight-back chair. "Now, George. Tell us what happened on

September seventeenth," Alban directed.

"Well, I was at Point Pleasant, West Virginia, crossin' over to Ohio on th' bridge when I noticed somethin' in the water."

"What did you see, George?" Alban inquired.

"I wasn't sure at first, so's I lassoed it and pulled it behind me over to Ohio an' dragged it up on shore. It was a body without a head. I rode to the constable's house to report it, an' we moved the body to th' courthouse. Th' constable said a coroner's hearing would be held."

"No further questions," Alban said.

"Cross examination?" Judge Guthrie asked.

"Where was the body when you first saw it?" Knowles inquired.

"Near th' bridge," the witness responded

"Where near the bridge?" Knowles asked, walking slowly towards the witness. The senator leaned over the man, making him uneasy.

"On th' side of th' bridge" replied Stone moving away from the imposing attorney.

"*Which* side of the bridge?" Knowles asked, leaning in closer

"Th'...th' north side," Stone replied.

"Was the body closer to Ohio or West Virginia?" Sen. Knowles pressed.

Stone stared down at the floor for several minutes in confused silence, then slowly responded, "I couldn't really say."

"Pass the witness." Knowles said walking briskly back to the defense table.

When the next state's witness took the stand, Col. Alban said, "Mister William Boyd. Please tell the jury what you know of this case."

"I am the Magistrate for Troy Township in Gallia County. On

September seventeenth, the constable arrived at my office. He told me of a body being found, and I immediately convened a jury. We noted the clothes of the deceased, the fact that his head was missing, and that the body was bound with a heavy chain to help it sink. There were no other wounds. He was a very large man, no boots, yet he had stockings on his feet. We noted his large hands as well. When we heard of the disappearance of Mister Eubanks, we contacted the family and his brother came down to identify the body a few days later. We had already buried the body so we dug it up for him to view. I kept all the clothing afterward, and here it is." He went on to identify each item of clothing taken from the body, and Judge Guthrie admitted them as evidence.

"Thank you Magistrate Boyd. That is all," Col. Alban said, passing the witness.

"Mister Boyd, did the body you examined have any tattoos?"

"No sir. And I know what tattoos look like. No old wounds or scars that I saw, either."

The rest of the morning, the prosecution introduced each of the men from the coroner's jury to confirm the same information as though by repetition the it would become fact. After lunch, the victim's brother, Robert P. Eubanks, took the stand.

"I saw the body down in Troy. It was my brother, of that I'm certain. He was a big man with big hands and owned a plaid shirt just like that one. It was odd that he wasn't wearing his boots. My brother, he practically lived in his cavalry boots. Still, I'm sure it was my brother. I haven't seen him since he left Boiling Springs with a guy named Bumgardner."

Hanson leaned over and whispered to Knowles, "I didn't pick anyone up in Boiling Springs. I met the wagon and Gollier at Belpre in the afternoon." Knowles nodded his understanding and made a note.

When asked if he'd met Bumgardner on any previous occasion, Eubanks rose from the witness chair and shouted, "I never met my brother's killer, but they tell me that's him sitting right there!" He forcefully pointed directly at Hanson as though pointing at him substituted for striking him with a fist.

"Objection," Knowles requested.

"Sustained. The witness will confine himself to speaking from his personal knowledge," Judge Guthrie admonished the grief-stricken brother.

"Did your brother have any tattoos, Mister Eubanks?" Knowles asked when it was the defense's turn.

"None, sir." Eubanks replied, and continued to glare at Hanson as he left the witness stand after being dismissed.

Mary Kyle, the victim's sister, testified next. "I made the pants that Mister Boyd has placed in evidence. I recognize my stitching as most would their handwriting. I made those pants for my brother, John Thomas Eubanks, as a gift. He had them on when last I saw him."

"My name is Samuel Guinn. I live in Parkersburg, West Virginia," the next witness responded. "On September thirteenth, I saw my long-time friend, John Eubanks, with a man on the highway east of Parkersburg. I don't remember what John was wearing, but the other man wore a black Plug hat. Eubanks said he was moving this man's family to Parkersburg from Gallipolis. They were stopped and checking, maybe even fixing, the wagon. It was between eleven o'clock and noon. I remember because Eubanks owed me money and opened his wallet. He only had a few small bills, but he paid me the ten he owed. The other man was the prisoner, I think. I never got a good look at him until I saw him in jail," he finished, nodding towards

Hanson.

"Mister Guinn. For the record, are you *positively certain* that this is the man you saw with Mister Eubanks?" Knowles asked.

"Well, the truth be told, I can not be *positively certain* he is the man I saw with John Eubanks, as he kept his distance and had his Plug hat pulled down over his eyes." Guinn squinted at Hanson as if in doing so, he might be more certain. "Nope, can't be *positively certain*, sir," he ended.

The next witness, George Hensley, testified that he, too, saw the same two men together. He personally knew John Eubanks, he said. John had called out to him, "Hello, George. Is that you?" He testified he talked with Eubanks, but under questioning by Knowles, Hensley also admitted he couldn't say *positively for certain* that Hanson was the second man he saw that day, "because the man wore a Plug hat and it hid his face."

The next witness, Samuel Robinson, stated, "John Eubanks was a boarder at m'house. He was a big man, yes, sir. An' he had a confederate munitions wagon I personally converted to haul oil barrels. He left sayin' someone wanted to hire him to move household goods. I remember, 'cause he said he liked that better'n haulin' oil. Said they was goin' to pay him twelve dollars a day! Anyways, he had on dark pants jus' like those, and a shirt jus' like that one over there when last I saw him. He never mentioned who he was movin', jus' he was movin' em' somewhere from Gallipolis."

Under cross-examination by Loomis, he admitted, "I never actually met th' prisoner before," and, "I never really ever saw Eubanks with th' prisoner."

Under oath, A.J. Snyder told the jurors, "I met the prisoner at Dye's Stable. He was leaving with another man in a large wagon. The prisoner asked didn't I think it was a fine rig, and I replied, I did. He gave me a look I thought suspicious and he had a cold manner about him that day," he testified. "I hurried off, anxious to be away from him."

On cross-examination by Sen. Knowles, Snyder stated, "The other man seemed to me more of average build, smaller than would comfortably wear the clothes on exhibit."

Al Miller testified, "I've known the Doc here, er, the prisoner, for well nigh on several years. I seen him near Dye's Stable and Livery with a team of five horses." He narrowed one eye suspiciously at Hanson. "They trailed one that looked sickly, a gray, but the others were in fine good shape. I recognized the team from last summer, but can't recall to whom they belonged then, 'though I know it wasn't the prisoner. There was another man with the prisoner of slight build. I barely noticed his clothes, but I think he wore light-colored pants. The prisoner wore a Plug hat that day like always. They seemed in a hurry to leave town."

Dugan Nolan squirmed uncomfortably on the hardwood witness chair as he testified, "I remember callin' to an oil wagon movin' along the pike I wanted to pass. As I passed, the prisoner looked to me to be in charge. The other man seemed cowered by him. The prisoner said his 'new rig'—those were his exact words—needed a new lead team. I knew of a reputable livery with a team in Gallipolis, so's I referred him there. He seemed in a powerful hurry, keeping up with my light rig for a while. The man with the prisoner was of average build. I'm certain about that. The prisoner wore a Plug hat, black as I recall."

"There being no further questions, the witness is dismissed," Judge Guthrie said. "Given the hour of the day, we will adjourn for the day and reconvene at the hour of nine tomorrow."

# Chapter Forty-One

The rain pounded on James Bumgardner and Gabriel Clem as each manned a wheel on either side of the wagon and pushed the wagon up the steep embankment of a normally placid creek. Sue slapped the reins against Banjo's back while the mule struggled, pulled, slipped, and resumed pulling in the wet mud. They finally crested the bank, and the men climbed back in to continue their journey.

Rain dripped from his hat as James said, "I hope this weather lets up. We don't have far to go, but the morning is almost gone, and the road so poor…" his voice trembled with genuine fear of failure.

Sue turned to see Clem digging in her purse, "There is nothing in there that belongs to you, Clem," she said pointedly.

"I was just looking for that bottle of elixir, er, tonic for my cough," he related. He held up the bottle of tonic and swallowed a double dose, then returned it to her bag.

Several miles passed in silence while the medicine took hold. Clem, turning his glazed-over eyes to Sue and James, admitted, "I'm sorry. I really hated Hanson, but it was for being everything I'm not. He's suave while I'm coarse. His intelligence shines, while I just get by. He has a beautiful wife and loving family, and I have no one. He has everything a man could want, yet wastes his life indulging in petty crime, and, yeah, I hate him for that, too. I've hated him for so long…" his voice trailed away.

"How did Woods fool everyone about Hanson killing Eubanks?" Sue questioned.

"Well, you see, it was all part of Woods' plan. I was the one who met John Eubanks in Boiling Springs, not Hanson. I rode with Eubanks through Virginia to the stable in Belpre, wearing a duster and Plug hat in order to make everyone seeing us think I was Hanson. Later, we stopped in a secluded area, where Woods joined us and got Eubanks drunk. The man Hanson met was, of course, Gollier, not Eubanks."

"What happened to Eubanks?" Sue asked, hoping Clem in his medicated state might reveal who really murdered the man.

"He's dead. He is the body they found. Woods cut off his head and was gonna carry it around like a trophy until I talked him out of it. Woods killed Gollier later that night, too, and we buried him together with Eubank's head in a riverbank in West Virginia. If anyone found Gollier's body in the river they might recognize the tattoo. I'll never know why Woods called Gollier here all the way from Texas just to kill him. It was probably another old grudge; Woods was someone who carried a lot of grudges."

"Tell me about the ferry accident." James was curious about the demise of the man who now seemed to reach out from the grave to take his brother's life.

"The sheriff kept Eubanks' wagon as evidence, so we 'acquired' a similar one to move the printing press. We knew this ferry that few folks use nowadays because it has such a low weight limit. The ferryman expressed reluctance to allow the wagon with the printing press and horses on the ferry. We convinced him it would work if we unhitched the horses, and emptied everything from the wagon except the press before it went on the ferry. The draught horses and I went without incident, and I waited on the riverbank while the ferryman, Woods and the wagon with the press inside started across the river. About halfway across, the bow of the ferry caught a wave and water splashed onto the barge causing it to rock. Suddenly, more waves came over it. It wasn't half a minute before the ferry sunk. The press sunk like a stone. The barge, men, and wagon were swept away." He paused, shaking his head as he recalled the scene. Looking up, his eyes fixed on another swollen creek and damaged bridge looming directly in front of them.

Banjo tossed his head and flicked his large ears as rain began falling again, and stopped at the wooden bridge. Water from the swollen creek had undercut the embankment at the far end. James walked the bridge and although he noted a few loose boards, thought it in fair and stable enough condition. Sue followed, leading Banjo, while Clem walked behind the wagon.

They had to stop near the end of the bridge where the rain-swollen creek had washed away the embankment leaving a gap four feet wide. The rift was too wide to jump over and the churning water too swift to ford.

"The next nearest crossing is miles out of our way…" Sue sobbed. James embraced Sue in the rain and she laid her head on his chest. "My dear Hanson…my dear Hanson…" she murmured, her tears mixing with the rain on her cheeks.

Clem watched fascinated by the show of love, his heart empty from living a loveless life. A knot rose in his throat at the sudden realization that he would always be denied such emotion.

James released Sue, head bowed, and girded himself for failure. Despondent over being unable to proceed, it was as if God Himself were impeding their progress to save his brother. Suddenly his thoughts were interrupted by a loud thud.

"I pulled some loose boards up from the bridge behind us. We can place them in front of us, and, if we hurry, we may yet be able to get to Marietta in time. They'll listen to me once we're there," Clem announced as he dropped a second board in place. Together they prepared the temporary overpass and carefully drove the rig over it.

On the other side, they climbed back into the wagon and pressed Banjo onward. The poor mule's back was foaming with sweat despite the rain.

"It must be well past noon," Sue agonized. "Hanson said the sheriff would wait as long as possible because the sheriff believes in his innocence. How long do you suppose they'll wait?"

"I don't know, Sue. How long do you think Hanson can stall them?" James replied, his brow furrowed with worry. Praying for a miracle, Sue noticed with apprehension the rain increasing in intensity as they pushed on.

# Chapter Forty-Two

Cold December winds blew as Hanson's trial continued. At nine o'clock sharp, the prosecution called Payne Lewis of Lewis' Dry Goods and Sundries. Lewis was obviously nervous about being thrust into the center of attention and his voice wavered as he spoke. "The... prisoner...came in the store that night...I know him well. Well enough to know that *somethin'* was different. He talked about having bought a new large rig. He asked for wine and I gave him a pint, which he swigged from. Then..." Lewis' vacillating voice shrank to an inaudible mumble.

"You must speak up so everyone can hear you," prompted the judge.

Lewis gulped audibly and continued. "Then he handed the pint to the deceased and insisted he drink, too. The man...the victim, I mean...took a drink and the prisoner bid him drink more. The prisoner then requests eggs...*two dozen* eggs, mind you...and from the glare in his eye, I dared not question the request." Lewis shuddered, then looked directly at the jury. "Then he demands *another* pint of wine and, of course, I produced it immediately. The other man, he bought a bottle of liniment, which he paid for..."

"Did you happen to hear the other man's name?" Knowles

interrupted.

"No, sir."

"Did you notice the other man's purse?"

"Yes, sir. I'm a merchant. I notice things like that." The courtroom tittered, while Lewis, unfazed, continued. "It was *stuffed full of money!* He told me he had nothin' smaller than a twenty. He was a nice man..." Muted murmurs rose from the visitor section of the courtroom.

"How would you describe his build?"

"Oh, everyone's large compared to me," the slightly-built storekeeper responded, bringing chuckles from the gallery.

The prosecution next called Roger Hill, who glanced at Hanson with reservation as he came forward. From the witness chair, he told the jury, "Hanson...the prisoner there...often rents a space from us, but normally he drives an apothecary wagon. On September fourteenth, he rents a space and pays, as usual, in cash. He returns to the house later that night requesting a large pan. He further demanded Missus Hill prepare coffee for him in the morning. Later, he again returned to rent my skiff, 'in order to wash some clothes,' he claimed. He stared at us with cold, merciless eyes..."

"Knowles, that is not the way it happened!" Hanson protested.

"Let it pass. The less we make of this the better," opined Knowles. "Hill is well-liked hereabouts, and hopefully the jury will see through his exaggerations."

Hill continued. "Later that night, I hears some loud splashes. Suspicious-like. Sounded like someone throwing something big in the river. Next morning, I sees the horses having a tough time pulling the rig onto the roadway from the landing. The prisoner was driving, whipping the horses madly as if the devil himself is chasing him. He chose a bad angle for the horses to pull the rig onto the pike. An experienced wagoner would have entered further down where the rise is easier. Seeing this, I calls to the prisoner, I says, 'Where's that partner of yours who knows how to drive the rig?' He growls back with a fierce look in his eye, 'Oh, he's gone' and makes a motion with his thumb across his throat." He looked with trepidation at Hanson, while nodding in agreement with himself.

Next to sit in the witness chair was David McLaughlin, the happy Irishman who today began, "Sure, 'tis true, I know th' prisoner. He came upon me tending me fences one morn' with as sickly a horse a man has ere seen. He enlisted me to assist in bleeding th' animal. At one point, th' frightened beast tossed his head and got blood all over the rig and the both of us. At that moment, th' prisoner's eyes were black as Satan's; looking at that horse he was angry, you know, wanting to be on his way an' all. We gave the ill-begotten animal a potion of red pepper tea to induce a bowel movement that was quite successful, leaving the animal joyfully tooting his gratitude." McLaughlin's description generated chortles in the crowd. "He stayed until the animal could travel, leaving between stops and starts of downpours, both from the heavens and the animal." More laughter followed.

Ed Fuller took the stand recounting his encounter with Hanson as a meeting with a, "tough guy, wearing a Plug hat, sliding his rig to a stop right next to mine. Neither of us could move because the Hocking River had overflowed the bridge. He was impatient, anxious to be out of the area, and offered to sell me a sickly gray horse for a hundred and fifty dollars, claiming he had raised it from a colt. I declined the offer. It seemed he was hiding something. There was blood on his shirt and rig, and when I pointed it out to him, he seemed surprisingly unconcerned. We visited for several hours while waiting for the river to recede. Even so, before the water was completely off the bridge, he took off in a powerful hurry."

"I found a wagon and a team of hobbled horses parked on my father's property," Jim Miller told the jury. "I rode up to the wagon and called to the prisoner, asking if he knew he was on my father's property. From inside the wagon I heard an outlandish curse like I 've never heard before, then the prisoner stuck his head out and demanded to know if he had to pay to park upon our land. I told him the only rent due was the courtesy of leaving it clean. He seemed a suspicious one to me. He offered to sell me the wagon he was in, which I thought remarkably odd, and after I declined, I asked his name. He said it was Yaruer, claiming it had a silent letter. I'd never heard a name like that, so I figured he was one to watch. The next day, I was relieved when I saw him leaving our property."

"Mister Miller, are you sure the name wasn't Bumgardner?" Loomis questioned on cross-examination.

"Sir, I am quite familiar with the Bumgardner name, and can say for certain that he did not say Bumgardner." Loomis correctly decided to drop the line of questioning.

A portly gentleman in an ill-fitting three-piece suit next sat in the witness chair. "I ran across the prisoner amid a crowd on Front Street in Pomeroy. He was trying to hawk a sickly horse. He claimed to be a veteran of the Ohio Volunteers, and said he needed money. I looked the horse over and could tell it was recovering from the colic. I offered one hundred dollars, knowing if he took the offer he was a thief and the animal most likely stolen. He declined and insisted on one hundred and fifty dollars, a price akin to thievery." George Hibbard drew laughter with the comment. "It was clear he was unfamiliar with the horse. He declined my higher offer of one hundred twenty five dollars, and as he pulled away, I determined to remember his name, Bumgardner, as the whole event was so remarkably suspicious," Hibbard related.

Dr. James Barton, whom Dr. Hanson had known for quite some time, took the stand next. "Doctor Hanson has lived in Addison for several years. He is a sober, righteous man. I met with him on Monday to claim debts he owed me, including ten dollars for a watch he pawned to my wife. Hanson acknowledged the debts, promised to square accounts on Tuesday, and did as he vowed. He stated the urge to move had come upon him suddenly but three hours before, and was evasive about his destination. He left Wednesday with his family and possessions on the heavy rig in question. I did not ask about the wagon, presuming he had acquired it lawfully. He offered to sell me the gray horse, but I hadn't need of one." The normally warm doctor was cold in his testimony and aloof, not once meeting eyes with Hanson or even looking in Sue's direction.

Ed Ramsey, on being sworn in, told about replacing the boards in the rig. "By the time I arrived, the old boards were removed an' disposed of. The prisoner said he could not stand to look upon them. Throughout the time we replaced the boards and did some other repairs, he seemed preoccupied, as if worried about something."

After begin duly sworn, the teamster Hanson hired testified, "I'm Robert Woolley. I live at Gallipolis, Ohio. On Wednesday, September nineteenth, the prisoner here hired me to drive his rig to Columbus. He said he and the family were relocating. It was clear to me that he was not adept at driving the rig, although he claimed to have hauled oil with it for some time. He mentioned he had just come from Burning Springs. We got a late start and ended the day in Thurman. As to his manners, I can tell you this: He is a callous man, for example, having paid for his family to stay in a bed and breakfast, he left me to sleep under the wagon." Disapproving murmurs filled the room.

"The next day, we made only a few miles. Heavy rains brought us to a halt at Richmond Dale. That night, we all shared the shelter of the wagon. On Friday morning, the prisoner sold his gray horse in Chillicothe and we headed on towards Frankfort. Before we got to Frankfort, a rider came up and warned the prisoner that an arrest warrant had been issued for him. The prisoner avowed he never killed anyone. The rider suggested he go west, but the prisoner refused to abandon his family. We went about three miles further before four constables caught up to us and arrested him. He didn't seem to me like a man who had committed murder," the wagoner testified.

"The name is David Davis. I'm the Constable for Washington County. I arrested the prisoner and later brought him from the jail in Chillicothe to here." The heavy constable's oversized moustache wiggled and waggled as he spoke, amusing some in the gallery. "Right after I arrested him, I asked where he obtained the wagon. He said he bought the wagon from a man named Gollier. When I inquired where the man was, he told me the man was to have met him at Point Pleasant, but had failed to show. I told him the man had indeed been on his way, but was caught without a head on." Davis laughed at his word play and was joined by others in the courtroom. Judge Guthrie allowed the chortling to die down on its own, then motioned for Davis to continue.

"The prisoner told me he paid this man, Gollier, eight hundred dollars for the rig. A minute later, he said he paid eleven hundred for it and claimed the man was to meet him to collect another three hundred cash, but never showed. The prisoner also claimed he gave Gollier a mortgage deed along with cash for the rig. He told all these different stories within a matter of minutes. During my investigation, I found blood on the tailgate of the wagon, and that several floor boards had been replaced in order to hide blood that was on them."

William T. Foley, the blacksmith, was called next. "I repaired th' chain that was later found on th' headless body. It was for John Eubanks. I'm positive it's th' same chain. Them are my hammer-marks."

A cobbler, Robert Neil, looked closely at the boots offered into evidence and testified, "I personally repaired these boots for John T. Eubanks. They are confederate cavalry boots, and if you look, you can see "JTE" carved inside. I replaced a heel on the left boot, but not the right boot. Look," he turned the boots over for the jury to inspect, "the heels don't match. Eubanks didn't want to spend the extra twenty-five cents for a matching heel."

Sheriff Jackson Hicks' testimony was long and detailed, essentially reviewing the route Hanson took and all the different people the sheriff spoke with while performing his own investigation. The sheriff also repeated the several stories Hanson told about the purchase of the wagon, with the prosecutor emphasizing Hanson's dishonest inconsistencies. Hicks further noted the newly-replaced floorboards and the blood on the tailgate of the wagon. Then, he read aloud a letter between Hanson and Sue, asking her to wait for his next letter. Sue, sitting in the gallery directly behind Hanson, reacted with some anxiety upon discovering their letters had been intercepted.

After a brief court recess, Knowles began Hanson's defense by recalling several of the witnesses, emphasizing the favorable aspects of their testimony. Then, he called his expert witness, Dr. George Hildreth.

"Severing a head without crushing a vertebra is nearly impossible," Dr. Hildreth testified. "It took great skill to remove the head from the body. A large man like the victim would have struggled even if attacked in his sleep. A smooth cut like the one on the body would have been extremely difficult for someone the defendant's size and physique. Furthermore, the body like this would be expected to surface, given the high river levels, in about three days. If Eubanks was killed on the night of the thirteenth, the body should have appeared much farther downstream than where it was discovered by Mister Stone."

Under cross-examination by Col. Alban, Dr. Hildreth admitted the body could, nonetheless, rise anywhere, "depending on blood loss and gas formation." Moreover, the doctor acknowledged that, yes; one could use alcohol or even medicinal chloroform to cause unconsciousness. In such a case the victim's head could have been severed without a struggle, resulting in a clean cut as the body exhibited.

In the late afternoon, both sides rested their case, and the judge adjourned court for the evening, slating the closing arguments for the next day.

The following morning, Mr. Ewart closed for the state. "Gentlemen of the jury, you will soon be deliberating to determine the answers to several questions: First, is John T. Eubanks dead? We have presented Eubanks' brother and sister who have testified as to the identity of the body found by George Stone. A cobbler, the victim's sister and a blacksmith all testified about his clothing, and the gruesome actions the prisoner took to hide the victim's identity and sink the body, all to thwart justice. Second: Did John T. Eubanks meet his demise by violence? We have listened as members of the coroner's jury described the mutilated condition of the body. There is no question John T. Eubanks died of violence. Third: If he met his death by violence, was Hanson Bumgardner the author of that violence?"

Pointing to an easel on which rested a map boldly marked with the last ride of Hanson Bumgardner in red, Mr. Ewart continued. "Many witnesses have testified that Hanson Bumgardner was the last person to be seen with Eubanks, and that he took Eubanks' possessions, namely his rig, clothes, and team, using them as his own as he followed this escape route from his crime. Fourth: Was the violence done to Mister Eubanks done with premeditated malice? The very method of disposal of the body demonstrates his premeditation. Remember, he had to go from Addison, Ohio, to Boiling Springs, West Virginia, and return with his victim until they camped south of Belpre. All the while he was calculating when would be the best time to strike, to kill for the wagon he so coveted. Yes, the case is circumstantial, as I am sure the defense will point out. But, when you hear hoof beats outside, it is reasonable to presume there are animals going by. Vote logically. Vote your conscience. Vote to convict. Thank you."

Mr. Loomis presented half of the defense's closing, reiterating the fact that the defense need not prove innocence; rather, "the prosecution must overcome the presumption of innocence," stating further, "The tally of witnesses for or against the defendant does not matter. What matters is that they cannot meet the burden of proof. They say Mister Eubanks is dead and, sadly, we agree. Did he meet his death by violence? I believe they have proved that point. But did Hanson Bumgardner do it? No, the best they can do is put pins on a board to show that Hanson drove his newly purchased rig home. No one was ever able to say without doubt that they saw Hanson with Eubanks. The people who saw Eubanks could not identify Hanson with assurance, and the people who knew or saw Hanson could not be certain that it was Eubanks they saw with him. Eubanks was a large man. All the witnesses agreed that the man that Hanson was travelling with was an average-to-slightly-built man. This is where the state's case falls apart. You *must* vote for acquittal. The prosecution, despite all of the circumstantial evidence presented, has failed to prove, beyond reasonable doubt, that any violence ever occurred between these two men."

# Chapter Forty-Three

The December trial rose to its climax as Senator Knowles stood for the second half of the defense's closing arguments.

"Gentlemen of the jury, the state has brought you nothing except proof that Dr. Hanson Bumgardner *rode a particular road*. The witness in Parkersburg, Mister Guinn, says he is uncertain that the man with Eubanks that day was Doctor Hanson Bumgardner. Moreover, he says Eubanks' wallet was nearly empty.

"George Hensley said, and I quote, 'I cannot positively say it was the prisoner.' Mister Robinson testified he never saw the deceased and Doctor Bumgardner together. Mister Miller, Mister Snyder, and Mister Nolan all disagree as to the description of the man Bumgardner was with and further, none of their descriptions match Eubanks, who was a large man by his own brother's testimony. Mister Nolan said the doctor told him it was 'his new rig' while discussing a mate for the gray horse. If the deceased, Thomas Eubanks, actually sat beside Hanson Bumgardner, why did he not dispute this claim? He did not, for my client had already purchased the rig, and the former owner had the money in his pocket. While the storekeeper could not confirm it was Eubanks at the store that night, he did confirm for us that the man Bumgardner was with had *a full wallet*, a twenty dollar bill being the smallest he could produce. Doesn't it make sense that the defendant paid the deceased for the wagon? What else could account for the sudden appearance of this money and the lack of comment about ownership of the rig?"

Knowles' voice rose, speaking with increasing authority as he continued reviewing the evidence. "Mister McLaughlin says he helped Hanson bleed the gray horse, which accounts for the blood on the wagon. Bob Woolley testified that Bumgardner firmly denied being involved in any murder when the rider came to warn him to flee, and appeared confused when told the victim was Eubanks. Instead, he refused to abandon his family, professed again his innocence, and has continued to proclaim such up to this very day.

"This scant circumstantial evidence is not enough to take a man's life. The law says he must be presumed innocent, as Mister Loomis has pointed out, until the state provides *proof, beyond any reasonable doubt,* that this man is guilty. That means you should presume him innocent and exercise reasonable doubt to the state's proof of nothing but a route which he rode. Look at the evidence carefully, vote not guilty, and release this innocent man." Knowles bowed slightly at the waist first towards the jury and then the judge.

Col. David Alban then stood and walked slowly from the attorney's table to stand in front of the jury for the state's final closing comment. "Gentlemen, you represent Washington County, Ohio. You represent the conscience of this city, this county this state. You have heard from your fellow citizens for three days how the prisoner followed this route..." he pointed to the map on the easel, and slowly ran his finger along its entire course, "...in order to suit his evil purposes. You have heard how George Stone found the body that began the investigation. You've seen the clothes Mister Boyd brought here, as well as the testimony of each member of the coroner's jury. The victim's brother, Robert Eubanks, confirmed the identity of the body as did the victim's sister, Mary Kyle, who *made the pants found on the body with her own hands*. Mister Guinn testified he met the accused and the victim outside Parkersburg as did George Hensley, Misters Miller Snyder. Mister Nolan described and identified the prisoner with the victim *on this very route*. The storekeeper, Payne Lewis, was intimidated by Bumgardner. Even Bumgardner's old acquaintance, Roger Hill, said the prisoner told him the next morning when asked about Eubanks, 'Oh he is gone'. Truer words were never spoken, for the prisoner had killed him.

"Jim Miller then told us that Hanson Bumgardner, while hiding on Miller's land, give a false name in an attempt to conceal himself the day after the murder. Bob Woolley testified later that the prisoner told him he had 'just come from Boiling Springs', exactly as we have alleged. *From the prisoner's own mouth*, you have sufficient basis for conviction. There is no mistaken identity here, gentlemen, nor any confusion as to who was *with* Bumgardner."

Walking slowly in front of the jury box, he made eye contact with each member. "The defendant claims he was flush with cash and purchased the rig. However, gentlemen, recall that he told many different stories about how much and in what manner he paid for the rig. I remind you of the unchallenged testimony of his landlord, Dr. Barton, that the prisoner was months behind on rent and even had to pawn a watch for cash.

"The sheriff and constable both testified to finding Hanson in possession of the stolen rig heading west as quickly as possible, with blood spattered on it. To each person he met, the prisoner told a different tale and you are no exception, gentlemen of the jury!"

Walking back to the table, he concluded, "It is time to end all these lies and convict Hanson Bumgardner for the murder he so obviously committed!"

On the gallows, Hanson Bumgardner looked down upon the official witnesses and pleaded, "...and, so, kind gentleman, this is the tale of how my name has come to be reviled, from one who has spent his life helping the afflicted, now, in return, wrongly convicted of murder."

Hanson's voice had become so hoarse, his ability to keep speaking was nearly at an end. He shook his head in frustration. "After my arrest, you heralded an escape attempt as further evidence of my guilt. Woe that you would not listen; I have said time and again, I was only trying to protect my wife and family from harm. A person unnamed brought me a horse that evening, and while playing 'Busted Bean' with a deputy, I kissed him on the head with a lump of coal. I ran through the jailhouse as quickly as I could, never suspecting a meeting of the sheriff and his fifteen deputies would be taking place there that very evening. I saw no benefit in resisting arrest this second time, but was nonetheless shot in the shoulder while I struggled with a deputy who leapt upon me." He could see by the rows of downcast eyes that his final pleadings were failing.

His eyes begging, he gazed upon those still standing on muddy planks waiting for his story to finish. Hanson saw that their patience had come to an end. In a low, raspy voice, tense and filled with desperation, he continued. "The judge gave instructions to the jury that they must determine for certain that the body was in Ohio when discovered. Stone testified he found it on the West Virginia side of the river and he dragged it to Ohio. For God's sake, extradite me that I may have time to find Woods, or Gollier, or Clem, any one of which can set me free with their testimony. I will gladly stand trial there."

He cleared his throat and swallowed dryly before continuing. "I agreed to be represented by Loomis and Knowles. Despite Senator Knowles' grand effort, my cause was lost to lies. It is inconceivable that an unbiased jury could convict a man to death on such scant evidence. They say I killed for the wagon, but I had already purchased it with counterfeit money. Why would I commit murder for something I already possessed through guile? It doesn't make sense!"

Hanson paced across the front of the gallows platform. "Why then have you convicted me? Over the fibs I told to sell a horse? How many of you have never once stretched the truth when selling a horse or wagon? On these so-called lies, I stand before you convicted, guilty of no more than the falsehoods of mercantile advertising. Yet, here I am, condemned to death, leaving a widow and three little boys to the mercy of this heartless uncaring world. I admit before God and man I am a sinner, but this crime of murder I did *not* commit. It is not good to condemn a man to death on circumstantial evidence alone, without an identified body or murder weapon. But even the governor will not hear my pleas, so it is remains in the hands of the Grand Judge of all things to proclaim my true innocence."

Hanson fell silent in dreadful realization that in just minutes he would be standing alone before that Almighty Judge. The clock in the square struck a single note as Hanson Bumgardner stood in gathering terror over what was about to transpire.

In his mind, he saw Sue and James with Woods, Gollier, and Clem in the wagon, crossing the river, hurrying to his rescue. He stretched his entire body, stood on his tiptoes, and looked east, but saw nothing. He sank back into his shoes, his body slumped forward, his eyes clouded with exhaustion, his heart grudgingly resigned to his fate.

The sheriff, seeing Hanson's expression, recognized it was over. Hanson had finished talking, spinning his tales as he always had. But now he had come to the end of his life's tale.

"Yup, it's about time, Hanson," said Sheriff Hicks firmly but compassionately.

"Yes, Sheriff, I suppose so," Hanson replied softly, finally abandoning any wisp of hope for a miraculous rescue. He drew in a long sigh while his pulse quickened. "Reverend, please," he asked, bowing his head. The Rev. Mullenix quietly said a prayer. The sheriff stood silently waiting alongside Deputy Thomas Hicks for the prayer to end.

"Amen," said Hanson at last. Hanson turned around and Sheriff Hicks motioned towards the trap door.

Hanson stoically walked a few paces and assumed a position in the center of the trap door. He placed his hands behind him so the deputy could bind them. Sheriff Hicks reclaimed the hood Hanson had left on the table earlier, and placed it over Hanson's head while Deputy Hicks cinched Hanson's legs together with rope. Sheriff Hicks' hands quivered as he placed the noose around Hanson's neck, drawing it snug and draping the measured length of rope upon Hanson's shoulder. He could hear Hanson breathing in fast short gulps through the thick canvas hood.

Hanson's sudden silence and the activity on the gallows drew the gathered witnesses back to the present. Some had allowed their mind to wander; others had been visiting in low voices while Hanson recited the details of his life. The moment they came to witness was about to happen. Moving about, each claimed a spot he deemed the best from which to observe the event.

Sheriff Hicks nodded to his deputy who backed away from the

trap door. The sheriff walked over to the lever set along the edge and grasped it in his shaking hands. Anxiety churned his stomach at the thought of the three possibilities that might occur when he pulled the lever. First, the drop might not be long enough, and the prisoner would strangle on the end of the line, a horrible experience for the prisoner as well as the witnesses. It could take as much as ten minutes to strangle the condemned to death. Sheriff Hicks' research indicated this could be prevented by leaving a length of rope on the prisoner's shoulder, as he had done. However, if he had allowed too much length, the second possibility could occur, and the falling body would drop too far, gaining so much speed that the yank of the rope would sever the head from the body. The latest scientific articles on hanging that the sheriff had consulted provided guidance based on the height and weight of the prisoner as to how far the condemned must drop for the third and preferred contingency: that of snapping the neck and causing instantaneous death. As Sheriff Hicks gritted his teeth this afternoon, he prayed he'd gotten it right.

Impulsively, Rev. Mullenix stepped onto the trap door next to Hanson, surprising everyone. The sheriff immediately pulled his hands away from the lever, perturbed but curious as to the pastor's intent.

"Hanson Bumgardner. Did you kill John Eubanks?" the Reverend asked loudly, hoping to give Hanson one last earthly chance to confess his crime before man and God.

"No sir! I did not!" declared Hanson from inside the hood.

The witnesses raised their eyebrows and exchanged glances at his final adamant declaration of innocence. The Reverend stepped away from the trap door and stood next to the deputy.

"Hanson Bumgardner. Are you ready?" Sheriff Hicks called out authoritatively as he again nervously gripped the lever.

"Yes, sir. I am read..."

The clank of the lever instantly releasing the trap door interrupted Hanson mid-word, the loss of support accelerating him swiftly downward. The resonant twang of the abruptly taut rope confirmed the successful execution. The crowd was caught mid-breath by the suddenness of it all. Sheriff Hicks sighed in relief that his fears had not materialized. He looked at his pocket watch, confirming aloud, "One forty post-noon, the execution of Hanson Bumgardner was carried out according to the order of the court."

Conversations slowly resumed, growing steadily in volume. The witnesses milled about for several minutes before meandering out in small groups of twos and threes. When only a few remained, Deputy Tom Hicks led a group of four deputies to take down Hanson's body and place it in the coffin waiting under the gallows. It was Deputy Hicks who removed the gallows hood from the body.

Hanson's handsome features were calm. The only evidence he was dead was the blue tinge about his lips. No longer would the sweepstakes smile or tales of adventure cross his lips. Hanson Bumgardner was dead, his reputation sullied forever as a murderer executed by the state for his crime.

Sheriff Hicks looked down on Hanson's body in the coffin, his face tense with sorrow, as he placed Hanson's signature black Plug hat on the man's unmoving chest. Deputy Hicks slid the coffin lid in place and nailed it shut.

The deputies carried the coffin out to the street to the war surplus caisson waiting and slid the casket on board. The driver, Bill Rider, carefully tied the coffin in place, then headed for the Ohio River Bridge on his way to the cemetery. People traveling the road stopped and stared at the coffin as it slowly passed

# Chapter Forty-Four

Miles away from the Ohio River, James was the first to see his old friend, Bill Rider, coming towards them along the muddied West Virginia pike. Rider drove solemnly up to them, and slowed. As the caisson came alongside, Banjo stopped. James placed his arm around Sue's shoulders while she sobbed. "Damn you, Clem. Damn you and Woods forever to hell," she cursed through her tears.

The three men removed the casket from the caisson and onto James and Sue's wagon. Bill Rider then handed Sue the letters Hanson penned earlier that morning. She nodded her thanks through her tears. James looked at Gabriel Clem, whose face was narrow, drawn taut as he coughed.

"You might as well go on back to Pocahontas, Clem. Go home, and learn from Hanson's death. Lead a sober and moral life," James recommended.

"Yeah, maybe," Clem said unconvincingly. Looking at Sue, he wanted to say something, anything, to make amends, but knew better.

They parted ways without further words.

Sue and James took Hanson's body back for interment in Ten Mile where the family returned after the war.

Back at Ten Mile, Sue discovered the bottle of tonic she had shared with Clem missing from her purse. Also missing was the unlabeled bottle of elixir with two X's cut in the cork. Hanson had planned to drink the poisonous elixir, rather than face the noose, were they unsuccessful in their appeal.

Sue later learned that Gabriel Clem died one day after Hanson Bumgardner, and wondered if his sudden death might have been caused by drinking a purloined bottle of elixir. Sue smiled at the thought that her Hanson may have had the last word after all.

Col. David Alban, having listened to Bumgardner's soliloquy, pointed out to the press that Bumgardner was a consummate liar. "I suggest you keep to reporting that, despite Hanson's emotional pleas and fairy tales, he was duly convicted on the evidence presented in court. I further remind you that the victim's body, when found, was without boots, and the cobbler identified the boots in evidence as belonging to John Thomas Eubanks, whom Bumgardner claimed never to have met. No doubt Hanson failed to mention this fact on the gallows, because *the reason the dead man's boots were available as evidence is that, when arrested, Hanson Bumgardner was wearing them."*

The following simple words in the February 21, 1867, edition of the *Marietta Times* well summarized the feeling of the townsfolk:

> *"Guilty or Not Guilty, Hanson Bumgardner has gone to a bar where his crimes are known; where they will be faithfully judged, and where just and true punishment will be meted in accordance therewith. As he asked for mercy, so may Almighty God have mercy upon him."*

If you enjoyed *The Hanging of Dr. Hanson,* consider *The Bahrain Conspiracy* also by Bentley Gates:

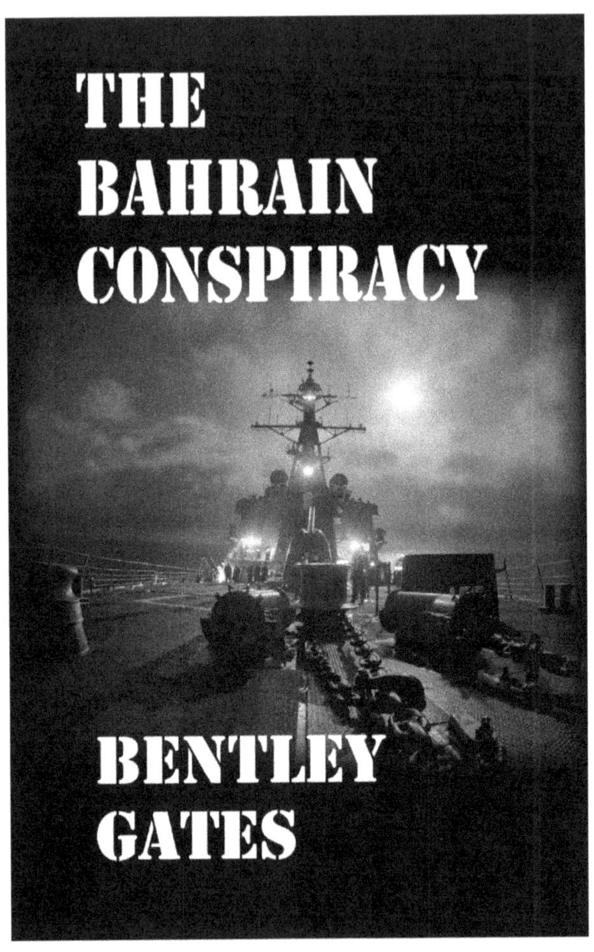


*Lieutenant Commander John Allen leads US Navy SEALs Team Six and a CIA agent against an alliance of Somali Pirates and Islamic Jihadists bent on using hijacked ships as weapons of mass destruction in a simultaneous attack on both US coasts.*

# About the Author

Novelist **Bentley Gates** brings a strong background in investigation, research, martial arts and education to the novels he writes, helping create the realism he is known for in his works. His previous novel, THE BAHRAIN CONSPIRACY (Savant 2009) was an Amazon Kindle Genre Bestseller. He has been awarded the prestigious "Editor/ Publisher Award" from the Journal of the National Association of Legal Investigators. Called a 'maverick' when working in the corporate environment, he left that setting to settle on the plains of Texas to write novels.

Author website at
http://www.thebahrainconspiracy.com

If you enjoyed *The Hanging of Dr. Hanson,* consider these other fine books from Savant Books and Publications:

*Essay, Essay, Essay* by Yasuo Kobachi
*Aloha from Coffee Island* by Walter Miyanari
*Footprints, Smiles and Little White Lies* by Daniel S. Janik
*The Illustrated Middle Earth* by Daniel S. Janik
*Last and Final Harvest* by Daniel S. Janik
*A Whale's Tale* by Daniel S. Janik
*Tropic of California* by R. Page Kaufman
*Tropic of California* (the companion music CD) by R. Page Kaufman
*The Village Curtain* by Tony Tame
*Dare to Love in Oz* by William Maltese
*The Interzone* by Tatsuyuki Kobayashi
*Today I Am a Man* by Larry Rodness
*The Bahrain Conspiracy* by Bentley Gates
*Called Home* by Gloria Schumann
*Kanaka Blues* by Mike Farris
*First Breath* edited by Z. M. Oliver
*Poor Rich* by Jean Blasiar
*The Jumper Chronicles* by W. C. Peever
*William Maltese's Flicker* by William Maltese
*My Unborn Child* by Orest Stocco
*Last Song of the Whales* by Four Arrows
*Perilous Panacea* by Ronald Klueh
*Falling but Fulfilled* by Zachary M. Oliver
*Mythical Voyage* by Robin Ymer
*Hello, Norma Jean* by Sue Dolleris
*Richer* by Jean Blasiar
*Manifest Intent* by Mike Farris
*Charlie No Face* by David B. Seaburn
*Number One Bestseller* by Brian Morley
*My Two Wives and Three Husbands* by S. Stanley Gordon
*In Dire Straits* by Jim Currie
*Wretched Land* by Mila Komarnisky
*Chan Kim* by Ilan Herman

*Who's Killing All the Lawyers?* by A. G. Hayes
*Ammon's Horn* by G. Amati
*Wavelengths* edited by Zachary M. Oliver
*Almost Paradise* by Laurie Hanan
*Communion* by Jean Blasiar and Jonathan Marcantoni
*The Oil Man* by Leon Puissegur
*Random Views of Asia from the Mid-Pacific* by William E. Sharp
*The Isla Vista Crucible* by Reilly Ridgell
*Blood Money* by Scott Mastro
*In the Himalayan Nights* by Anoop Chandola
*On My Behalf* by Helen Doan
*Traveler's Rest* by Jonathan Marcantoni
*Keys in the River* by Tendai Mwanaka
*Chimney Bluffs* by David B. Seaburn
*The Loons* by Sue Dolleris
*Light Surfer* by David Allan Williams
*The Judas List* by A. G. Hayes
*Path of the Templar - Book 2 of The Jumper Chronicles* by W. C. Peever
*The Desperate Cycle* by Tony Tame
*Shutterbug* by Buz Sawyer
*Blessed are the Peacekeepers* by Tom Donnelly and Mike Munger
*The Bellwether Messages* edited by D. S. Janik
*The Turtle Dances* by Daniel S. Janik
*The Lazarus Conspiracies* by Richard Rose
*Purple Haze* by George B. Hudson
*Imminent Danger* by A. G. Hayes
*Lullaby Moon* (CD) by Malia Elliott of Leon & Malia
*Volutions* edited by Suzanne Langford
*In the Eyes of the Son* by Hans Brinckmann

Coming Soon:
*More More Time* by David B. Seaburn
*Elaine of Corbenic* by Tima Z. Newman
*Flight of Destiny* by Francis Powell

http://www.savantbooksandpublications.com

www.ingramcontent.com/pod-product-compliance
Lightning Source LLC
Chambersburg PA
CBHW051239260626
47162CB00002B/515
*9780988664067*